SONNET TO
A DEAD CONTESSA

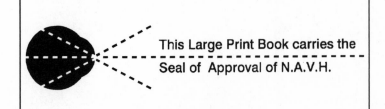

This Large Print Book carries the
Seal of Approval of N.A.V.H.

SONNET TO
A DEAD CONTESSA

GILBERT MORRIS

THORNDIKE PRESS

A part of Gale, Cengage Learning

GALE
CENGAGE Learning

Detroit • New York • San Francisco • New Haven, Conn • Waterville, Maine • London

GALE
CENGAGE Learning™

LIBRARY OF CONGRESS CATALOGING-IN-PUBLICATION DATA

Morris, Gilbert.
    Sonnet to a dead contessa / by Gilbert Morris.
        p. cm. — (Thorndike Press large print Christian historical fiction) (A Lady Trent mystery ; bk. 3)
    ISBN-13: 978-1-4104-1887-6 (alk. paper)
    ISBN-10: 1-4104-1887-1 (alk. paper)
        1. Women private investigators—England—Fiction. 2. Aristocracy (Social class)—England—Fiction. 3. Large type books. I. Title.
    PS3563.O8742S675 2009b
    813'.54—dc22   2009018872

Published in 2009 by arrangement with Thomas Nelson, Inc.

Printed in the United States of America
1 2 3 4 5 6 7 13 12 11 10 09

To Gale Towne
Thanks for the memories!

ONE

Lady Stephanie Welles entered the Blue Room, paused, and at once noted that almost every man in the room was looking at her. She was pleased, but not surprised, for she had long known that her ability to draw attention was highly developed. She was wearing a crimson gown with such a breathtakingly wide skirt that it made her waist look as if a man could span it with his hands and overlap his fingers. Her eyes and her lips gave a hint of her will and her pride. She was tall and shapely in a manner that would draw any man's eyes. Aware of the effect her entrance had on those who watched her, she tilted up her head in an imperious manner and then turned toward the three women who were waiting for her.

Marchioness Rachel Reis rose and moved across the room, her raven black hair framing her face, her Jewish blood evident in her features. She was an attractive woman of twenty-eight, not tall but with a good carriage. She came to stand in front of Lady Welles.

"I'm glad you were able to come, Lady Stephanie. It's a good cause we're working for," she said, smiling, and waited for a reply.

A caustic humour touched Lady Stephanie's eyes. "Of course — and I'm always anxious to do my bit for a good cause." She saw the expression on Lady Reis's face and laughed. "You find that amusing? Well, I have to do some good works, or I won't get into heaven, will I?"

"You will be able to add your contribution to the London Festival of Arts. The profits will go to help the poor of our city."

"I'm not sure what I can do to help."

"There will be work enough for us all — but just your name and your support are greatly appreciated. Come and we'll get started."

The two high-society women made their way over to a table where two other women of superior status were seated. "I'm amazed that Stephanie has volunteered to help with the festival," said Baroness Danielle De-Main, a tall woman with a fine figure and aristocratic features. "She's not known for her good works, is she, Margaret?"

"Now, Danielle, don't be harsh." Countess Margaret Acton was a short, rather well-padded woman of thirty-three. She had a wealth of light brown hair and a pair of warm brown eyes. "She just wants to help, I'm sure."

Lady DeMain smiled. "You'd speak well of Judas Iscariot — or of the devil himself, Margaret. And I'm not sure that Stephanie isn't the devil — no, the devil is a male. But Stephanie must be one of his demons."

"Shh! She'll hear you, Danielle!" She rose and smiled, saying, "I'm so glad you've decided to join us, Lady Stephanie."

"Why, as I just remarked to Rachel, I'm always available for good works." She paused and smiled thinly. "I see skepticism in your faces. Well, you are right. I'm not given to holy causes — if that's what the festival is. I always thought it was about greedy artists trying to gouge more money out of buyers."

Lady DeMain laughed. "You are right, Stephanie, to some degree. But as you know, 25 percent of all sales will go to help the poor."

The four women ordered lunch and discussed ways to entice more influential citizens to join them. Suddenly Lady De-Main exclaimed, "Look at that!" Her three companions turned to see what she meant, and Lady Welles laughed. "I thought this was an exclusive restaurant. What in the world are those women doing here?"

"I know one of them," Rachel Reis said, her voice strained. "Her name is Martha Bingham. She's been after me to join her organization. She's really quite a bore."

"What organization?" Stephanie asked, eyeing the trio. "Not a crusade to wear the ugliest clothing in England, is it?"

Indeed, the three women advanced toward their table. The leader was a tall, strongly built woman with a squarish face, a prow of a chin, and dark brown hair. She pulled up in front of the seated women and stridently said, "My name is Martha Bingham. I have come to enlist your aid in helping the women of England assume their rightful place in our society. This young woman is my aide. Her name is Miss Jeanne St. Clair. And this is Miss Violet Bates, my secretary. They will be glad to assist you in filling out papers that will enable you to join us. We have a place for each of you."

"And what is that place, Miss Bingham?" asked Lady DeMain. She was amused at the woman but at the same time annoyed that they had invaded the restaurant.

"I am founder and president of Equality

for Women," Miss Bingham said. "I believe you have all received my invitation?"

"Oh dear, yes," Lady Welles said. "I think I remember something of the sort. Please send no more. My wastebasket is full of such 'invitations.' "

A young woman to Miss Bingham's left suddenly took a step forward. She had blue eyes and reddish-blonde hair. She was wearing a plain black taffeta dress that revealed a trim and rather athletic figure. Her voice was low, but a thread of anger tinted her words. "You call yourselves women? Fah! You're nothing but slaves to men who bargained with your parents for rights to your bodies! I despise you!"

"Now, that will do!" Lady Welles said angrily. "You know nothing about us! You have no idea what nobility means!"

"Do I not?"

Margaret Acton was shocked at the vehemence in Jeanne St. Clair's face. There was something almost feral in her expression, and her voice throbbed as she spat out the words, "Noblemen can be full of evil! You don't know what's happened to me. A member of Parliament" — she broke off in angry sobs — "he went to church every Sunday . . . It was wrong, I tell you, wrong what he did to me! Is that what nobility is?"

"That will do!" Lady DeMain said loudly. She saw that the manager had approached and said, "Howard, show these women out!"

Mr. Howard, a tall, thin man, had been watching the scene nervously, and now he scurried forward, saying, "I must ask you ladies to leave."

Martha Bingham's face reddened. "I will not leave until I have spoken to these women."

"Howard, get rid of them!" Lady Welles said. "Call a policeman if necessary."

"I trust that will not be necessary. You must leave." He nodded to a burly man who had been watching. "Joseph, help these ladies out, please."

"Yes, Mr. Howard." The man advanced, reached out, and took the arm of Martha Bingham. Then, at that instant, Miss Bingham's secretary began to weep. Joseph pulled at Miss Bingham's arm, but Jeanne St. Clair leapt forward and struck him a powerful blow in the throat. He stepped back, his face crimson, and began to gag.

Chaos took over. Martha Bingham shouted her message; the manager ran from the room but soon returned with a policeman. He was a broad-shouldered fellow, and when Jeanne tried to hit him, he simply shoved her to the floor and took Martha

Bingham's arm. "You're under arrest for disturbing the peace. Come along now. Don't make things worse."

Margaret Acton was shaken by the event. She watched them leave, and when they were at the door, Martha Bingham turned and shouted, "You're unfit to live! Slaves, that's all you are! But that will change! We don't need you or your fancy title . . . !" Margaret then saw the large woman turn and put her arm around the younger secretary. She patted her back and spoke soothingly to her.

"She's got some affection in her," Margaret said in a murmur.

"I suppose even wild beasts in the jungle have some sort of tender feelings for their offspring," Lady DeMain said. "But that other one, she's as wild as any tiger!"

"What a fine dinner!" Lady Welles said. "The entertainment was very exciting. Well, I must go. Not," she added, "to enlist in Miss Bingham's organization. There are ways to master men without force. They're weak creatures, after all."

Three days after the scene with Martha Bingham, Lady Stephanie Welles had almost forgotten it. She had told her husband, Lord Herbert, of the affair and he had grunted.

"Old biddy ought to be locked up!"

"I'm going out tonight, Herbert." Stephanie noted that her husband was not interested enough to ask where she was going, but she was accustomed to this. She dressed and got into her carriage, saying, "Take me to the Old Vic Theatre, Alvin."

"Yes'm, Lady Stephanie." He spoke to the horses and soon they were on Drury Lane. As always, the area was bustling with activity even as the sun went down over London. Although it was one of the better sections of the city, Lady Welles was slightly on edge, as always, for even here good and evil mingled. Side by side with noble ladies dressed in the finest of clothing, prostitutes with painted faces and gaudy attire paced in the flow of traffic. One expected to find harlots in the Seven Dials District or London's notorious St. Jiles District, known as the Rookery, but here in the heart of London, the evil seemed somehow out of place to Lady Welles. The theatre crowd filled the street, all headed toward one of several playhouses. For most the destination was the Old Vic. As her carriage drew up in a line in front of the theatre, Lady Welles waited until the driver hopped down and opened the door for her. "Here we are, ma'am."

"Very good, Alvin. You'll have to watch when the crowd comes out and be sure you don't park too far away."

"Oh no, ma'am. I'll be on watch for you."

Lady Welles reached into her reticule, pulled out a coin, and handed it to him. "Buy yourself a good dinner. It's rather a long play, I understand." Without waiting for a reply, she turned and moved down the street toward the entrance of the Old Vic. A line was waiting to buy tickets, but she simply walked by them, and when she reached the door, she handed the man a reservation and a one-pound note.

"Yes, ma'am, you're just in time." The doorman smiled, a tall, sallow-faced man with badly fitting false teeth. "Shall I show you to your seat?"

"That won't be necessary, thank you."

As she joined the flow of people moving through the large foyer, Lady Welles attracted the eyes of both men and women. She was a graceful and strikingly beautiful woman elegantly dressed tonight in a polished blue-and-grey-striped taffeta skirt with a white silk blouse and lace ascot with a small pearl stick pin. She wore a sapphire comb in her hair and a sapphire and diamond necklace that glittered under the gaslight as she moved. Men's eyes seemed drawn to her, but she paid no heed as she made her way. The theatre was filling rapidly, but as she moved toward her seat, she was conscious of the chandeliers blazing so brightly one could barely look at them. The women everywhere wore glamourous jewels that sparkled on arms and throats and wrists, and the colourful dresses of silk, taffeta, voile, and velvet, along with the warmth of peach- and rose-tinted costumes, gave a flaring vibrancy to the room.

She took her seat amidst the rustle and the whisper of the fabric of her dress, conscious of the voices and of the bursts of laughter that broke out from time to time. She turned at once to the woman who was seated next to her, and as she sat down, she said with surprise, "Why, Helen, I didn't expect to see you here."

Lady Helen Maddox was a short, rather dumpy woman but made every attempt to compensate for her lack of graceful figure by expensive dress. She wore a crimson gown that did nothing for her rather ashen complexion, but it was beautifully cut, the full sleeves ostentatiously decorated with blue velvet bows at the shoulders. She had a pair of lively grey eyes, and when she smiled and greeted Lady Welles, there was genuine pleasure in her voice. "Why, it's you, Stephanie," she exclaimed. "What a pleasant surprise! I was afraid I'd have to sit by a bricklayer or some other impossible being."

"Then both of us are happy. I was dreading that I might have to sit beside a ranting Methodist and be preached at."

The two women sat there chatting, for they were old friends. Both of them were of the nobility. Lady Stephanie's husband, Sir Herbert Welles, was a member of the House of Lords. Lady Maddox's husband was a mere baronet whose title would cease to exist when he did the same himself. Nevertheless, they were both addressed by the title "Lady."

"Look over there, Stephanie," Helen said, her eyes glittering with excitement. "Up there in the first balcony." Stephanie looked up and at once saw what Helen was so excited about. "The Prince of Wales," she murmured.

"Yes, and look at that woman with him. One of his mistresses, no doubt."

"No doubt."

"I think it's terrible!" Helen exclaimed, not taking her eyes from the heavyset man with the pointed beard and the woman who sat beside him. "The Queen is terribly disappointed in the Prince. He's nothing but a wastrel."

"So the gossip goes."

"Oh, dear me, it's not gossip! He has all sorts of women, some of them noble, if you can believe it. I think the one with him is an actress."

Stephanie took a closer look. "She's attractive. Rather gaudy, I should say, but better than his usual choices, I would guess."

The two women sat there talking about the royal family, for Queen Victoria and her husband, Prince Albert, were symbols of the solidarity of the British Empire. It was well known that Victoria had fallen madly in love with the German prince, and that even after they had produced a house full of children, she was still as much in love with him as ever. Somehow this union pleased the British public. They were more accustomed to their rulers being either without morals or able to conceal their baser doings adeptly. But Queen Victoria was, indeed, a most moral and upright woman. She had none of the flamboyance of Queen Elizabeth, but she was better at this point in time for England than that redheaded, almost manlike woman had been.

The crowd grew noisier, and nobility and working persons were strewn throughout the audience. True, some of the better seats were more expensive, but many commoners afforded them, and a duke might find himself sitting next to a mere shopkeeper. Stephanie turned to ask, "I suppose you've seen *Macbeth*?"

"Oh, indeed, I have! I've been to this production three times."

"Why in the world would you do that?"

Helen shook her head. "You'll see when the play starts. It's Dylan Tremayne who plays the leading role. He's simply *divine!* I do believe he's the best-looking man in England!"

Stephanie was rather bored and shrugged her shoulders. "That's part of a stock in trade of actors, isn't it? They're supposed to be good-looking."

"Oh, he's more than fine-looking!" Helen insisted. She leaned over and talked with excitement. "He has something about him that draws your attention the minute he comes onstage, and he's exactly the same offstage."

"You mean he's sexually alluring?"

Helen stared at Lady Stephanie. "Well, I wouldn't have put it in exactly those words, but in a way I suppose you're right. Women just can't resist him."

"I shall do my best to keep from leaping out of my seat and running up and throwing myself at his feet."

Helen laughed. "You're making fun of me, but you wait and you'll see!"

Five minutes later the curtain parted, and the play began. Stephanie had seen *Macbeth* performed several times, and in all truth had been rather bored with the main character. She had told her husband, "Herbert, that character Macbeth in the play by Shakespeare, he bores me to tears. He has no pluck. His wife has all the courage."

Lord Herbert had smiled at her. "His wife loses her courage, remember?"

"Of course she does. Women always have to bear their husbands' shortcomings."

Herbert had laughed. "I wonder what Shakespeare would say to that."

As the play unfolded, Stephanie kept her eye on Dylan Tremayne mostly because of what Helen had told her. She had been prepared to dislike him, for as a rule, pretty men, overly handsome ones, were rather hollow on the inside. But as Dylan Tremayne moved across the stage, there was virility and a strength in his motions, and when he turned to look out over the audience, his eyes were the bluest she had ever seen. Indeed, he was handsome, but as Helen had insisted, Tremayne was more than just a fine-looking man.

There was one intermission, and both

Lady Helen and Lady Stephanie were uncomfortably warm. It was the beginning of summer, and there were no windows to admit a breeze, so each of them had brought a handkerchief to mop her brow.

"Well, what do you think now?" Helen asked, turning to give Stephanie an enquiring look. "Isn't he everything I said he would be?"

"I give you this, he *is* fine-looking — and he does have a certain flair."

"A certain flair? Come now, Stephanie, admit it. You couldn't take your eyes off him, could you?"

Stephanie suddenly laughed. "He does have whatever it is that some people have. Women have it sometimes. Men can't take their eyes off of them. There can be twenty women in a room, but when a woman with this quality appears — every man turns to stare at her."

"That's exactly the way it is with Tremayne, only it's the women staring."

"What do you know about him, his private life, I mean? He's very successful, isn't he?"

"Not really," Helen said quickly. "Not until recently. Hamlet was his first leading role, and that was awhile back. Before that he was only in minor roles. Of course, he also has an interesting background."

"What sort of background?"

"He was a coal miner in Wales, then he ran away from his master and came to England. He joined the army and served well, I understand, and when he came out he had no profession, so he somehow became attracted to the theatre. He took what he could get, of course, and *Hamlet* was his first real opportunity, which led to *Macbeth.* He can have any role he pleases, Stephanie. The city is mad about him." She turned and whispered, although there was no need for it. "Look down the row in front of us at the end. Do you see that woman?"

"Yes. Who is she?"

"She's the Viscountess Serafina Trent."

"I've heard of her."

"She's gained quite a reputation as a detective."

"A detective?" Stephanie leaned forward and stared at the woman. "Whatever can you mean, Helen? Women aren't detectives."

"Well, she's not like most women. Her father is a very famous scientist — Septimus Isaac Newton, very well-to-do."

"Is he a nobleman?"

"Oh no. Serafina married a viscount, Charles Trent. It was a short marriage, for he died rather shockingly. There's some scandal about it."

"What sort of scandal?"

"Well, I shouldn't say this, for you know how I *hate* to gossip." She lowered her voice to a whisper. "Some say his death wasn't entirely natural and that his wife had a hand in it."

Stephanie turned and studied the face of the woman in question. She was, indeed, an attractive woman with strawberry blonde hair, and when she turned in Stephanie's direction, it became obvious that she had a wide, sensuous mouth and a squarish face. There was a look of determination on her features that one did not often see in a woman.

"What does she have to do with Tremayne?"

"He's her protégé, you might say. As I say, she's done some work helping the police solve some crimes, and Dylan Tremayne worked for her. They're very close, so my information tells me."

"Very close? Does that mean they're having an affair?"

"Oh, no one actually has any evidence of that, but she'd be a fool if she didn't," Helen said, laughing and shaking her head. "And he'd be a fool if he turned her down. Isn't every day an actor gets the chance to have — a relationship, I might say — with a viscountess."

Stephanie encouraged Lady Helen to talk more about the actor and found her completely willing.

Finally Helen said, "If you go backstage after the play is over, you'll find women practically *throwing* themselves at him! It's disgraceful!"

Stephanie suddenly smiled. "Did you throw yourself, Helen?"

Helen was an honest enough woman. She had a marriage of convenience, and her ways were well known to Stephanie. "Well, I tried, but he had younger women, some of them with titles. Besides, from what I hear, he's as pure as the driven snow."

"What do you mean?"

"He's a religious fellow, so my information goes. He doesn't drink, and he doesn't have anything to do with women."

"How do you know that?"

"Why, Lady Margaret Acton told me. She's the best friend of Lady Trent. That's her sitting beside her now. You see? She said Lady Trent has told her that Tremayne is not interested in those women who clamour after him, but I find that hard to believe."

The curtain opened then, and the two women sat through the drama. After the play ended, Dylan Tremayne was brought back five times as the audience, mostly women, applauded until their hands must have ached. Tremayne seemed rather awkward, as if this were something he had to endure as part of his profession. Stephanie studied him. He was at least six feet tall and had coal black hair, glossy, with a slight curl that usually fell over his forehead. He had a wedge-shaped face, a wide mouth, and a cleft chin, and his striking blue eyes were the colour of the cornflowers that one could find in any British field.

"Isn't he a dream?" Helen whispered.

"He can't be as pure as he's rumoured to be," Stephanie said. "I'll join the adoring women."

Helen stared at her, then laughed. "Well, you be sure and let me know how it turns out."

Stephanie merely smiled and remained in her seat. The crowd filed out until there were only a few left. She waited still longer, but when she arose and went backstage, she found Tremayne still with a small group of women, only four, but they surrounded him. Stephanie saw at once that he was being patient but would like to end the conversation. She waited as he broke free from the last one and then quickly entered and shut the door of his dressing room. Without delay, Stephanie walked over and tapped on the door. It opened almost at once, and she saw Tremayne frown — but immediately his mobile features formed into a smile of sorts.

"Yes, madam?"

"I'm Lady Stephanie Welles, Mr. Tremayne. Could you spare me a few moments?"

"Why —" Tremayne hesitated and then shrugged. "Come in, Lady Stephanie."

Stephanie stepped inside and glanced around the room. It was cluttered with the paraphernalia of the acting trade, costumes hanging from hooks, a large dressing table with a square mirror illuminated the gaslight. She turned suddenly and said, "I know you must be weary of hearing this, but I simply had to come and tell you how much I enjoyed your performance."

"Very kind of you to say so."

The words were really a dismissal, Stephanie knew, but she was an accomplished woman where men were concerned. There was a way to gain this man's attention, and she set out to find it. She became aware that he was being patient, that she was just another stagestruck woman to him. This angered her for some reason, but she persisted.

Finally a knock sounded at the door, and

Tremayne said, "Excuse me, Lady Stephanie." He went to the door, opened it, and began a short conversation with a man about the lighting for the next performance. Stephanie saw that he had taken off the belt with the dagger and jewelled scabbard. It was hanging now on a hook almost hidden by his black cloak. Quickly she reached out, removed the knife, and concealed it in her reticule. When he turned back, she said quickly, "I've taken enough of your time, Mr. Tremayne. My congratulations on your success."

Relief showed itself in Tremayne's face. "Very handsome of you to say so. I'm glad you enjoyed the performance. It's really a fine company."

"Yes, it is. Good evening, sir."

"Good evening."

She reached the door, then turned and said, "My husband and I are having a dinner for a few people at our home on Sunday night. Let me invite you."

"I would be happy to, Lady Stephanie, but I'm sorry to tell you I already have an engagement."

"Well then, perhaps another time." Stephanie smiled and left the room. She made her way out of the theatre, and she found her carriage waiting. She took the

27

coachman's hand, got inside, and immediately took the dagger out and looked at it. It was a handsome, rather fancy knife with jewels in the handle. She held it all the way to her home on Park Lane, the most fashionable address in London, bordering Hyde Park. She got out of the carriage and went in the house, and her maid Marie was waiting for her. Marie had orders always to wait up even when her mistress stayed out late.

"I'm tired, Marie. Help me get ready for bed."

"Yes, ma'am."

Lady Stephanie climbed the winding stairs and asked as Marie followed her, "Did anyone call?"

"No, ma'am, not tonight."

Going into her bedroom, which was quite overwhelmed with ribbons and laces, velvets, swags, tassels, ruffles, and broaches, she began to undress. She washed her face, and Marie fixed her hair for the night and helped her put on her nightgown. "That'll be all for tonight, Marie."

"Yes, ma'am. I put your sleeping potion there on the table."

"Thank you, Marie. You may go now."

As soon as the maid left, Lady Stephanie turned and took the knife out of the drawer where she had slipped it. She looked at it for a long time and then smiled. "He's a man," she said softly. "He can't be as holy as Helen says, but I'll find out, won't I?" She put the knife down on the dressing table, picked up the sleeping potion, and drank it off. She took it every night, for she did not sleep well.

Getting into bed, she lay there and waited until finally the potion began to take effect. It was a pleasant sensation, as if she were floating somehow suspended and motion- less. She fell asleep, or at least into that twilight zone that precedes sleep, and as she did, a strange dream formed in her mind. She often dreamt, and unlike most people she always remembered her dreams the next morning.

This dream was about Dylan Tremayne. Her lips turned upward in a smile as she lay between the silken sheets, and she saw Dylan approaching her. She felt a sensuous pleasure as he came forward, his dark eyes gleaming and his mouth wide in a smile. Then she saw a shadow surround Dylan, and it troubled her. It came forward, and she closed her eyes and actually lifted her arm, for the sleep was not complete. She fully expected to dream that he would take her in his arms, but instead, suddenly she felt something on her throat as hot as a branding iron and as cold as ice.

Lady Stephanie Welles opened her eyes, and when she saw the face close to hers and felt the blood running down her neck and over her shoulders, her last thought was, *This is no dream . . . !*

TWO

The theatre was not one of Serafina Trent's favourite activities. She would much prefer to be in a laboratory dissecting a corpse. At least, that had been her preference at one time. Since she had met Dylan Tremayne, however, the theatre had taken on a new dimension for her, and now as she sat in the Old Vic watching the play unfold, she wondered at herself. *I've changed so much since I met Dylan. I never thought a man would be able to have such an effect on me, but he has. I don't know if that's good or bad, but he's like no other man I ever met — whatever that means.*

"Look, I think it's almost time for the second half." Lady Margaret Acton, who was sitting beside Serafina, was studying the viscountess carefully. Lady Margaret was Serafina's closest friend. Part of that was due to the fact that she had two children, Charles and Roger, who were favourite playmates of Serafina's son, David. But Margaret and her boys had been away for a while, visiting Margaret's ailing mother, and David had sorely missed them. Serafina had missed Margaret even more than she expected. She fondly looked at her friend's clear brown eyes and thick brown hair. She was very lively and vivacious, far more outgoing than Serafina herself, and Serafina admired her immensely.

"I'm enjoying this play," Margaret said, "but I must confess I can't watch anyone but Dylan. He's such a handsome fellow!"

"Oh yes, he is," Serafina said, nodding her agreement, "but I don't believe he ever thinks about that."

"Well, that's very rare. Usually good-looking men are proud as peacocks. Can't pass a mirror without preening."

"Dylan doesn't even think to get his hair cut. I have to remind him sometimes." Serafina leaned back in her seat and ran her eyes over the audience, then turned back to Margaret. "So nice that we're able to go out and do this. We owe it all to Irene."

"Yes, she's the best sister anyone could ever have. She's been so sad — unable to have children and then losing her husband." Margaret shook her head, and grief passed her eyes briefly. "She's thrown herself into

taking care of Charles and Roger. Sometimes I think she's more of a mother to
them than I am."

"Don't say that," Serafina said quickly.
"You're just different, that's all. She likes to
stay home, and you like to go out — and
you enjoy so many things."

"Yes, I suppose I do. Too bad that Fredrick doesn't."

Serafina was surprised. Margaret seldom
mentioned her husband, Count Fredrick
Acton. It was obvious to most that the two
did not have a good marriage. Fredrick
stayed on long hunting trips to the south of
England and often went to France. He was
actually home very little, and Serafina was
aware that this hurt Margaret. There was
nothing to say about it, however, for Fredrick was not about to change his habits nor
modify his drinking problem. Margaret
moved uncomfortably and looked up.
"There's the Prince of Wales and that
American actress with him. He doesn't have
any shame about appearing with his mistresses. Makes no secret of his affairs at all."

"I'm sure the Queen and Prince Albert
are terribly hurt by him."

"I feel sorry for the poor man."

"For who?"

"For the Prince of Wales, of course. Queen

Victoria is a young woman. She could live to be an old lady, and until she dies the Prince has really nothing to do."

"He could find something useful to do if he wanted to."

"I suppose so, but what he's interested in mostly is gambling and races and fast horses — and faster women." Margaret winked roguishly. "That's the sort of man we can look forward to as king one day."

Serafina stirred restlessly in her seat. She was enjoying the play. She had read it and had seen it twice performed. She was well aware that Dylan dominated the role and also the audience.

"It is strange the way you got interested in Tremayne. Half the women in London are chasing around after him now, and you have him all to yourself."

A slight flush touched Serafina's cheeks. Although she had no real beauty, she did somehow have a sensual quality that did not pair with her scientific mind. She was of average height, and at the age of twenty-seven still had the figure of a much younger woman. She had dressed more carefully than usual, though she cared little for fancy attire. She wore a modest pearl grey skirt and jacket with dark green buttons and accents on the hem of the skirt and the sleeves and lapels of her jacket. A touch of delicate white lace edged with green showed at the opening of the tight-fitting jacket, and she had a peach cameo pinned to the lace at her throat. As she had been dressing that evening, she suddenly realised she had not paid so much attention to her attire in years, and it disturbed her and made her wonder if she had an interest in Dylan Tremayne that went beyond the ordinary.

"Women fall all over themselves for him. I heard he can't walk down the street without some brazen hussy making up to him."

"I know," Serafina said, "but he doesn't have anything to do with them."

"That's hard to believe."

"He's very religious, Margaret. I'm not, as you know, so it's amazing that the two of us have gotten along so well."

"Does he preach at you?"

"Not exactly. He talks about the things in the Bible, and he'll say something some-times like 'The Lord told me to go to the mission,' which is a little bit frightening to me."

"You think God really talks to him?"

"Oh, not in an audible voice. He's got a lot of Methodist friends, although I'm not certain he's a part of it, but they believe like the Quakers in being led by the Spirit."

"Well, he doesn't look like a preacher."

The curtain opened then, and the two women sat through the second half of the play. Lady Margaret was enamoured and insisted on whispering comments to Serafina as the play went on. Serafina disliked this, but she could not afford to offend Margaret, her best friend, so she endured it. Finally the play was over, and Margaret applauded as Dylan came back for several curtain calls. "He's beautiful, Serafina! Look at those tights! No wonder every woman in London is dreaming of him — and you have him!"

Serafina could not keep the sharp tone from her voice. "I don't *have* him, Margaret!"

"Well, he comes to your house all the time."

"Some of that was because we were working on cases together. He helped me clear my brother, Clive, when he was charged with murder. I could never have done it without him. He took me into the worst parts of London you can imagine to find the real murderer. The other thing is, it's David he comes to see."

"Really?"

"Yes. He plays with him as if he were David's age. I've seen him sitting on the floor sprawled out playing with toy soldiers for hours."

"I'll be happy to let him come to see Charles and Roger if you'll share him with me."

Serafina could not help laughing at the roguish expression. "You are just *awful*, Margaret!"

"I suppose so," Margaret sighed, "but, dear me, just look at those tights!"

Finally the curtain calls were over, but during one of them Dylan Tremayne had spotted Serafina and had smiled directly at her and bowed. Everyone in the theatre craned their necks to see who the actor was smiling at, and Margaret said, "Every woman in this theatre hates you, Serafina."

"Don't be boorish. We're different in every way. Come along."

"But those tights, Serafina. Couldn't you bend a little bit for those tights?"

"We're going home now. We have a full day with the children tomorrow."

"You're not going backstage?"

"Certainly not!"

"I suppose it would do me no good to go, but if you weren't here, I think I'd take my chances."

Serafina laughed. "You'd be wasting your time. I tell you, Dylan Tremayne is not interested in women. He's interested in God."

Margaret sighed. "That's too bad, isn't it?"

Breakfast at Serafina's home was a rather large but informal affair. The table was more crowded than usual with Margaret and her children. Septimus and Alberta sat at opposite ends of the table, and Aldora, Serafina's younger sister, sat at her father's right. They had filled their plates, and the maid continued to bring food to them. The sideboard was laden with chafing dishes filled with eggs, meat, vegetables, and various pastries and breads. On the table were frequently renewed pots of tea, dishes of preserves, butter, fresh fruits, and sweetmeats. David was sitting next to Serafina, as he always did, and he was demolishing the fairy cakes that he loved and that the cook, Nessa Douglas, insisted on making for him. Serafina had warned Nessa she was spoiling the boy, and Nessa had said, "Nonsense! He deserves the best I can give him, the sweet little fellow."

The three children had been carrying the burden of the conversation, talking about the games they had been playing and the activities they had engaged in while their mothers had gone to the theatre, but David suddenly looked up and said, "Mum, is Mr. Dylan coming today?"

"Not today. He's in his play, you know. He'll be here next Sunday."

"Will he stay long?"

"Well, there's no performance on Sunday, so he'll spend the night."

Aldora, whom family and friends called Dora, spoke up quickly. "Matthew is coming too." Matthew Grant had fallen in love with Dora practically at first sight. It had been a difficult thing, for women of Dora Newton's station did not marry mere policemen — a fact that Lady Bertha Mulvane now spoke to as she often did. She was the older sister of Alberta Newton and, at the age of sixty, was heavyset with blunt features and overbearing manners. She was possibly the most selfish, ambitious, and greedy person who had ever sat at the table at Trentwood House, home of the Trents and of Septimus Isaac Newton and his wife, Alberta.

"I'm ashamed of you, Dora!"

"Ashamed of me? Why is that, Aunt Bertha?"

"You know why it is." Bertha shook her head, and the wattles on the sides of her neck shook and trembled. "Because you persist on letting that *policeman* become engaged to you."

"But I love him, Aunt Bertha."

"Nonsense!"

"It's nonsense to be in love?" Lady Margaret spoke up. "I can't believe you said that, Lady Mulvane."

Bertha Mulvane had been the wife of a baron, and when he had died, the title passed with him. She had no right to be called "Lady," but she insisted on the title.

"It's a shame that we have to have actors and policemen invading our home."

Serafina wondered why it was suddenly "*our* home" when Lady Bertha had her own place. She forced herself to listen as Lady Bertha continued to speak, and once again Serafina could not understand the woman. She had watched her earlier steal a spoon — there was no other way to put it. She had slipped it into a bag she carried with her, and Serafina knew that somehow she had managed to take many things from the Newton household. Even some of their furniture had mysteriously disappeared and reappeared at Lady Bertha's small cottage.

Margaret finally turned and, ignoring Lady Bertha, said, "Why do you like Mr. Tremayne so much, David?"

"Oh, because he plays with me all the time. He does all the things I like to do. He can play soldiers up in the attic. He goes with me to find birds' eggs. He takes me fishing. And he tells the most wonderful stories!"

"He tells the most fanciful stories I ever heard of," Serafina said wryly. "I tried to get David to see that they're not good for him, but, of course, Dylan tells them so well it's like seeing them unfold. He reads him fanciful books too."

"But he's so much fun." David turned and said to Lady Margaret, "If Mum would marry him, he could play with me all the time."

Serafina's cheeks suddenly burned. "I'm not marrying a man just so you have someone to play with."

"Well, there are worse reasons for marrying a man," Margaret said. "Men marry women for their money and then pay them no attention. Women marry men for their titles and have no love for them at all. I would say those are worse reasons than marrying to get a playmate for such a good boy. You ought to think about it, Serafina."

Serafina glared at Margaret and knew she was being teased. She said quickly, "Children, go get ready."

"What are we going to do, Mum?" David asked.

"We're going to play croquet, and then we're going for a ride, and then for a picnic on the river. We'll have all day. Now, go."

After the company broke up, Serafina remained long enough to have a word with her aunt. She came and looked directly at her with an intensity that made Lady Bertha nervous. "Aunt Bertha," Serafina said evenly, "I'm going to have to ask you to stop talking about Matthew Grant in front of Dora."

"Why, I don't —"

"I'm not going to debate this with you, Aunt Bertha. The two are in love, and Matthew Grant is a fine man. He doesn't have a title, but I know plenty of men with titles who don't have his honesty and goodness."

"It's a disgrace!"

"This is a warning. You force me to speak plainly, Aunt Bertha. If I ever hear you speak slightingly of Matthew Grant or criticise Dora for her decision to marry him, you will not be welcome in this house. Do you understand me?" Serafina had used this threat before, and it usually had the effect of corralling Bertha — at least for a while.

Lady Bertha understood very well and swallowed hard, her face turning crimson.

She well knew she could not sacrifice her position in this household and her visiting privileges for anything. She could not speak but nodded shortly.

"Very well," Serafina said. "That will be the last we hear of this."

The day had been spent in every activity that would please the children. Serafina and Margaret were saying good-bye as the children were walking toward the carriage. Serafina suddenly reached out and said, "You're my best friend, Margaret. We must do this very often."

"I'm always willing. Perhaps you'll invite me sometime to meet the famous Dylan Tremayne."

"Of course. He'll be here Sunday night. You come. Bring the children, and you'll get to meet the famous Dylan Tremayne."

Margaret hugged Serafina and laughed. "He won't even see me."

She got into the coach, aided by the footman. When the door closed, the coachman spoke and the carriage moved away. Serafina's father came to stand beside her. He was a tall, gangling man, awkward in all of his ways — except with a scalpel or any other medical or scientific equipment. He had wild, fine white hair that would not lie down, a large head, and a very broad forehead. He usually forgot to shave and sometimes even to dress. He turned to the carriage and said, "That's a fine woman. Very fine children."

"I feel sorry for Margaret, Father."

"Why? They're doing very well, aren't they?"

"Her husband doesn't love her or the children. That's a load for any woman."

Septimus stared at his daughter, and he knew at that instant that she was speaking not of Margaret Acton's problems but of her marriage to Charles Trent. Both Septimus and his wife knew that the marriage had not been a happy one, but they had never learnt any of the details. He found nothing to say for a moment, and then he said, "I'm going to learn how to play croquet. I've got to learn to be more active in David's life."

Serafina knew her father was trying to make up the vacancy in her own life and that of David's, who longed for a father. "That will be wonderful," she said. "Come now. Let's go into the house."

THREE

"Superintendent Grant wishes to speak with you, Lady Trent." Serafina looked up from her book with surprise. "Superintendent Grant? Are you sure he doesn't want to see Dora?"

James Barden, tall and dignified, never showed surprise. He was one of the most certain people Serafina had ever known. "No, ma'am, he specifically asked for you."

"Well, would you show him in, please, James?"

"Certainly."

Serafina was puzzled, for she could not imagine why Grant would come to see her. Putting her book down, she rose and waited until he stepped through the door. She saw at once that he was troubled. "Is there something wrong, Matthew?"

"Could I talk to you for a moment, Lady Trent?"

"Not unless you call me Serafina. We're

45

going to be family, Matthew, so no more titles."

Matthew smiled. "That will be a little bit difficult for me, but I'll do my best." Grant ran his hand through his hair, which was thick and glossy and a beautiful silver colour. It was very attractive, although he did not think of it like that. He had sharp, penetrating hazel eyes, but Serafina could tell that he was disturbed.

"What is it, Matthew?"

The two were standing in the study where Serafina often retired to read. It was not a large room; most of the walls were covered with bookcases that reached to the high ceiling. Serafina had read most of the books. The huge marble fireplace sat dormant and imposing across from Serafina.

Matthew cleared his throat and said bluntly, "I've just come from a murder scene. Lady Stephanie Welles was killed in her home in her own bedroom sometime last night. It's a difficult matter, and I would like for your father to serve as the medical examiner."

"Well, I will go get him at once."

"And," Matthew said quickly, "I would like for you to come, if you would."

"Me? Whatever for?"

Matthew smiled slightly. "This is no

46

ordinary murder. It's the slaughter of a member of the aristocracy."

Serafina stared at him. "Her husband's in the House of Lords, isn't he?"

"Yes. His name is Lord Herbert Welles, and he's demanding we catch the murderer immediately."

"That doesn't usually happen."

"Of course not, but Lord Herbert's accustomed to having his own way. And the newspaper chaps are swarming. The public is demanding instant action. So — I can use all the help I can get." Matthew paused and looked at Serafina directly. "Besides, your reputation as a detective is becoming quite impressive."

"Oh, Matthew, you know better than that."

"No, I'm afraid I don't. There are some things I would like to have your advice about, if you wouldn't mind coming with your father to the scene of the crime."

Serafina was surprised, but she at once agreed.

"Good. I have a carriage outside," Matthew said. "I'll take you and your father to the scene and have you brought back. It's a matter of some urgency, you understand."

Septimus straightened up and gave Grant a

sharp look. "There's no mystery here about the cause of death, Superintendent. Her throat was cut. The murder weapon was left behind. I can't say if that was a slip on the killer's part or if he is daring us to find him." Septimus, who occasionally served as a medical examiner for the police or Scotland Yard, showed no emotion as he delivered this analysis.

"Yes, but in case it comes to trial, I would want to call you as a witness. Would you make any notes you need to, anything unusual about the murder? It would be very helpful. One thing that troubles us is that there were people in the house — servants, of course — but no one heard a sound. Wouldn't she have screamed if she were attacked?"

"That might have been impossible." Septimus shook his head and looked down at the body. "Look, the knife would have severed the vocal cords."

"I see. Well, we'll have the body taken to your home where you can do a complete autopsy."

Matthew supervised the transfer of the body into a vehicle driven by a brawny member of the police force. Septimus left at once to go with him. When Matthew returned, he said to Serafina, "I'm sure your father will do all that can be done in the medical sense, but I want you to look at the crime scene." He shook his head with something like despair. "It's confusing. I've never seen anything like it. Too many clues. I've made a list. Look, it's going to be a nightmare to follow up on these things." He handed her a sheet of paper, and she ran her eyes down the list:

- gold cuff link with the initials H. W.
- two ticket stubs, one to a circus performance, the other to a performance of Macbeth
- Victoria Cross medal
- woman's handkerchief with "Violet" embroidered on it
- one playing card, the queen of hearts
- two pennies with different dates
- picture cut from a book, of a woman in armour driving a chariot
- assortment of small bottles of all shapes and sizes
- poem on a scrap of paper

Serafina shook her head. "Some of these might be traced, but some would be impossible — these small bottles, for example."

"I know, but we have to try. What do you make of this picture of the woman wearing

49

armour and driving a war chariot?"

"It's a picture of Boadicea."

"Who was she?"

"She was an early queen in Britain, from a tribe called Iceni. When the Romans attacked her people and raped her two daughters, she raised an army and led them to battle against them. A very courageous woman, heroic, I might say."

She picked up other items seemingly at random, mentioning one from time to time. "Well, here's something," she said, picking up a gold cuff link.

"I noticed that. It's a very valuable one, solid gold, I would think."

"Yes, with the initials H. W. Probably belongs to her husband, Herbert, but it should be easy enough to trace."

She went from item to item and then moved about the room, her eyes going over the carpets and the wall. Finally she bent over and said, "Look at this, Matthew."

"What is it?"

"Some sort of white powder. Just a trace, but I'd like to know what it is."

Grant studied the tiny smear of white and said, "Could be something the servants use to clean the room."

"I don't think so. Look, there's a tiny bit of it on this Victoria Cross."

"You're right. But what does it mean?"

"I'm not sure, but we'd better search for any other traces of it."

The two went over the room but found no more of the powder. "Maybe it's a cosmetic, but I don't recognise it." Serafina frowned. "But then, I don't use a great deal of cosmetics. It seems the murderer is leaving a series of items here to confuse the police."

"Yes, and it will take weeks to sort all these things out, I'm afraid. But here, notice this." He removed an envelope from his pocket and gave her the single slip of paper. "This is the note that the killer left. It's a poem of sorts, though I'm no judge of poetry. See what you make of it."

Serafina took the paper and read the poem aloud:

Is this a dagger that I see for me?
This blood is not the last you will see!
Count the clues but no matter how you try
The lady will be the next to die!
Catch me if you can — you stupid weak
    policeman.

"Not much of a poem, Matthew," Serafina said as she studied it. "It's printed in block letters. It would be impossible to match it to anyone's handwriting."

"Yes, and the contents of it are frightening. 'Catch me if you can,' the murderer says, 'you stupid weak policeman.' I suppose that's me."

The two studied the poem, and Serafina made a copy and gave the original back to Grant. As she did, she said, "He's challenging you to find him." Serafina looked down. "And the next victim will be a lady."

"So he says. You'll need protection, Serafina."

For a time Serafina did not move. Then she lifted her eyes to meet Matthew's and said quietly, "You can't protect every lady in England, Matthew."

Grant quickly discovered that he had not underestimated the difficulties that lay ahead of him in pursuing the investigation into the death of Lady Welles. He had had two interviews with Lord Herbert Welles, neither of them pleasant. He was preparing for another when the Lord walked into his office, this time accompanied by none other than the home secretary.

"Good afternoon, Lord Herbert, and to you, Mr. Secretary."

"What have you found out, Superintendent?" Welles asked at once.

"The investigation is in its preliminary stages, sir," Matthew said carefully. "We're having particular difficulties because of the method of the killer."

"What sort of difficulties?" Welles demanded.

"As I told you earlier, sir, the killer has adopted a method of concealing his identity that no one at the Yard has ever heard of."

"What might that be?" the secretary asked.

"He brought objects and items of all sorts. As far as we know, most of them are unrelated to Lady Stephanie. We have to run each of them down, and it's a long list. But we're doing our best."

"Well, your best isn't good enough!" Welles replied. He continued to insult Matthew, and finally he shouted as he walked away, "If you can't handle a case like this, I'm sure Scotland Yard needs another superintendent!"

The home secretary, Gerald Ramsey, was a tall, imposing man but with a rather gentle manner. He nodded toward Welles. "I'm sure you'll understand, Superintendent, he's not himself."

"Quite understandable, sir."

"I never heard of anything like this. I don't know much about investigations, but what sort of items were you mentioning?"

"Items like these, Mr. Secretary." Matthew pulled the list from his pocket and watched as the secretary scanned it. "You see, most of these are rather ordinary items. Some of them are clues, perhaps, but many others are simply to throw us off the track."

"Well, Superintendent, this is not a very auspicious beginning to your career as superintendent."

"No, sir, it isn't. It will be very difficult."

"Do you have any suspects at all?"

Grant gave the secretary a direct look. "We have one, sir."

"You do?" Ramsey was surprised. "Who is it?"

"Sir Herbert Welles," Grant said lowly.

The home secretary's body jerked, his eyes opening wide. "Why — why, you can't possibly think that!"

"Most of the time, sir, when a wife is killed, the husband is the murderer. Those are the facts."

"For heaven's sake, Grant, be certain you don't say such a thing to anyone! The newspapers are already screaming for action. If they discover you're looking at her husband, it would be terrible."

"Yes, sir. I have all my available men out, each one trying to trace one of the objects you saw on that list, so far with no results.

Of course, it's early yet."

"It's not early for the newspapers." Ramsey shook his head sadly. "They're already starting, and they won't quit. You know that, I'm sure."

"Yes, sir, I certainly know that."

It was later in the day after the unpleasant interview with Welles and the home secretary that Sergeant Sandy Kenzie came in. He was a spare man of below-average height with sandy hair and a neat moustache. His speech branded him as a Scot the moment he opened his mouth. He had an odd look on his face, and he said, "Sir, I have something that may be helpful."

"One of the clues has been ferreted out?"

"Yes, sir. Here it is. The military medal that we found is numbered. You know the Victoria Cross is new. The Queen herself devised the decoration, the highest in the military. Several have been made, but they're all numbered."

"And who received the medal, Kenzie?"

"I regret to tell you that it belongs to General Leo Hunter."

"Oh my! That's a bad one!"

"I knew you'd think so." Kenzie clucked his tongue and shook his head. "It would be hard to arrest a national treasure. Ever since he performed so heroically in the Crimea, he's been the idol of the nation. I certainly hope he's not the guilty man."

"National treasure he may be," Grant said, his voice hard-edged, "but I'm sure he treasures that medal from the Queen herself, and it was found in the room of a murdered woman. I'll go see him at once. I'll be at his home if I'm needed."

"Come in, sir." The general stepped aside for Grant to enter. He looked elegant in a long black frock coat, a spotless white shirt, a simply tied black cravat with a small diamond stud, black breeches pressed to a knife crease, and black boots.

Grant stepped into the opulent drawing room of General Leo Hunter. The room was large, with windows along one side, and yet at first glance it did not seem so. The huge mantel dominated one wall and was flanked by bookcases to the ceiling. Dark upholstered armchairs were supplemented by very beautiful chairs with carved wooden backs like church windows. Everywhere there were ornaments, tapestries, and potted plants. Two magnificent bronzes stood on a low bookcase, and a marble ormolu-mounted clock sat on the mantel.

"Sit down there, sir," General Hunter

said. "Will you have tea, perhaps?"

"No, General." Matthew took his seat and wondered how to approach the situation. He stared at Hunter, who, at the age of fifty-six, looked ten years younger. He was a tall man with broad shoulders; dark hair, silver at the temples; and the most piercing dark blue eyes that Matthew had seen in any man. He looked the role of a hero, and he had been a hero in the Crimean War. The public adored him, and before making his visit, Grant had enquired quietly about what sort of man he was. He discovered several interesting facts. One, the general could be charming when he chose; two, he enjoyed women; and three, he was a widower. His wife, Roberta, was dead, and Grant found it particularly interesting that she was murdered by a burglar who was never apprehended.

"I have never entertained a superintendent from Scotland Yard."

"Well, I have never had a meeting with a general." Matthew tried to smile. He was trying to put into his mind a way he could approach the general, and finally he decided that the straightforward way was the best. "I'll get right to my point, General. Do you recognise this?"

Hunter took the object and held it up.

"Why, it's the Victoria Cross."

"Yes, sir. Very few of these have been passed out."

"Yes, I understand that. I was quite honoured to receive it."

"The medal was found in the bedroom of Lady Stephanie Welles, General."

"Preposterous!" Either Hunter was an extraordinary actor or he was truly surprised, for shock ran across his face. "There can't be too many of these around."

"No, sir, there aren't. This particular medal is yours. They are numbered, as you probably know."

"This is my medal? It can't be!"

"I'm afraid it is, General."

Hunter stared at Grant, then got up and walked across the room. He opened a drawer to a secretary desk and stared at it blankly. When he turned around, amazement and shock were written across his features. "My medal was right in this drawer. I always keep it there."

"When was the last time you saw it, General Hunter?"

"Why, I don't know. I don't look at it every day. I thought I would have it mounted, perhaps, when I had time." Suddenly Hunter drew himself up. "Does this mean I'm a suspect?"

"That's a rather strong way to put it, General, but we do need to know how your medal got into the murdered woman's room."

"Well, of course I would never wear this medal. That would be ostentatious, even for me."

"Could anyone have come in and taken it?"

"Well, certainly. The servants are in and out all the time. I have a great deal of company, and there are times, if they knew where the medal was, they could have taken it."

"Would you mind if I question your servants?"

Suddenly the general smiled rather grimly. "What if I did object?"

Grant did not hesitate. "Then, sir, I would have to do it anyway."

The general laughed. "Go at it, Superintendent. I hope you catch this fellow. Am I the only suspect, by the way?"

"No, there were many other items in the room. Evidently the killer was clever enough to get unrelated items. A few, like yours, were rare."

"Well, I hope you catch the fellow. I knew Lady Stephanie. A very fine woman, and her husband, I've met him several times too.

How's he taking it?"

"Not well."

"Too bad. Too bad. I'd appreciate it if you would let me know. I suppose you have to keep the medal."

"Just for now, General. It will be returned to you. Thank you for seeing me."

"Certainly. Keep me informed, if you will."

The attempts to sort out the meaningless items continued with Scotland Yard working around the clock. Kenzie came in late one afternoon and said, "Well, we identified this white powder. It's rosin. Acrobats use it to make their grips firmer."

"Yes, but what's it doing in Lady Stephanie's bedroom? She was no acrobat."

"Well, there was a ticket, sir, you remember, to the circus, where the fellow Henley does the performance on the tightrope and that horizontal metal bar. Perhaps we should go talk to him."

"So we have rosin and a ticket stub. Yes, talk to Mr. Henley and the other acrobats."

"Yes, sir."

Grant turned to his work, but he was aware that Kenzie had not left the room. "What is it, Kenzie?"

"We've got something else, sir. You won't like it."

"I like nothing about this case. What is it?"

Grant listened and saw at once that Kenzie was having a difficult time. When the man finally finished, Grant looked down at his hands and was silent for a moment. Kenzie didn't move or speak. At last Grant looked up. "You take Henley. I'll take care of this."

"Probably a good decision, sir."

Kenzie left, and for a long time Grant sat at his desk looking at the report that Kenzie had left. Then in an uncharacteristic gesture he picked up a paperweight and threw it across the room. It hit the wall, and Matthew Grant stared at the mark it made. He then rose, and the expression on his face was that of a man going to his own execution.

FOUR

The morning sun came streaming in through the open window, casting a pale yellow light on Serafina as she sat at her desk. She had been staring down at a sheet of paper for some time, but now she looked up and noted the tiny motes that seemed to do a fantastic dance in the beam of sunlight. The only sound in her room was the ticking of the large grandfather clock over to her left. She looked again at the sheet of paper, and her brow furrowed as she studied it. The list was composed of the items that had been left by the murderer of Lady Stephanie Welles. As Matthew had asked, she had pored over it and tried to impose some order upon it, but the murderer had been clever and there was no relationship between the items. Grant had every available man from Scotland Yard working on the case, and the newspapers were already having a field day — it was a sensational case, as it always is when a member of the aristocracy is brutally murdered.

Finally, with a sigh, she rose from her desk and left the room. She made her way to the nursery, David's playroom, and as she approached, she could hear Dylan's voice and David's laughter at something he had said. She passed through the doorway and saw Dylan sitting cross-legged on the floor, working on what appeared to be a kite. "What are you up to?" she asked.

"Dylan's making a kite, and we're going to fly it," David piped up. His eyes were alight with pleasure, and he nodded confidently. "And Dylan says I can fly it myself."

"It's *Mr.* Dylan, David."

"Mr. Dylan says I can fly it myself."

Serafina smiled and moved over to sit in a chair that was placed with its back against the wall. The room itself was stuffed with toys, and it was David's favourite room in the entire house.

She watched as Dylan began putting what appeared to be strips of paper on the framework of a kite. It was in the shape of a cross with an upright piece of very thin wood and the crosspiece not quite so long.

She knew Dylan was clever with his hands, and she asked, "How did you learn to make kites, Dylan?"

"Oh, I learnt when I was just a lad no older than David here. Made many a kite to fly high in the air, I have."

"Mr. Dylan, finish the story you started," David implored.

"Why, how do you expect me to make a kite and tell a story at the same time?"

"You can do it. I know you can. Tell it now, please, sir, please?"

Dylan cast a look at Serafina. He grinned at her, and a lock of his coal black hair fell across his forehead. He turned his head to one side and whispered loudly enough for her to hear, "Your mother doesn't like me to tell you those fairy tales."

"She won't mind, will you, Mum?"

"Go ahead. You'll tell it anyhow when I'm out of sight."

"You cut me to the heart, Viscountess," Dylan said, putting his hand over his heart in a gesture of overacting. "Strike me down like a dagger, your words do!"

"It would take a sledgehammer to strike your heart down! Go on and tell the story. David will give you no peace until you do."

"Right, you! As I was saying, David, when King Arthur was just a boy, nobody knew he was to be king of all of England, not even he himself. There was a deep mystery about his birth, and he had been raised by a wizard named Merlin."

"Was he a good boy like me?" David grinned mischievously.

"Oh, much better than you," Dylan said, winking slyly at Serafina. "He was a fine boy indeed. Always minded when he was told to do something. Never argued. So you see you've got a way to go before you're anything like the young King Arthur."

"Well, how did he get to be king if nobody knew who he was?"

"It's very simple. There was a huge stone, and there was a sword plunged into it, and everyone in England at that time knew that whoever could pull the sword out of the stone was to be the rightful king over the whole land."

Serafina listened as Dylan put the finished kite aside and now began to gesture, and his face was alight as he told the story. *He's a marvelous storyteller,* Serafina thought, *but I suppose that goes with being an actor.*

"Everybody came from miles around, David, strong men. There were knights of courage and boldness and strength in those days, so all the knights came, and all of them wanted to be king, of course. So they would all go to the stone and grasp the handle of the sword and try to pull it out, but none of them could do it."

"Not even the strongest one?"

"Not even the strongest one. There's more to pulling a sword out of the stone than you may think."

"What about Arthur?"

"Well, everyone had tried, and people were going home. Arthur saw that sword in the stone, and he walked over to it and something seemed to whisper inside his very head. *Pull the sword out of the stone, for you are the rightful king of England!*"

"And did he do it?"

"Yes, he did. He reached down, and the sword slid out of that big rock like it was made of butter. Someone cried out, and they all gathered around and stared at Arthur. One of the knights said, 'This can't be the king of England; he's only a boy.' But he had pulled the sword out of the stone, so he *was* the rightful king of England. Then all the people gathered around and began to shout, 'Long live the king! Long live the king!'"

Dylan leaned back on his hands, stuck his legs out, and nodded wisely. "That's how a boy named Arthur got to be king of England. But you see, God had chosen Arthur to be king, so there was nothing anyone could do about it. When God makes up his mind what a fellow is to do, why, it will be done."

"Is God only interested in kings?"

"Of course not. God is interested in everyone. Don't you remember, I told you when we were out hunting birds' eggs that God knows every sparrow that falls to the ground. He has a plan for all of them." Serafina watched David's face. It was an animated face indeed, giving promise of a handsome man in the years to come. His eyes were dark blue, and he had a way of staring at people silently at times, as if he were studying them for some reason. He was watching Dylan right now in that way, and she wondered what he would say.

"How will I know what God wants me to be?"

"Ah," Dylan said, nodding sagely, "that's where you have to search for God. There's a verse in the Bible that I think you ought to know. It says, 'It is the glory of God to conceal a thing: but the honour of kings is to search out a matter.'"

"I don't understand what that means."

"It's very simple. We're all put here in this world for a purpose, but God doesn't always tell us what it is, so we have to search for it." He leaned over and ruffled David's hair and smiled. "You remember how we looked for days trying to find a bluebird's egg?"

"Yes, I thought we would never find one."

"But we didn't give up, did we? When we didn't find one the first day, we went the second day and the third day, and we got very tired of looking for that particular egg. But we found it, didn't we?"

"Yes, we did, and it's there in my collection." Jumping up, David ran over and pulled an egg from a group. He said, "Look, Mum, here it is. It was so hard to find."

"It's a beautiful egg." Serafina smiled. "I know you worked hard to find it."

"Well," Dylan said, "if you and I would hunt so hard for a bird's egg, think how much harder we ought to search to find out what God wants us to do during our time on this earth."

"Is that what you do, Mr. Dylan?"

"Yes, indeed, David, and I want you to do the same thing. God has a wonderful plan for your life, and all you have to do is find it." He turned suddenly and faced Serafina, who was watching him in fascination. "There you are, Serafina Trent, another fanciful story from an actor fellow who has no right to be instructing others. I know you don't like fanciful stories, but I like them."

"I like them too, Mum," David piped up.

Serafina suddenly smiled. "I liked that one

myself."

"Come on. Let's go fly the kite," David said.

"All right, old man, we'll do it." Dylan got to his feet in one smooth, easy-flowing motion. He was, Serafina thought, one of the most graceful men she had ever seen. He was strong and well built, muscular, but still he moved so easily in all of his motions. She watched as the two left the room, Dylan carrying the kite, and David a huge ball of string. Napoleon, the enormous mastiff who guarded David as if he were the crown jewels, happily lumbered along beside them.

She moved over to the window, and soon they emerged from the big house and out onto the spacious green lawn. The trees had been cut back, so there was little danger of a kite being lost. She watched them and could hear their voices plainly. David asking question after question, and Dylan patiently answering them. Finally they were ready, and she smiled as Dylan manoeuvred the kite up into the air as David held on to the string. "Let out more string, Davey boy, let it out!" Dylan called, and then he moved quickly over to stand beside David. Serafina watched as the kite flew higher and higher, and the two voices made a pleasant sound on the summer air.

"What are you watching, Serafina?" Dora asked.

"It's Dylan and David. Dylan made that kite himself, and now he's teaching David how to fly it."

"He's a gifted man, isn't he?"

"Yes, he is. I don't know much about acting, but those who know say he's one of the best to ever grace the stage here in England. But I'm far more impressed," she said, "at how he won David's confidence and how the two have grown to be such fast friends."

The two women stood there watching, and finally Dora said, "I'm a little troubled. Could I talk to you?"

"Why, of course you can." Serafina turned and put her back to the window and studied her sister's face. Dora was a slender young woman, well formed, with a wealth of auburn hair and warm brown eyes. She was nearly nineteen and had always seemed almost childlike in her ways, but now Serafina knew she was coming into womanhood and had fallen in love with Matthew Grant.

"What is it, Dora?"

"Well, it's about love." She suddenly blushed and ran her hand over her hair in a nervous gesture. "It's just like magic to me the way I love Matthew and he loves me." Her voice grew warm and her eyes lit up as she began to speak of how she had been afraid of Matthew at first, but had discovered that beneath a rather stern exterior he had the gentleness she desired in a man. Finally she looked down and said, "But I don't know anything about love: What I'm supposed to do. How I'm supposed to act. I'm going to marry Matthew, but I don't know how to be a wife. Will you tell me, Serafina?"

Serafina could not speak for a moment. This was the one question she had hoped Dora would not put to her, but she had suspected it would come. She had been her younger sister's confidante for years, and now at this moment she would have given a great deal to have a ready answer. Her own marriage had been so terrible that she had nothing to share along those lines, and finally she said gently, "You'll find your way, Dora. You have a good, loving heart, and Matthew is a good man. So the two of you are going to have a wonderful life together."

Dora listened as Serafina spoke another minute, encouraging her sister. Finally, when Serafina finished, Dora said, "What about you, Serafina? Will you ever fall in love again?"

The question caught Serafina with the suddenness of a blow. "Oh, I don't think about things like that."

Dora's face showed disappointment, but she smiled and, after a few minutes more, excused herself.

Serafina returned to the window and stared down. She could hear the voices of Dylan and David as they flew the kite higher and higher, but a question suddenly had come to her. *Will I ever have love?* Ever since her marriage ended, she had tried to block out this question, to throw herself into science and into the work with her father, but now as she stood there, the thought came, *What would it be like to be married to Dylan?*

It was a question she had never thought she would ask, for viscountesses didn't marry stage actors. *Aunt Bertha would die of shame,* she thought, *and many others too.*

As she stood there, she fixed her eyes on Dylan, and a memory came back to her. Twice since she had known Dylan they had come to moments that she had not forgotten. In one of those instances she had been terribly troubled and shaken. Dylan had embraced her and just held her. She still remembered, even though it had been months ago, what it had been like to be held in his arms and comforted. The other memory was the time he had simply kissed her, and as she stood there, she remembered how she had surrendered to his embrace and how she had had to fight to pull herself back from any intimacy. She knew she was afraid of love, or perhaps it wasn't love that she was afraid of but just men. Charles had been a vicious man under a smiling exterior. He could be charming, and usually was in public, but she had dark memories of the intimacy of her married life with him. As she stood there at the window, her eyes followed Dylan's movements, and she realised that she had a longing for something in her life. Someone, perhaps, to share it with. She had always pushed away from any sort of surrender of this kind, and although there had been men who had come to woo her, she had never once been excited or tempted to marry anyone else. But now as she stood there at the window, she knew that if Dylan Tremayne moved out of their lives here at Trentwood House, David would not be the only one who would grieve.

"What were the two of you playing at so hard, Dylan? David went right to sleep. He hasn't taken a nap in ages."

"I think he's the one who tired me out," Dylan said. He was in the study looking at the books when Serafina returned from taking David to his room. "Did he seem okay?"

"Yes, but he was so tired he crawled into bed and went right to sleep."

"He's such a fine boy, Serafina, and he's going to be a fine man."

Serafina hesitated, then said, "You've meant a great deal to David, Dylan," and then almost involuntarily the next words came out, "and to me too."

"You say that now? Well, pleased I am that you feel that way."

The two were suddenly caught in a moment that neither of them could explain. It had happened before, and Serafina understood well that it was because they felt an attraction, but one that she thought could never amount to anything. There was too much space between them, too many differences — her bad marriage, Dylan's faith, and his uncertainty about his career. So Serafina was glad when Ellie Calder, the tweeny maid, came to the door and said, "There's a lady to see you, ma'am."

"Who is it, Ellie?"

"She gave me this card for you." Serafina saw that it was a plain white card with a single name on it: MARTHA BINGHAM.

"Do you know who she is, Dylan?"

"Never heard of her. Who is she?"

Serafina made a face. "She's a woman who's lecturing all over the country now saying that women need to have equal rights with men. She's been to see Lady Margaret, trying to enlist her in 'The Cause.' "

"Whatever can she want with you?"

Serafina smiled suddenly. "I imagine she's come to get me to join forces with her to put you men in your proper places."

"Sounds dreadful."

Serafina laughed. "Well, I'll still see her, I suppose. Show her in, Ellie."

"Yes, ma'am."

The two waited, and in a short time a woman came through the door. "Lady Trent, my name is Martha Bingham." The woman was rather striking. She was taller than average and had a fine figure. She was attractive, but her voice had a strident quality to it. "I apologise for coming without an appointment, but I felt I had to see you."

"That's quite all right, Miss Bingham. My good friend Lady Margaret Acton has told me of your work. Would you have a seat? This is Mr. Dylan Tremayne."

"How do you do, Mr. Tremayne?"

"I'm happy to meet you, Miss Bingham."

Martha Bingham, Serafina saw, had fixed her eyes on Dylan. She was accustomed to women looking at Dylan with all sorts of emotion. Most of them were overwhelmed by his good looks and his stature as an actor, but there was nothing in this woman of admiration. She eyed Dylan instead as one would eye an opponent.

"Shall I have tea brought in, Miss Bingham?"

"No, I would much rather get right down to business." She suddenly turned and said, "I prefer to see you alone, but if your friend here wants to stay, I have no objection."

"Well, perhaps it would be just as well if you state your business," Serafina said.

"Are you familiar with our movement?"

"I have read a little in the newspapers."

"Then you must understand how anxious I am to have women like you join our forces."

"What exactly do you hope to accomplish, Miss Bingham?"

Miss Bingham put her gaze on Serafina. She had strange, slate-coloured eyes, a hue that Serafina had never seen before. There was a forcefulness in her that could not be denied. Perhaps the fact that she was physically larger and obviously stronger than most women revealed some of the inner force.

"Women in our country are no more than slaves."

"Isn't that a little extreme?" Serafina said.

"No, it isn't. Why, we don't even get to

choose our names. I was given my father's name."

Dylan suddenly spoke up. "So was I."

The woman gave Dylan a quick glance and then shrugged. "Men just have no understanding of these things. A woman can't even own property here in this country without a lot of legal manoeuvring. Men can do anything they please, but women are kept at home to bear children and do housework."

Serafina listened as the woman continued to speak. There was an anger in her, she could see that, and also a strength that was undeniable. But finally she heard her say, "I was hoping you would come to our rally tomorrow in Hyde Park. It would be very helpful if I could introduce you as being a supporter of our movement."

"I'm sorry, Miss Bingham, but I will be unable to attend."

The woman's slate-coloured eyes seemed to glow, and her lips drew into a straight line. "I will hope you change your mind, Lady Trent. You'll always be welcome." She rose and nodded slightly to Dylan, then moved out of the room.

As soon as she was gone, Dylan smiled. "I take it you won't be joining the lady's army."

"Well, she has a point. Women are abused,

and there are some rights — the right to vote, for example — that I believe that women should have."

"I believe that too. I'm sure many men do."

"Not so many as you might think," Serafina said. "Women have a difficult time in many ways."

Suddenly Ellie was back. "Superintendent Grant is here, ma'am. He wants to see you and Mr. Tremayne."

Serafina and Dylan exchanged glances. "Show him in at once, will you?"

"Yes, ma'am."

As soon as Matthew Grant entered, Serafina saw that he was troubled. "What is it, Matthew? Is it a new development in the murder case?"

Matthew sighed and shook his head. "I'm afraid so, and this is not a pleasant one. It's you I've come to see, really, Dylan. I was told you would be here."

"To see me? About what?"

"We have been running down this multitude of clues, and we made a rather unpleasant discovery."

"Unpleasant? In what way?" Dylan asked.

"The knife that killed Lady Welles belonged to you," Matthew said directly. "It's the knife that you use in the play, you know, when Macbeth kills the king."

Serafina sat alert, and she turned to Dylan. "Where'd you keep the knife?"

"Why, with the other costumes. It was missing a few nights ago. I don't remember exactly when. I was ready to go onstage, and suddenly I realised that the knife was gone, and I had to get the prop man to find me another one quickly."

"Will he testify to that?"

"Why, of course he will."

"You surely don't suspect Dylan, Matthew?"

"No, of course not. It's just another one of these fantastic things. First we find the Victoria Cross belonging to a national hero at the crime scene, and now a prominent actor's knife is found there."

"Anyone could have taken that knife. The door's not locked, and people do come and take souvenirs."

"Well, the unfortunate thing is," Matthew said grimly, "a fool of a policeman let it slip that the knife belonged to you, that it was part of the costume you wear in the play. So you can depend on it — tomorrow you will be in the news, and then I'll have to contend with Lord Herbert, who is raving like a maniac for an arrest already."

"Are you going to arrest me?"

"Certainly not, but I just wanted to prepare you for what's going to come." He turned to say, "Lady Trent, have you made any headway with that list I gave you?"

"No, not really. If I ever saw a random list in my life, that was it. Whoever killed the woman had to have collected these things and brought them, somehow, when he came to do the murder."

"He must be insane," Matthew said, "but then, I suppose in some way all murderers are not quite sane."

The three stood there talking as Matthew asked the standard questions. Then he turned and said, "I'd like to see Dora before I leave."

"She's out in the back in the garden, Matthew. Let us know if anything happens."

"Of course I will."

As soon as Matthew left, Serafina turned to Dylan and said with a troubled look on her face, "This is bad, Dylan. You know how the newspapers are."

"And the public. Nothing more fickle than the public. A hero today, a murder suspect tomorrow."

"This murderer has already drawn two suspects: General Hunter and you. I wish it hadn't happened."

"God will sort it all out."

Serafina was struck, as she always was, at Dylan's calm insistence that God was in everything that happened to him. She did not argue any longer and had actually learnt to admire his steadfast conviction. Now she shook her head and said, "What I'm worried about is that in the note he left, he said he'd strike again. That will be hanging over our heads."

The two stood there for a moment, and then Dylan said heavily, "I think I'd better be going. Tomorrow won't be very enjoyable after the papers come out."

"Come back when you can. David misses you constantly."

"Yes, I'll do that." He suddenly reached out his hand in an unusual gesture, and she took it. He squeezed it slightly and said, "Be cautious, Serafina, but don't worry. God's going to take care of all of us."

FIVE

The face of Sir Herbert Welles was flushed with anger, and his voice was pitched high as he spoke to Matthew Grant. He had come into Grant's office making demands again, this time about Tremayne, and Grant, knowing the power in the hands of members of the House of Lords, had managed to keep his temper.

"Your work is not acceptable, Superintendent," Welles said, biting the words off as sharply as if he used a knife. "You should have made an arrest by this time. What have you been doing sitting in your office while a murderer is roaming the streets of London?"

"Perhaps you don't understand how difficult the situation is, Lord Herbert. It's always difficult to catch a murderer like this, but this one is especially a problem."

"What's the problem? You found the murder weapon, and you found the man who owns it," Welles shouted, his voice tight with strain. "Arrest the man! I demand it!"

Carefully Grant spoke, keeping his voice on an even plane. "I know you've been reading the newspapers, and I'm well aware that they are agitating for us to arrest Dylan Tremayne. But I can't do that, sir."

"You made that very obvious, and it's clear enough why you won't arrest him."

"I won't arrest him because there's not enough evidence to do so."

"That's not true, and you bloody well know it! You won't arrest him because he's your friend." Welles nodded vehemently. "You think I didn't know about that? Well, I do! He even stayed at your house for a time. That's the reason you won't arrest him."

"I would arrest anyone if I had sufficient evidence."

"You have evidence."

"No, sir, I do not."

"The knife belonged to the man. You've proven that. I read that in the papers."

"Yes, the knife belonged to him, or at least it belonged to the theatrical company of which he is a member. They own all of the costumes and all of the 'props,' as they are called. It was not a personal possession."

"But he had access to it. He carried it on the stage."

"Yes, Sir Herbert, he carried it on the

stage. That's what it was there for. I spoke to Mr. Elliot, the producer of the play. The knife actually belonged to his brother, Thomas. He had borrowed it for use in the play that Mr. Tremayne is now acting in."

"But it was in his possession."

"Not in the sense you mean."

"What are you talking about? He had the knife. Everybody knows that."

"The reporters of newspapers are rather simplistic, so let me explain —"

"You had better. I've been talking to the home secretary, and I've demanded action on this. Now, what have you to say for yourself?"

"In the first place, Sir Herbert, the knife was kept in Tremayne's dressing room, and the door was never locked. Anyone could have come in at almost any time and taken that knife, and I'm convinced that's what happened."

"You have no evidence of that."

"No, but I do have evidence of where Dylan Tremayne was on the night that your wife was murdered." He waited for Welles to speak, and when Welles simply stared at him in disbelief, he said, "We checked his movements very carefully. He was, of course, on stage until ten o'clock, at which time the play was over. He went out to eat with some of his fellow actors, and they were together until eleven thirty."

"They have lied for him, of course."

"No, sir, they would not lie for him, not those that I have mentioned. We checked not only the actors but others who were present. One of them was Lord Cherbourg. I'm sure you're familiar with his record. Lord Cherbourg said that Mr. Tremayne was with him until eleven thirty."

"But the papers say that my wife was killed sometime between midnight and eight in the morning."

"That's true."

"Then this actor fellow would have had plenty of time to come to my house, break in, and kill my wife."

"What would his motive be?"

"He's a maniac. I've had threats before, Superintendent."

"Well, as far as I can ascertain, there was no motive. Your wife did go backstage and congratulate Tremayne, but she remained only for a few moments and then left. That's when Tremayne went out for supper."

"But after the supper he would have had plenty of time."

"Yes, sir, he would have had time, but we know exactly where he was all that night."

"What does the man claim? I suppose he

has some lying actors, low-class people, to swear he was with them."

Grant ground his teeth together. "He was at the Water Street Mission from midnight until the next morning."

"The Water Street Mission? That's some sort of work carried on for drunks and harlots, isn't it?"

"It's a Christian organization. They try to feed and care for those who are unfortunate, yes."

"I refuse to believe that you are such a simpleton, Grant! You're going to take the word of those people? You're not fit to be superintendent of Scotland Yard!"

"Dr. Able Matson was there all night. I have his sworn statement that Dylan Tremayne never left the side of a dying man that Dr. Matson was treating. I suppose you have heard of Dr. Matson?"

Sir Herbert opened his mouth to speak but found that he had nothing to say. Dr. Able Matson was a nobleman and actually could have the title "Sir" before his name, but he preferred "Dr." All of London knew of his work, and his reputation was spotless.

"I refuse to accept this. I'm going to look into it further. I'll have a word with Dr. Matson myself."

"If you choose. I have his sworn statement

if you'd care to read that."

"I'll speak to the doctor himself, and I'm warning you. I'm expecting results from you, Superintendent, and soon!"

The door slammed as Welles left, and Matthew Grant went slowly back to his desk and sat down. He would have liked to have struck a mighty blow right between the eyes of Sir Herbert Welles, but he had more control of himself than that. He sat there waiting until finally he calmed and then went to the door and called out, "Kenzie, come in here, please."

He went back to his seat as Sergeant Kenzie entered and said, "I heard most of what was said. It was rather stupid, if you ask me."

"Don't let the reporters hear you say that about a member of the House of Lords — however true it might be."

"Of course not, sir."

Grant leaned forward and said quietly, "Kenzie, I'm giving you an assignment. I want you to go find out everything you can about Lord Herbert Welles and about his wife. Dig deep. Talk to the servants. Anyone who might know something."

Kenzie nodded at once. "You suspect him?"

"I think he's overreacting, Kenzie. A man

would be upset about the death of his wife, but from all I've heard of Sir Herbert Welles, this behaviour is not typical. I think he's putting on some kind of a show, and I want to know why. Get right to it."

"Tell us about the knife, Mr. Tremayne!"

Dylan had just stepped out of his carriage in front of the Old Vic. He found himself surrounded by a group of reporters, all of them shouting questions at him. This was not new, but he was sick of the whole thing. "No comment!" he snapped and pushed his way through the crowd, ignoring the pleas.

As soon as he stepped inside, he was greeted by Charles Elliot, the producer of the play. "I suppose you're sick of all that, Dylan." Elliot shook his head. "The newspapers wouldn't know truth if it bit them on the nose."

"I suppose that's the way they make their living."

Elliot was staring at Dylan cautiously. "I wasn't at all sure you'd come."

"Why would you think that?"

"Because it's going to be embarrassing when you go on the stage after the stories in the paper. We've already sold out every ticket, and they're not coming to see *Macbeth* either. They're coming to see the man to whom the newspapers have done every-thing but called 'The Slasher.' " Elliot came forward and put his hand on Tremayne's shoulder. "Are you sure you can do it, Dylan? It's going to be like throwing you to the wolves."

Dylan shrugged. "I'm the same man I was. It's my job, and I'll do it."

"Well, I've assigned some people to keep them away from your dressing room at least — the reporters, I mean."

"Thanks, Charles, that'll be a help." Dylan turned and started toward his dressing room. He stepped inside, but before he could even remove his coat, a woman came in. Lilly Clairmont, who played the role of Lady Macbeth, was older than she looked. She had cared for herself, so she was still able to act in younger roles.

"Hello, Dylan."

"Hello, Lilly."

"I saw the reporters out there like a pack of wolves. Why don't you deck a couple of them? That would discourage the others."

Dylan suddenly smiled. He liked Lilly. She was no better than she should be as far as men were concerned, but she was a good actress, and after trying Dylan's virtue, she had settled for friendship.

"I don't think that would be the answer."

Lilly came forward, and there was concern on her face. "We have a full house."

"So Charles told me."

"They won't be lovers of Shakespeare either, most of them. Can you do it, Dylan?"

"I'll do my best. It's my job."

"Have they found out where you live yet?"

"Oh yes, I can't get to the place. They hide and jump out popping questions at me."

"Come and stay at my place. They'll never guess you're there."

Dylan smiled, and Lilly could not help but notice how she herself was weakened by the smile. "Thanks, Lilly, you're a good friend. But God will take care of me."

As soon as possible, Grant called for a press conference, more or less. The reporters, sniffing the possibility of news, had gathered around, and Grant had said quietly but firmly, "I know you fellows are just doing your job, but you're not helping your newspapers any. You're going to have to print some retractions and make an apology, all of you."

Dave Ripton of the *London News* said, "Why should we do that, Superintendent?"

"Because, as I've tried to tell you, there's absolutely no possibility that Dylan Tremayne could be the Slasher."

"But the knife was his."

"The knife belonged to the theatrical company. Anyone could have taken it. You could have taken it, Henry." He had turned to a small man with a moon face and a pair of sharp grey eyes.

"But I didn't take it, so why should we print a retraction?"

"Because I have evidence from a most reliable witness that during the time the murder of Lady Stephanie Welles was committed, Dylan Tremayne was in the company of a very reputable witness: Dr. Able Matson." A murmur went around the crowd, and Grant felt a quick satisfaction. "So I want to keep you gentlemen informed and give you news as I can, but for anyone who doesn't print a retraction and an apology to Mr. Tremayne, I will see to it that he never hears anything from me again."

That did the trick. The papers apologised, some with rather poor grace, but at least it was done. The playhouse was still selling out, and the show was doing well, and Tremayne felt a great relief. He had never been afraid that he would be charged, for he well knew that there was no evidence against him, no motive, and he had an impeccable witness who would testify.

By Thursday morning, he could freely

come and go from his own quarters, and he was about to leave when he heard a knock at the door. *Who could that be? Not a reporter, I hope.* He went at once to the door and opened it and was pleased to see two women, Lady Serafina Trent and Lady Margaret Acton.

"Hello, Dylan, we've come to kidnap you."

"I can't imagine a more pleasant form of kidnapping."

"Lady Margaret, may I present Dylan Tremayne. Dylan, this is Lady Margaret Acton, one of your most ardent fans."

"Yes, indeed," Margaret said. Her brown eyes were sparkling, and she put out her hand, which Dylan took not knowing whether to shake it or kiss it, so he settled for a firm handshake. "The kidnapping was my idea. We're going to have tea with a rather select group of people — namely, Serafina and myself — and we want you to come with us."

"Why, I would be most happy to, Lady Margaret. Shall we leave now?"

"Yes," Serafina said, "the carriage is outside."

"Let me get my coat and hat and we're off." He turned but then wheeled back around. "I do have to make one stop. It may be out of your way. It's in the Seven Dials

District."

"Oh, we have time for that," Serafina said. "More of your admirers, I suppose."

"No, it's actually two old friends of yours, Lorenzo and Gyp."

"What perfectly charming names." Margaret smiled, her eyes sparkling. "They sound absolutely sinful."

"Well, they were at one time, Lady Margaret. They're both ex-criminals, but they've given their hearts to the Lord now and are serving him among the poorer people of London. Gyp could open any safe in London in less time than it would take you to powder your nose, and as for Lorenzo, he can become invisible, and I believe he could make his way through a keyhole. They were both very good at their jobs, but praise the Lord, they've given it up now."

"Well, I'd be happy to see them again." Serafina smiled. "I liked them very much."

"Very well," Dylan said. He picked up a lightweight coat, put it on, and then plucked his hat off of a peg and carried it in his hand. "We're off, then."

Lady Margaret sat fascinated during the carriage ride. She fired question after question at Dylan, and it embarrassed Serafina when she said, "I just love you in those tights. I think it's sad that English gentlemen don't wear them anymore."

Dylan laughed out loud. "I'm glad they gave you some pleasure, Lady Margaret."

When they arrived at the home of Lorenzo and Gyp, Margaret said, "I must meet these gentlemen."

Dylan hesitated. "It's a bit rough, ma'am."

"Good."

Dylan assisted the two ladies down and they turned. When he knocked on the door, it was opened at once by Lorenzo. The huge, burly man's blunt features broke into a broad smile, and his voice boomed, "Well, praise be to God and the Lamb forever, my dear brother Dylan. And who are these lovely ladies? Oh, I see Lady Trent. So good to see you again."

"How are you, Lorenzo?"

"The Lord has been good and gracious as always, and this lovely lady is . . . ?"

"This is Lady Margaret Acton. She's very anxious to meet you and Gyp. I've told her about your former activities, and she is delighted to hear that you have reformed."

"Reformed? No, indeed! Not reformed, Lady Margaret. Regenerated! Washed in the blood of the Lamb! Made pure in the garments of Jesus Christ himself!"

Dylan and Serafina exchanged smiles.

They were accustomed to Lorenzo's eloquent and florid descriptions of his spiritual condition, but they both could tell Lady Margaret was overwhelmed. They were waiting for the question, and shortly it came. "And may I ask, Lady Margaret, have you been born again? Are you on the way to glory?"

Lady Margaret was taken aback, but she said at once, "Yes, I've been a Christian for many years. Not as good a one as you, I'm sure, but I love the Lord."

"Gyp, do you hear that? Come out and meet these ladies." He performed the introduction, and the dark-skinned Gyp with a gold earring pleased Lady Margaret a great deal. Finally it was Dylan who said, "We'd like to stay and visit longer, but these ladies are taking me to tea. You sent for me, Lorenzo?"

"Indeed, I did. I sent for you because an old friend of yours is here."

"An old friend? Who is it?"

Lorenzo was smiling broadly. "You wait right here, brother, and you shall see." He disappeared into the dark recesses of the room, and Lady Margaret asked Gyp innocently, "Are you in fact a gypsy?"

"Yes, ma'am, and proud I am of my heritage."

"I think gypsies are so romantic."

Gyp suddenly laughed. "Well, the gypsy life is not quite as romantic as one reads of. It can be hard. Many people see gypsies only as thieves."

"I'm sure that's not true."

Dylan was waiting, and when the door opened he was surprised to see a woman come through. For some reason he had been expecting a man, but the woman who must have been in her late twenties was holding a small child, and she came at once to stand before him. He took her in quickly, for she had hair as black as his own and blue eyes. Her face was heart-shaped, and she was a shapely woman, her form not hidden by the cheap dress that she wore. Serafina was looking at the woman too, and her eyes narrowed when the woman said in a clear voice, "A good day to you, Dylan. It's been a long time."

Dylan could not think of a simple reply, and Serafina, who was accustomed to Dylan being quick-witted, saw that he was totally baffled by the young woman's words.

Suddenly the young woman laughed, and a dimple appeared in each cheek. "It's all alike you men are. You forget a girl the moment her back is turned."

"I'm sorry," Dylan said. "Would you

refresh my memory?"

"Forgetful, you are! Why, Dylan, you gave me your first kiss — or so you said — down at the deep pool in the river."

Lady Margaret was leaning forward, avidly taking all this in, and Serafina also was studying Dylan's face intently. Suddenly she saw his eyes open wide, and a smile came to his lips. "Why, it's you, Meredith Evans!"

"No, Meredith Brice now. I married Lewis Brice."

"My best friend! I'm so delighted to see you again, Meredith. Forgive me for not knowing you, but it's been a long time. Where's Lewis? Is he with you?"

"No, Lewis is in the cemetery next to his father and his mother."

A cloud crossed Dylan's face. "Sorry I am to hear that."

"He was the pastor of a small church, and I did what I could to help. We were planning to go as missionaries and proclaim the gospel of Jesus, but God saw fit to take him from me."

"I'm so sorry, Meredith," he said quietly, "but it is a delight to see you again. And who is this little one?"

"This is Guinivere. She's almost two now."

"Well, let me see this fine lady." Dylan reached forward and took the child, held her up, and stared into her face. Serafina could see the youngster staring with large eyes, and suddenly the little girl smiled. Dylan exclaimed, "There's a fine girl, you are!" He put the girl in the crook of his arm and said, "I'm so sorry about Lewis. May I ask what you're doing in London?"

She looked down at her hands. "Things have been hard in Wales. I came to stay with my sister Angharad, but we hadn't heard from her for a long time. We had had a few letters, and she seemed to be doing well. We had no place to go, so I finally got enough money saved to make the journey, but I haven't been able to find her."

"Meredith came to one of our services, Brother Dylan," Lorenzo said, "and she's been staying here."

"I've imposed on these gentlemen, but I've got to find work until I can find Angharad. I have a little one to care for, don't I?"

Dylan, still holding the child, said to Serafina and Margaret, "Ladies, I'm so sorry, but I must see what I can do about this."

"Of course, Mr. Tremayne," Margaret said. "If we can be of any assistance, you'll let us know."

"That I will, Lady Margaret. Lady Serafina, I know you'll understand."

"Yes, of course." She turned to Meredith and said, "As Lady Margaret says, we'll do anything we can to help you and your beautiful daughter."

"Oh, there's kind you are, all of you!" Meredith exclaimed, and her face lit up. "I — I must admit my faith was growing a bit weak. Lorenzo and Gyp have been so kind, but I've been an imposition."

"Not a bit of it, not a bit!" Lorenzo boomed. "But I'm telling you this: your old friend Dylan is quite a detective, and Lady Serafina there, why, she could go to work for Scotland Yard if she put her mind to it."

Serafina and Margaret made their good-byes and left the house. They got into the carriage, and as soon as they moved forward, Margaret began talking excitedly. "What a romantic thing! Isn't she a beautiful woman?"

"Very attractive."

Margaret stared at her. "What's wrong? You seem discouraged."

"Dylan is easily swayed. He tends to jump into things sometimes."

"You think the woman is going to impose on him? She didn't seem like that kind to me."

"Well, Dylan is so emotional."

"They were childhood sweethearts apparently."

Serafina smiled, but her smile was not altogether easy. "I wonder, Margaret, if he would have been so quick if she had been a plain woman instead of the beauty she is."

"Shame on you, Serafina! I think he would. He just seems like that kind of man."

Serafina was quiet while Margaret spoke on, and finally she burst out, "She's too attractive to be a minister's wife."

Margaret suddenly laughed. "Well, dear, she can't help it if she's attractive. So she got Mr. Tremayne's first kiss and maybe not the last one."

"Oh, don't be foolish! He's as you say — that kind of man. Always wanting to help everybody. So he'll help her find her sister, and that will be it."

Margaret knew her friend very well. "You seem jealous."

"Don't be silly, Margaret! That's the most foolish thing I ever heard you say. That was a long time ago. They were just children."

"Well," Margaret said, tapping her chin thoughtfully, "she's not a child any longer, is she?"

Six

Superintendent Matthew Grant greeted his three visitors, or rather two and a half visitors, with curiosity. Dylan brought a young woman who was holding the hand of a child with black, curly hair and brown eyes, and for one moment the thought sprang to Grant's mind that Dylan had found a lost wife. He got this idea primarily because of the proprietary air that the young woman cast on Dylan. *She is a good looker,* Grant thought, *but good-looking women are always drawn to Dylan.*

"Good afternoon, Dylan. What can I do for you?"

Dylan shifted his feet and said rather quickly in a tone more nervous than usual for him, "I have someone I want you to meet, Superintendent. This is Meredith Brice, and this fine young lady is Guinivere, known as Guin for short."

Matthew nodded toward the young

woman and managed to conceal his curiosity. "I'm happy to know you, Mrs. Brice."

"Thank you, Superintendent." She smiled, and two dimples appeared — one on each cheek.

"Mrs. Brice is an old friend of mine from Wales," Dylan said quickly. "She came over to live with her sister, but she hasn't been able to find her. I thought, Superintendent, that you might be able to give us a hand."

"Well, I'll certainly do what I can. Sit down, Mrs. Brice, and let me get a few of the facts."

Dylan said, "Come here, little one. Sit on my lap, and I can admire you."

The child smiled and came to him easily. Matthew had always noticed the easy way Dylan had with children. They seemed as drawn to him as good-looking women. He began to ask questions about Meredith's sister, last known address, description, full name, married state, and finally he nodded and said, "Well, that will give us something to go on, Mrs. Brice. When was the last time you saw your sister?"

"Oh, it's been five years, sir. She is a little older than I am, and she left to marry."

"Have you heard from her recently?"

"No, sir, not recently. She did write when she first got here, but then the letters seemed to fade away. Very worried about her, I am."

"I'll see what I can do. I'll see that your description of her is given to all the policemen on the street."

"Thanks, Matthew," said Dylan. "If you'll wait in the carriage, Meredith, I need to speak with the superintendent for a moment."

"Of course, Dylan. Come along, Guin."

As soon as the woman and child were outside, Grant gave Dylan a wicked smile. "So — are you going to be comforting the widow Brice, Dylan?"

"Don't talk like a fool."

"Well, if you do, Lady Serafina will be jealous."

Dylan's face flushed, and he glared at Matthew angrily. He turned around and walked off, ignoring Grant's laugh that followed him.

As soon as the man was gone, Kenzie entered and cast a look after the pair. "Who was that with Mr. Tremayne?"

"Long-lost sweetheart. A widow now. We're supposed to see if we can find her sister. Here's all the information. Print it up and give it to all the men on the streets."

"Fine-looking woman."

"Oh, Dylan never fools with a woman unless she's absolutely beautiful. What do you have for me, Kenzie?"

"Well, sir . . . ," Kenzie said deliberately. He had a habit of twisting his square frame into some sort of snakelike appearance and of running his hands through his sandy hair. He did so now, and there was a smile on his face. "I have a bit of news for you, Superintendent. You remember you asked me to look into Lord Herbert and his wife?"

"Yes." Grant was instantly all attention. "What have you found out?"

"Nothing for a while. I'm afraid I had to be a bit of a deceiver."

"You, a deceiver! I can't believe it. A good Presbyterian like you, Kenzie?"

"It's part of the job, don't you see, Superintendent? In any case, the cook at the Welles household is a fine woman. I sat in her kitchen, and we had quite an interesting talk along with some of the best angel cake I ever had in my life."

"What did you find out?"

"It wasn't too easy. Alice Taylor is not a loose talker. I had to be very clever to get it out of her, romance her a little, you know."

"I didn't know this was in your character, Kenzie." Matthew Grant was amused. He knew Kenzie had a sharp, penetrating mind, but he was, in fact, an ardent Presbyterian and, as far as Grant could discover, had never done anything deceitful since he had known him. "What did you find out?"

"Well, I got it out of Alice that Lady Welles was not altogether a moral woman."

"Not a good Presbyterian, eh?"

"No, indeed, sir. As a matter of fact, she hinted on the first talk we had that the woman had no morals where men were concerned. Then on the next talk she came right out and admitted it."

"Anything else?"

"Yes, sir. A few nights before the murder, Lady Welles and her husband had a furious argument. Alice said she was afraid they were going to shoot each other. It was very bad, she said. Apparently they both have quite a temper."

"I see." Grant stood quietly for a moment assimilating the information. His mind was like a machine, in a way, taking facts in, never forgetting them, and in some way putting them together in a way that made sense to him. "I think you're going to have to do a little more romancing, Kenzie."

"How's that, sir?"

"We need to know the name, or names perhaps, of any men that Lady Welles was seeing."

"I'll do my best, sir."

"Perhaps you need to take Miss Alice some flowers or some small gift like that."

"Oh, that would not be at all in keeping . . ."

"Then tell her she has pretty eyes. With a ladies' man like you, Kenzie, I certainly don't need to give you any advice."

"I'll do my best, sir."

"Too bad he's a Presbyterian," Grant said as soon as Kenzie left. "He needs a little bit more deceit in him than a good Presbyterian is supposed to have."

David's eyes glowed with excitement, and he came running up to grab his mother by the hand. "Mum, can I take some of my toys with me?" The morning sun slanted through the window, illuminating his face and emphasizing the eagerness in his bright blue eyes.

"No, indeed, I'm sure Lady Margaret's children will have all the toys you need."

"How long are we going to stay?" David demanded. He had been excited when his mother told him they were going for a visit to Lady Margaret's house, and had piled questions on her.

"Just until late afternoon. They'll be coming to spend the weekend with us next week."

"Lady Trent, the carriage is waiting," Louisa Toft, Serafina's maid, came to say.

"Oh, tell them we'll be right there, Louisa."

"Yes, ma'am."

"Come along, David. We don't want to keep Miss Margaret waiting."

The two had made all preparations, and Peter Grimes helped them into the carriage, saying, "Have a good visit, Lady Trent."

"Thank you, Peter. You keep an eye on things while I'm gone."

"Oh yes, ma'am, I surely will."

David talked steadily all the way to the Acton town house, and as soon as the carriage stopped, he was greeted by the Acton children, Charles and Roger. They pulled him off at once, and Margaret laughed. "We won't be troubled with entertaining them, I think. Come inside, Serafina. I'm dying for tea."

The two entered the house and soon were being served tea by a pretty maid. The room was pleasant, furnished in cool greens and filled with sunshine. There was a large fireplace of polished marble, and on the walls were Dutch pastoral scenes with cows. The two women talked as they sipped their tea and nibbled at tiny fairy cakes. Serafina felt comfortable in the room and with Margaret's company as she did no other place outside her own home.

Margaret said, "I thought we might go by Lorenzo's. I've collected some clothes that I thought he and Gyp might find some use for."

Serafina smiled. "I'm sure that's a fine idea. I have done the same in the past. They are always helping women among the poor classes."

"They are really very interesting men. Were they really criminals?"

"Dylan says they were. Gyp was the best safecracker in England, he said, and Lorenzo, he won't even speak about his wrongdoing. But that's all over now. Come along. We'll pay them a visit."

They left the children in the charge of Irene, Margaret's sister, and soon arrived at Lorenzo and Gyp's door. As usual, Lorenzo's voice was booming, and he was full of all sorts of Christian greetings. "Well, bless the Lord, O my soul!" he said with a broad grin. "Glory be to God and the Lamb forever! Good to see you two ladies."

He ushered them inside, and Gyp was cooking something on the stove. "Hello, Gyp," Serafina said.

"Good day, Lady Trent, and to you, Lady Margaret."

"I brought some clothing that I thought someone might be able to use," Lady Margaret said.

"It's very kind of you to think of the poor," Lorenzo said sonorously. "I'm sure the ladies will be most grateful."

"I didn't bring any clothes this time, but I have a gift here in cash. Perhaps you can put it to good use."

"Yes, indeed! Praise the Lord, and thank you, Lady Trent. Gyp, we might know of someone who is in dire need."

"Always folks in dire need."

The door opened, and the two women turned to see Dylan stepping aside to allow Meredith to enter. Dylan was holding the little girl and said at once, "Why, Lady Margaret, it's good to see you, and as always, you too, Lady Trent."

"It's good to see you, Mr. Tremayne," Margaret said, "and you, Mrs. Brice."

"Thank you, ma'am." Meredith's face lit up with a smile, and she put her hand with a sort of possessiveness on Dylan's arm. "You'll not believe what this man has done."

"I think I might believe anything of him," Serafina said, eyeing the gesture carefully. "What is it?"

"He's found me a place to live and paid for it and given me money for food for myself and my little one."

"Now, Meredith, don't be trumpeting all that about. You're not supposed to let people know that."

"Oh, but, Dylan, so grateful I am to you. I didn't know what I was going to do." She looked up at him with something like adoration, and Dylan gave her a bright smile. "Well, I'm glad I was able to do something." He turned and said, "We've come for Meredith's things, and Guin's too."

"I'll go get them right now," Meredith said. She started to take Guin with her, but Dylan smiled and said, "I'll just hold this beautiful lady."

The child looked shy, but she reached up and put her hand on Dylan's cheek. She pulled his head down and whispered something, and he laughed. "I'll see about that." He winked and said, "She's interested in candy. Can you believe it?"

The two women waited, and Meredith returned rather quickly. She moved to stand by Dylan and gave him an adoring look.

"We'll have to run along now," Dylan said. "I want to get Meredith and Guin settled before dark."

"So good to see you again, Lady Trent, and you, Lady Margaret."

The two left, with Serafina and Margaret

following behind them.

Irene was preparing David for the trip home as Margaret and Serafina enjoyed a few more minutes together. Margaret leaned over and picked up a cup and drained it. "Those three children can tire a person out. If we didn't have servants to help — and Irene, of course — I couldn't handle it."

"Well, they are a handful," Serafina said. "It's so nice of you to invite us over. While you were away, David was so lonely for playmates."

"We're going to have to see that our children have more opportunities now that we're back." Margaret put the cup down and gave her a critical look. "Did you notice how that woman hung on to Dylan?"

"Yes, I noticed."

"Rather peculiar, wasn't it?"

"Women are always drawn to him, Lady Margaret. You saw them at the play."

"Maybe Welshwomen are just more free with men."

"That may well be."

Margaret saw that Serafina did not want to talk about it. She had her own thoughts about this woman whom she dearly loved, and she half suspected that there was more to Serafina's feelings for Dylan than she would admit to. Finally she stretched and said, "I admire Dylan's religion and his friends the same, Lorenzo and Gyp. What a strange name — Gyp."

"You admire that? They're really enthusiasts."

"I think sometimes I would like to be a Methodist and do some shouting. I get so bored sometimes with our services in the Church of England, don't you?"

"You know I don't have much religion. My father has educated most of that out of me."

Margaret leaned forward, and a serious light came into her face. "I think I need more of God like those people have."

Serafina was not able to answer. She, too, had been affected by the warmth of Dylan and his friends and the obvious pleasure they got out of worshipping and serving God. Usually when she thought of this, she put it aside quickly, for she had long ago put God out of her scheme of things.

Margaret was not finished, however, and for the next fifteen minutes she sat there talking about how she longed for a walk with God, and she finally said, "I'm going to one of the services at the house there to listen to Lorenzo preach. I think I would like it."

"Well, you'll certainly *hear* it. He's very loud, but he is a fine man. They helped me greatly when I thought David was in danger. They gave up everything and came and stood guard over him."

"That is wonderful. I wish you didn't have to go, Serafina, but I know you're tired." She got up, and Serafina rose with her. Suddenly Margaret came forward, embraced Serafina, and kissed her on the cheek. "You're my dearest friend, Serafina. I treasure our friendship more than you'll ever know."

Serafina was touched. She smiled and said, "That's the way I feel, Margaret."

David came in, begging to stay for the night, but Serafina said firmly, "Charles and Roger are coming to spend the entire weekend with you next week. Come along now."

The two of them left, with Margaret going out to the carriage to see them off. She gave Serafina a hug. "Good night, my dear."

"Good night, Margaret. It's been a wonderful day."

"Indeed, it has! We'll do it again next week."

Serafina got into the carriage with David and leaned out the window to wave to her friend. "I'll see you soon," she called out, and was rewarded with a smile from Margaret. She settled down in her seat and felt a sudden thankfulness that she had such a friend. But her next thought was of Meredith Brice and how she had looked with such adoration at Dylan.

Seven

A bar of golden sunlight streamed through the window from Serafina's right, illuminating the study with its clear, pure light. She glanced around and thought, not for the first time, how pleasant this room was. She loved books, and the study had been one of her favourite rooms since early childhood.

Two walls were lined with books from floor to ceiling. In front of that wall was a large oak desk with an orderly stack of papers on it and a small plain lamp. A green leather wing chair was nearly drawn up to it, two others on the far side of the desk. On each side of the fireplace was a massive portrait. One was of her father in full dress with his hair combed, for once. The other was of her mother, who wore a long, sweeping green gown and stood by a short Corinthian column that held a vase of red roses. Both portraits were excellent likenesses and expertly done.

A small sound from David caused Serafina to turn her head quickly and study the boy. Even as she did, she thought of how this world held nothing more treasured to her heart than this small boy. She smiled at the studious look that wrinkled his brow, and, as usual when he was thinking deeply, he took his right earlobe and tugged at it as if trying to separate his ear from his head.

The ormolu clock on the mantel over the fireplace sounded its steady ticking, and from outside the sound of a sweet birdsong drifted in, mellow and soft. The only other sound was the voice of one of the maids, dimmed by the closed door, and from far off the sound of a dog, probably Napoleon, barking steadily.

Finally David reached out tentatively and moved one of the draughts. He loved the game of draughts, known to the Americans as checkers, and he suddenly looked up at her and smiled brilliantly. "I've got you, Mum!" he cried.

For one instant Serafina could not speak. He looked so much like his father, and, as always, a slight fear touched her spirit as she had a faint premonition that he might turn out to be like the man she had married. But then he smiled, and the sweetness of it drove the fear from her heart. "Well, I

116

don't think you do. I'll just move here."

Instantly David crowed and, reaching out, took two of her pieces. "There! You see? You might as well give up, Mum. You've only got one piece left, and I've got three kings."

"Never give up, David." Serafina smiled. "No matter how hopeless it looks."

"Really? But it seems like such a waste of time."

"You never know what will happen."

"Go ahead, then." David watched the board intently, and with a few swift moves, managed to pin Serafina's remaining piece. "Now," he said triumphantly, "I win!"

"Yes, you do. You're a fine player."

David smiled brilliantly at her, and she admired him.

"You ought to write a book on how to win at draughts."

"I'd rather write a story about a princess who is captured by an evil knight."

"And I suppose she gets rescued by a very handsome, courageous knight."

"Yes, that's the kind of story I like."

"You've been listening to Dylan's stories too much."

"No, I haven't, Mum. He tells *great* stories. They always end happily."

"But life isn't like that, I'm afraid, David."

David looked at her steadily, and finally

he said in an altered tone that she seldom heard, "Was my father good at games?"

"You mean like draughts?"

"Yes, like that."

"He didn't play games much. I expect he would have been good if he had put his mind to it."

"Did you ever play with him?"

Suddenly one of the bad memories that lay dormant in Serafina's mind surfaced. The memory was as clear as a painting on the wall. She had been sitting across from Charles and had just beaten him at a game of chess. His face had turned red, and he had reached out and swept the chess pieces in a gesture of anger. Then he had slapped her face. His eyes had been blazing with fury, and she could resurrect the feeling the imprint of his hand on her cheek had left, although that had been years ago.

"Not very often."

David was silent for a time, and Serafina could see his mind working. She knew him so well. She was afraid at times, for this boy now fully occupied her heart and mind and soul. She waited for him to speak, and finally he said, "It might be nice to have a father."

"I suppose that would be good."

"Do you think —"

"Do I think what?" Serafina asked when he broke off.

"Do you think you might ever marry again?"

It was not the first time David had broached this question. She had seen it rise to his lips more than once, and now she knew that it had been something deep in his heart, and something he had thought about for a long time. It frightened her what deep thoughts he had at times, and she had no idea what to answer until finally she struggled to come up with one. "Your grandfather is like a father to you."

"No, he's like a grandfather."

Another thought seemed to be birthed within David's head, and she finally said, "What is it, son?"

The words came out reluctantly and almost as if they had to be pried loose. "Dylan is like a father." He was watching her eyes, Serafina saw, and he spoke quickly. "He takes me places, and he plays games with me — and he tells me stories. He's always ready to help me when I need something. That's what a father does, isn't it?"

Once again Serafina could not find an answer that seemed satisfactory. "I suppose so. Dylan is a good friend to you." Quickly she rose, saying, "That's three games you've beaten me. I refuse to be beaten again! Come along. Let's go see how the roses are doing . . ."

Septimus's hand moved with precision and firmness. The scalpel opened the body on the table in front of them, and Serafina quickly tied back the flesh with sutures. They worked quickly and easily; the dead body might have been a melon or a piece of cake for the emotion that didn't show in either of their faces. There must have been a time when Serafina was apprehensive about cutting into human flesh (even though it was dead), but that had been long ago. She had long since steeled herself to take no thought of what the human being had been like before death. It had been part of the process of learning that she had received from her father, and she often felt a wave of thanksgiving that she had had this man to teach her all that she knew.

"Does David ever talk to you about Charles?"

Serafina's head lifted, and she blinked with surprise. It was like her father, she thought suddenly, to come out with something totally unrelated to the affair at hand. She had thought his attention was totally on the body of the middle-aged man that lay before him, and the question had disturbed her and had caught her off guard. She looked up and studied her father. As usual, he wore a dirty white smock, and his hair was waving wildly as if in a stiff breeze. His eyes were dreamy, as they often were when he was dissecting. But she was so uncomfortable that she could not answer, and finally Septimus spoke again. "Your mother and I knew you weren't happy with Charles, but you've never told either of us what the problem was."

Indeed, Serafina had told her parents little of the horror that her marriage to Charles had been. They had been excited when she met Count Charles Trent, for he had all that a man should have — at least on the surface. He was handsome, cultured, wealthy, positioned, titled, and, of course, he had been pursued by half the women in the English court. She herself had looked forward with great excitement to becoming a bride, but the romance had never come. She thought of his cruelties and of the twisted part of his mind that he always kept hidden from others, allowing it to come out only when he was with her. She did not like to speak of these things and could not think of a proper answer. Finally she said, "He was not a good man. Not what I thought he was."

Septimus responded, "Well, your mother and I thought it would be a good match for you."

"So did I, Father. I had a rather romantic fantasy about marriage. I found out that I was very wrong."

"I'm sorry, my dear. I can see that you don't like to speak of it."

"It's best not to. Memories like that shouldn't be paraded, and I appreciate you and Mother not pressing me."

Septimus studied her and finally gave a weary sigh and turned his head to one side. "Do you think, daughter, you will ever marry again?"

"I doubt it. It's too big a gamble." Serafina was glad when the door opened and Barden, the butler, said, "Lady Trent, Superintendent Grant would like to see you."

Relieved to get away from the conversation that had shaken her, Serafina said quickly, "Take him to the study, Barden. Tell him I'll be right there."

"Yes, madam."

Grant rose as Serafina came into the room. He wore a soft, white silk shirt, a plain black cravat tied meticulously, and a casual jacket. His trousers were a rich brown and had a razor-sharp crease, and his black boots gleamed as if made out of glass instead of leather. Serafina thought, *He's one of the best-dressed men I've ever seen. No one would ever take him for a superintendent of Scotland Yard.* But his haggard expression countered the rest of his appearance.

"How are you, Matthew?"

"Well, not too well, I'm afraid." Matthew hung his head, not meeting Serafina's eyes.

Serafina looked surprised. "What's the trouble?"

"I'm afraid I'm the bearer of bad news."

Serafina blinked for a moment. "What is it? Is someone ill?"

"Worse than that, I'm afraid. It's about your friend Lady Acton."

"Why, she was all right when I saw her yesterday."

Matthew Grant was a plainspoken man, and in most situations had no difficulty conveying information. He was well aware, however, of the close friendship of Lady Margaret Acton and Serafina Trent. He had been surprised to find that the relationship between high-class noble-born ladies could be so firm and so very real. He had marked it often, although he had never commented on it, and now he wished that he were anyplace in the world except in this room, facing the woman in front of him. Finally he gave a slight shrug of his shoulders as if shaking off a burden. "I'm sorry to have to be the one to tell you this, but Lady Acton is dead."

For a moment Serafina did not understand him. The liveliness of Margaret on their last meeting leapt into her memory, and she was in a state of shock. She felt as if she had been struck.

"How can she be dead? Was she ill?"

"I'm afraid not, Lady Trent. She was murdered in her bedroom — exactly like Lady Welles."

"Murdered?" The word hardly would say itself, for Serafina's mouth felt dry and her lips seemed almost paralysed. She had been shocked by the murder of Lady Welles, but Margaret was more than an acquaintance. The two were almost like sisters, and now she stared at Grant, willing him to unsay his words. Finally she cleared her throat.

"You're certain, of course — but it's hard for me to believe."

Grant dropped his head and studied the carpet. "Well, you'll believe it when you see her, Lady Trent."

"See her? Why should I?"

"Because I need you. You knew her better, perhaps, than anyone else, and there are strange circumstances. I have little faith in the imagination of the average Scotland Yard inspector, and what we have here is something out of a nightmare. I hate to ask you to do this, but I'm sure you want to have her killer brought to justice."

"Certainly. Do you want me to go now?"

"If you would."

"Should I ask my father to accompany us? He's in the middle of an autopsy."

"No, not right now."

"Let me change clothes."

She moved quickly out of the room without another word, went to her own room, and changed to a simpler dress. She put on a rather severe chocolate brown velvet dress with a chatelaine pin as the only ornament. When she returned, Matthew was waiting for her, and the two walked out to the carriage he had brought. "Shall I order my own carriage, Matthew?"

"No, I'll bring you back when we're finished."

She took Matthew's hand as he assisted her into the carriage, and then he walked around and entered from the other door. He sat down beside her, and after he spoke to the driver, the carriage lurched forward. For a time neither of them spoke, until finally Matthew said, "What sort of a marriage did Lady Acton and her husband have?"

Turning quickly, Serafina had a strange feeling. He was questioning her as if she had special information. She and Dylan had asked that sort of question of many suspects, and although Matthew was aware that she could not be the Slasher, as the murderer had been called, she could not answer for a moment. Finally she said, "They didn't get along too well. That's no secret, Matthew. Everyone knew that."

"What was the trouble?"

"They never should have married in the first place. She had money, and he had none. So, after they married, for some reason, he felt obliged to bully her."

"You mean physically?"

"Yes, I'm afraid I do. I had seen bruises on her face that she tried to cover up but could not. When he came into a room, she would almost physically flinch."

"And everyone knew about this?"

"Their close friends did. He was sly about it though. He appeared to be very careful of her well-being and was always asking her if she needed another coat to keep warm or was there too much breeze. But the smiles that he gave her never reached his eyes. I think he eventually just grew tired of her and treated her like she didn't exist. Then she left to stay with her ailing mother for a while. Now that she is . . . was . . . back in town, he rarely is." Serafina paused and said forcefully, "I can't stand the man, Matthew."

"Do you think he's capable of committing a murder?"

The wheels were rumbling over the gravel and broken rocks in the road, and the carriage lurched from side to side as it hit holes created by the rain two days earlier. Serafina thought and tried to make herself as objective as she could. "I suppose most of us are capable of murder if the circumstances are right."

"That's an evasion, Serafina."

She did not notice that he used her first name. "I suppose it is," she said wearily. She sat back and looked out the window, and he questioned her no further.

The Acton town house was large and extremely gracious. The furniture was Regency and Georgian in keeping with the architecture of the house itself. As the two entered, admitted by a rotund butler with the mundane name of Smith, Matthew Grant asked a smaller man who was waiting, "Kenzie, has anyone called?"

"No, sir." Kenzie shrugged and said, "I didn't expect anyone, sir."

"Come along, Lady Trent," Matthew said shortly.

They climbed a winding staircase, and skylights gave the stairs excellent clarity, or would have during the brilliant sunlight. It was late now, and the darkness seemed oppressive to Serafina. They entered the room, and although Serafina had steeled herself against the sight she knew awaited her, still when she saw her friend lying in her bed laced with crimson blood, her eyes opened wide and a silent scream issued from her mouth. Margaret's throat was cut, and other slashes soaked the snow white shift she wore as if she had been in a slaughterhouse.

She moved closer and forced herself to look down. "The vocal cords were cut. She couldn't have cried out."

"The same as Lady Welles. I'm afraid there seems to be a pattern here."

Serafina tore her eyes away from the body, unable to look at it. Her training seemed to have flown out the window. "Why would you say that?"

"It would be better if there were no patterns. This proves that the killer is methodical. If there are two murders, there may be three or half a dozen. There have been other serial killers, as they're called, in England, like William Palmer, who poisoned a number of people."

Serafina said, "I remember reading about that trial at the Old Bailey. He was convicted and executed by hanging, wasn't he?" She shook her head and looked around the room, noticing what appeared to be unrelated items scattered over the floor. "Have you examined all these pieces of evidence?"

"I don't know as you could call them that," Matthew said grimly, his face set. "It's the same as when Lady Welles was murdered. They're all sorts of things that have no place here. I've made you a copy of a list that we compiled."

Serafina took the paper and studied it:

- small cameo of a woman
- newspaper article about Gerhard Von Ritter
- silver spoon
- silver snuff box
- fine handkerchief with "Violet" sewn in
- small kitchen knife
- small key
- queen of hearts playing card
- autographed picture of two circus performers, signed "To our good friend

Lady Acton"
- drawing of a woman holding a hammer and a spike

Serafina looked up from the list, a thoughtful expression on her face. "Some of the articles are duplicates, the handkerchiefs with 'Violet' on them. That must mean something, but what?"

"I noticed that, and there's the playing card, the queen of hearts. What does that mean?"

"I'm not sure. It may be just a trick to confuse us. I don't understand the picture of the woman."

"No, I don't either. We'll have to ask around." He held up a piece of paper. "And here's the poem."

"Another poem?"

"Yes, just like Lady Welles's murder. See if you can make anything out of it."

Serafina took it, and her eyes ran over it.

Hath not a Jew eyes?
If you prick us, do we not die?
The world is full of traitors,
And highborn women mere impersonators!
Better if they were off the earth —
Even those of noble birth!

"What do you make of it, Lady Trent?"

"It's like the other note. Terrible poetry, I think, although I'm no expert. That first line sounds familiar, but I can't place it."

"I can. It's from Shakespeare's play *The Merchant of Venice.* I don't know what it means though."

"Who said the line?"

"The merchant himself. A Jewish merchant. Mean enough fellow, but one felt sorry for him."

"Notice how the killer has put in a reference to 'highborn women.' And the two victims were both that, women with titles."

"Evidently the Slasher has a hatred for women who are titled." He gave her a quick glance. "You'll have to take precautions, Serafina."

The two talked about the clues, and finally he said, "I'll have Kenzie make a diagram of the room. And, if your father agrees, we'll move the body to his laboratory for the autopsy."

"Yes, please do. He will do it."

Matthew came forward, took her hand, and held it. It was an unusual gesture for him. "I'm sorry to put you through this, Serafina, but unless we catch this fellow, he'll kill again."

"We will find him, Matthew."

They walked out of the room, and the

butler, Smith, was waiting. "Where is your master, Smith?"

"He's at his club, sir, I understand."

"You're not expecting him home?"

"No, he stays there whenever he is in town."

This was no shock to Serafina, but Matthew's eyes narrowed, and he said, "Thank you." He turned. "I'll go break the news to him."

"I'd better stay here, Matthew. The children have to be told. It might be best if I do it rather than a man from Scotland Yard."

"What will happen to them?"

"She has a sister, Irene, who takes care of them. She never married. She's very devoted. I expect she will stay here as housekeeper and nanny for the children. But they loved their mother. They're going to have a hard time."

Matthew's eyes closed, and he shook his head. "What an inhuman beast!"

"*Inhuman* is exactly the word I'd use. You'd better go, Matthew." She watched as he left the house and went at once into the kitchen, where she made herself tea and set to thinking up a way to break the news to Margaret's children — but there was, she knew well, no good way to tell two children their mother was dead.

EIGHT

Serafina and her family arrived at St. Mary's Church, which was only a short distance from Prince's Road. Other members of the funeral party were filing in, all with the same pinched expression on their faces that one sees at a funeral. Several members of Parliament were in attendance, and Lord Herbert Welles, the widower of the murdered Lady Stephanie Welles, was seated in front of Serafina's family. Marchioness Rachel Reis and her husband, the marquis, were there. The marquis himself was a short man with black hair and black eyes that seemed too small for his frame. He was a successful arms manufacturer, but his wealth showed more in the dress of the marchioness than in his own. She was a striking woman of average height with black hair and grey eyes. Next to them were Baron Jacques DeMain and Baroness Danielle DeMain. They were of French descent. Serafina was surprised, however, to see Miss Martha Bingham, who sat in a group of women all plainly dressed, and all of them had a rather predatory look about them.

She was very much aware of Dylan, who had entered quietly. She was taken aback to see Meredith Brice sitting beside him. For some reason the sight irritated her, for the woman did not know Margaret Acton. Dylan had come to support Serafina, who had told Dylan much about her meaningful friendship with Margaret. Somehow, however, she was angered by the sight of the Welshwoman. Mrs. Brice was wearing a black dress, apparently new, and somehow managed to look very seductive even in such circumstance and in such costume. The family came in and took their seats, and Serafina's heart went out to Charles and Roger, both dressed as miniature adults in suits of solemn black. Count Fredrick Acton had a stricken expression on his face, though Serafina could not discern whether it was because he expected this day or was shocked by its arrival.

The service began and continued, as it seemed to Serafina, interminably. The Church of England certainly knew how to hold a funeral — if length and a solemn air were the prime requirements. On and on droned the speakers, and at one point Serafina wanted to jump up and scream, *This is Margaret! She's my friend. She was a lovely person, and I see none of her in what is happening in this church today.*

Somewhat shocked at her impulse, Serafina looked down to see that she was squeezing David's hand so hard he was wincing. She immediately released her grip, put her arm around the back of his shoulders, and whispered, "I'm sorry, Davey boy."

"It's all right, Mum." He managed a smile, but his face was pale. He had been worried about what would happen to his companions, the children of Margaret Acton, and seemingly nothing Serafina could do would calm his nerves. She had promised him that they would visit the boys every week, would have them over to stay for the weekend, and this had swayed his anxiety somewhat. But still, as the funeral droned on, his eyes went again and again to his two youthful companions. Serafina could read his expression. *What if that were me and I had lost my mother?* He had an open simplicity that she loved, and she dreaded to see the day when he became sophisticated enough to hide behind fashionable faces and expressions.

Finally the service was over, and the

tedious and painful second act of the funeral began. Serafina had always hated funerals, especially this part. She led David outside, and the sun was high in the sky as the hearse drawn by four black horses with black plumes passed. It had glass sides, and she could see the coffin inside covered with flowers. Obviously a small fortune had been spent on them, and for some reason the thought incensed Serafina. She felt David's hand tightening on hers and saw that he was staring at the coffin. Putting her arm around him, she stooped and held him close. "Don't mind it," she whispered. "That's not really our Margaret."

"Who is it, Mum?"

"I mean," Serafina stammered, "that the soul of Margaret isn't in there."

"Where is it, then, Mum?"

At this simple, straightforward question, Lady Serafina Trent was speechless. She had little religious faith, but she discovered that her acquaintance with Dylan had brought something there. She tried to speak and finally said, "She's gone to be with God."

"In heaven, Mum?"

"Yes, David, in heaven." She was amazed at the ease with which she said such a thing, for her religious life had been dead. But now she found something blooming there. A faint hope like a tiny bud was just beginning to open, and she found to her shock and amazement that there was a joy that was not there before. The idea of Margaret being forever gone, never existing anywhere, was abhorrent to her. But the idea of her friend being in heaven, as Dylan believed and was attempting to get her to believe, was a good and pure and powerful force within her breast. She stood there and watched as three other carriages packed with mourners all in black followed the hearse, and then she led David to their own carriage. She helped him in, and then she got in and waited as Albert Givins, the coachman, skilfully guided the carriage into the line that followed the hearse. Peter Grimes, the footman, was standing behind the carriage along with Danny Spears, all dressed in suits of solemn black.

The trip to the cemetery seemed to take forever. There was another service there, but finally it was all over, and with a sigh of relief, Serafina went forward and knelt beside the two boys. She embraced Charles, then Roger, and whispered to each of them, "I'm so sorry. Your mother was such a dear friend of mine. You must come and be with David and me often." She saw a light of joy in both faces as if the news had come straight from heaven. She stood up and turned to Count Acton and said, "Lord Fredrick, I can only offer you my grief. She was my best friend."

Count Fredrick Acton had the heavy features of a drinker, and even now she could smell the alcohol on his breath. He muttered what people mutter at such times, and quickly Serafina turned and went back to the carriage.

As they made their way home, David was very quiet. Only once did he speak. "Are you sure that Lady Margaret is in heaven?"

"Yes, I'm very sure."

Serafina was shocked and amazed at how easily the answer seemed to come. There were tears in her eyes because of the loss, and she could not help that, but there was a hope also that had not been there before. And along with that hope came the thought: *There is a heaven, and if Margaret is there, I would not see her if I were to die.* This concept occupied her mind as the carriage rumbled down the highway, and it brought her to an area of thought that she had carefully kept closed off before.

Serafina and David spent the rest of the day together. They played draughts and other games, but later they went outside to go for a ride. David rode his pony, Patches, and Serafina, her mare. She rode very slowly, keeping up with him, and was pleased to know that he seemed more cheerful and the colour had come back into his face. They paused by the creek to water their mounts, and David said, "This is where Charles and Roger like to come. Charles caught a big fish right over there by those willows."

"Yes, I remember. He was so proud of it."

"Roger was jealous because he didn't catch anything."

"But you remember that he caught a big turtle there one time. He wanted to eat it."

David suddenly laughed. "Yes, it didn't look like it would be very good, and Cook wouldn't have anything to do with it."

The water made a sibilant noise under the horses' front feet as they turned back toward the house. "It's getting late," she said. "We'll have to let Danny rub your pony down and the mare too."

"I could help him do it."

"If you'd like, you can. You like Danny, don't you?"

"Yes. He was my best friend — until Dylan came. I mean Mr. Dylan." He shot her a quick look. "I know you want me to call him Mr. Dylan. He says I don't have to if there's no one there but the two of us."

"Then that would be perfectly all right, but it's good manners for young people to address their seniors with respect."

"I respect him."

"I know you do, dear, and so do I."

"Do you really like him, Mum?"

"Why, of course I do. He's become a very good friend."

"He talked to me a little bit about Lady Margaret."

"What did he say?" Serafina was curious, and she turned to face the boy. She saw that he had a very serious look on his face.

"He said that death wasn't anything to be afraid of. That Jesus died and rose from the dead so that all of us who love him would go to heaven. That's what I want to do, Mum. I talked to Dylan about it."

"And what did he say?"

"Oh, he told me about how when he was a boy about my age he felt the same way. And he said that at some point, very soon now, I could make sure that I'd go to heaven."

"And how did he say you'd do that?"

"It's really simple," David said earnestly. "You have to tell God you've committed a sin."

"Just one sin?"

"No, all the sins you ever committed."

"Well, that wouldn't be too many for you."

He looked at her and shook his head solemnly. "More than you might think. Anyway, he also said after I told God I had sinned and I was sorry that I should ask Jesus to come into my heart and live there forever."

Serafina was aware that this was what Dylan believed. It was the typical nonconformist view of salvation. She was aware that other groups that were called "high church" had more rules. There were strict ceremonies to be observed. Something happened when a child was baptised. It sounded suspiciously like the child was saved, but Dylan had told her once that he had no confidence in that. Neither did she, for that matter. She knew that Dylan's religion was simple, as was that of Lorenzo and Gyp and others she had met in that circle. As they approached the stable, she was aware that David was very quiet.

"Is that all, David?" she asked.

"He said I ought to pray and say my prayers every day, and that I ought to listen to the sermons at church. He said that one day Jesus would come knocking at my door."

"He said that?"

"He read it from his Bible. He asked me

to memorise it, and I did."

"Can you say it for me, David?"

"Yes. Jesus said, 'Behold, I stand at the door, and knock: if any man hear my voice, and open the door, I will come in to him, and will sup with him, and he with me.' "

"That's a very beautiful thought."

After they arrived at the stables, Danny took the horses and said, "I'll take good care of that pony of yours, Master David, and your mare too, Lady Trent."

The two smiled at him and went upstairs. David went to his room, and she followed him. He went over to the heavy wardrobe, rummaged around in it, and came out with a New Testament. "Here it is, Mum." He pointed at the verse, then said, "I hope I don't die before Jesus comes into my heart."

Serafina's heart went out to the boy, and she put her arms around him. "No, you're not going to die for a long time."

"But, Mum, nobody knows about that. Lady Margaret didn't know she was going to die. That's why Dylan said we ought to have Jesus come into our lives as soon as we can." He looked at her and said, "Did Jesus ever come into your heart, Mum?"

Serafina Trent could not answer. She ignored the question and squeezed him and said, "Let's go see if we can find something to eat before supper." She saw he was disappointed at her answer, but she had no other answer to give this son of hers.

A few days after the funeral, Dylan arrived at the apartment he had found for Meredith and Guin. She opened the door to his knock and he smiled at her. "It's the delivery man. I found some good things at the greengrocer's."

"Come in, Dylan." Meredith smiled. She wore a pearl grey skirt and jacket with dark green buttons. Dainty accents adorned the sleeves and lapels and the skirt hem. Delicate white lace edged with green showed at the opening of the tight-fitting jacket.

"New dress?" he said as he entered with the groceries in his arm.

"It was one of Lady Trent's, I think. She brought some of her things to Lorenzo, and he let me have first pick. Do you like it?" She turned around and smiled winsomely at him.

"Very nice."

"Did you ever see her wear it?"

"I don't think so, but it's notoriously bad at women's fashion, I am."

"Bring the groceries in here." He followed her over toward a counter and set the box down, and she began to take out the items, exclaiming over each of them. "Oh, strawberries! Aren't they lovely. We've got to have those right away. They're just ready to eat. And look at this! What beautiful cucumbers. Suppose I make us some cucumber sandwiches, and then we have some strawberries. I even have a little cream, I think."

"That sounds good to me."

"You sit right there and tell me about the play while I fix us a snack."

Dylan sat down in a chair and leaned back. He clasped his hands together and told her the details of theatre life, which she loved to hear. Once she turned to him and said, "Oh, I'd love to be an actress."

"Well, you could be, you know."

Meredith turned and stared at him, her eyes going wide. "You're making fun of me."

"Why, not at all," Dylan said, shrugging his shoulders. "You've got the looks for it. I don't think there's a better-looking woman on the stage."

Suddenly she laughed. "You always were a flatterer even when we were children. Remember down by the creek when you told me I was the prettiest girl in school?"

"Nothing but the truth, it was."

She was slicing cucumbers now, and he noticed how attractive her hands were. He studied her without appearing to do so. The sunlight through the window threw its pale gleams on the satin skin at her throat. Her lips lay softly together, and light danced in her eyes as they met his glance. He saw, beneath her expression, fullness waiting, and the fullness was a promise and a temptation that he had not expected. She was watching him, and her expression grew smooth and tight, and a disturbed breathing lifted her breast. Her glance held him for a moment, and warmth ran between them, and the knowledge of a swift and common thought suddenly connected them. Dylan was disturbed and rose to look out the window.

"Did you have any word about your sister, Angharad?"

"No, not yet."

Her answer was brief, and he looked around suddenly. "Where's Guin?"

"She's asleep. Come, I've got the sandwiches made and the strawberries ready. Let's take them out in the backyard. There's a table and bench there and a fence to give privacy."

"All right."

The two of them carried the snack outside on trays, and there the garden was blooming in full. "Beautiful garden," he said.

"Someone cared for flowers very much,"

she agreed. "Here, put our things here and sit down."

He sat down on the bench, and she sat beside him so close that he could smell the fragrance she wore in her hair. Her arm brushed against his lightly, and she said, "Not much of a cook, I am, Dylan, but anyone can make cucumber sandwiches."

Dylan bit into the sandwich and said, "Fine! Fine! Nothing better than a cucumber sandwich."

"Unless it's an eel pie. That always sounded terrible to me, but you loved them when you were a boy."

"I remember. We bought some once at the fair. I don't know where I got the money."

The two ate the lunch, and she raved over the strawberries. When they finished, he said, "You have some cream there on your lip."

She turned to him. "I'm a messy eater. Take it away, will you now?"

He reached into his pocket, got a handkerchief, and brushed it across her lips. "There," he said.

"You have to take care of me in every way, it seems. I don't know what I would have done if you hadn't come along."

They sat there talking, and he was aware of the warmth of her body as she leaned against him momentarily. "We used to sit like this down by the river. You remember?"

"Yes, I do."

"You remember you were too bold with me once, and I shoved you in?"

Dylan laughed. "I haven't thought of that in years, but I deserved it."

"You weren't a bad boy. Just curious."

"An impudent dog I was!"

"No, you were always a good boy. Tell me about your career."

The two sat there, and, as always, she wanted to hear about acting and the theatre. He was aware that many women were curious about that, so he spoke for a time, drawing out many experiences.

"What about all the women? What do you do with all of them?"

"Nothing."

"Nothing? That must be hard on a man. Some of them are very attractive."

"They're not interested in me."

Meredith frowned. "Why, of course they are. I've heard they crowd around you after your performance."

"They're interested in a celebrity. If I were a footman, they would never look at me."

"What a thought!" She laughed. "So you don't give any of them any encouragement, not ever?"

"Not now. Maybe I did once, but things are different now."

The two sat there talking, and she asked him finally, "If you're not interested in those women crowding around you, what sort of women are you interested in?"

Dylan had thought a great deal about this, but had never spoken of it. "Meredith, all men worship beauty. Some men never see the real thing. But some men find a woman, and they see her and have her and never regret it. I've seen elements of a woman in many women put together. The attractiveness physically of one, the charm of another, the sweetness of a third, the strength of another. Put them all together." He smiled here, and his lips were broad, and his eyes were steady on her. "That's what all men are looking for."

"That's hard on a woman, for there would never be a woman with all those qualities."

"I suppose not, so we all have to take what we can get." He found himself drawn to her then and did not know how it came, but something drew him. Her hair was as black as a crow at midnight, and her mouth was wide and self-possessed. Her figure was smooth and rounded within the dress she wore, and her nearness set off its shocks within him. Without being aware of it, he suddenly put his arms around her, and she came to him, and he felt her lips come up quick and eager. It was like falling into layers of softness and softness, all of it closing around him, warm and painfully good. The feeling of it was a sustained wave to him and the same goodness without shame. And when he moved away, he heard her release a small sigh, and he saw that she was smiling. Her fingertip brushed against his lip, and she swayed against him. "You're a man of wonder, Dylan Tremayne."

"Excuse me."

Both Dylan and Meredith started. Dylan twisted his neck and saw that Matthew Grant had come through a gate that led to the front yard. He jumped to his feet, his face flaming. "Hello, Matthew. I didn't expect to see you here."

"Neither did I," Meredith said. Her face was angry. "You could knock at the door."

"I did, but no one answered. I thought I heard voices around here."

"What is it you want?" Meredith asked.

"I have come to see if you have a painting, even a miniature of your sister. We're not getting anywhere with our search."

"No, I have not."

"Then could you give me a more complete description?"

"I've already done that."

Matthew Grant was aware that he had behaved improperly. "Sorry to intrude," he said. "I just thought I could —"

"The next time you stand at the front until someone comes to the door, Superintendent."

"Of course, Mrs. Brice."

He turned to go when suddenly Dylan said, "I'll go with you, Matthew. I'd like to know what's going on with the Slasher cases."

"Do you have to leave now? Guin will be waking up soon. She loves to see you."

"I can come back later."

"Thank you for the groceries." She reached out and touched his chest lightly, and he turned quickly and left the backyard, accompanied by Matthew. As soon as they were outside, Grant said, "Comforting the widow Brice, are you, Dylan?"

"Keep your nose out of other people's business!"

Grant did not speak for a moment, and then he said, "I'm sorry. I didn't mean to intrude. I really didn't, but we're not finding a woman that looks anything like the brief description we have. She was rather vague about it."

"Well, she hasn't seen the woman in years.

Her appearance has probably changed."

"I suppose you're right, but I apologise for intruding, and no more teasing about Mrs. Brice. All right?"

"Of course." Dylan's anger dissipated, and when Grant suggested that they go to a pub for a snack, he went along. He was not actually hungry, but he wanted to find out what was going on with the case.

Matthew ordered a steak and kidney pudding, and afterward some spotted dick made with suet and lots of raisins and cream. Dylan had some steaming treacle pudding with brandy sauce and scalding hot tea. As the two men ate, Grant told Dylan what he had discovered.

"It's either someone trying to make this murder look like Lady Welles's murder, or it's the same man who killed Lady Welles, as I told Lady Trent."

"Why would someone try to make this murder look like Lady Welles's?"

"Well, it's not unheard of. Someone starts killing people in a very rigid, routine fashion, and if a man wants to get rid of his wife, he follows that pattern. Everyone thinks it's the same killer who's already struck. People take advantage of the killer's notoriety to get rid of unwanted wives and sweethearts. That's what happened after

151

William Palmer, a doctor, was convicted for killing several people by poisoning them."

"I see where they are calling this murderer the Slasher."

A grimness came to Matthew's face, and he said, "Yes, that's what they call him, and that's what he is."

"You think you'll catch him, then?"

"We'd better! The politicians and newspapers are howling for some action. But this fellow is clever. He left a lot of meaningless clues."

"How do you know they're meaningless?"

"There are so many of them." He took a list out of his pocket and said, "I've got men working on all of these."

Dylan looked over the list. "Anything I can do to help?"

"Maybe. One of the clues is a picture of a woman, a rather strange picture of a woman holding a hammer and a spike. Look at it," he said, taking an envelope from his pocket. "Neither Serafina nor I can make anything of it."

Dylan looked at it and then said instantly, "Why, this is a woman named Jael."

Grant stared at Dylan. "Who was she? And how do you know her?"

"Her story is in the Bible."

"The Bible? I don't remember any woman

named that in the Bible."

"Well, she's not as famous as some. You can read about it in the book of Judges, one of the early chapters."

"Tell me what you know, then I'll read it for myself when I get a Bible."

"The book of Judges records the history of Israel before they had a king. God called men to lead the people in time of war, men and women called judges. A king named Sisera brought his army to destroy the Jews; God called on two judges to save the nation, a man called Barak and a woman called Deborah. There was a battle, and General Sisera fled. He found shelter at the home of a man named Heber, but he met his fate there: Heber's wife, Jael. She knew that Sisera was the enemy of Israel. She fed him and got him to sleep, promising him that she would not let an enemy find him." Dylan rubbed his chin and said slowly, "Those were violent times, Matthew, and Jael did what Eastern peoples would despise. They believed that when even an enemy took shelter in your home, you had a sacred obligation to keep him safe."

"I take it Jael didn't do that."

"No, she waited until he was asleep, then she took a spike and a hammer. She put the tip of the spike to his temple, then drove it into his skull with a blow of the hammer."

"A rough woman indeed!"

"Those were terrible times."

"This is some help. In the first murder, the Slasher left a picture of a warrior queen, and now we have another woman who will kill to get what is needed."

"What does that mean?"

"I'm not sure, Dylan, but there's a killer loose who's ready to kill, just as he killed those other two women!" The men talked a bit longer about the case, then rose to leave.

"Where you headed for now?"

"I'm going out to see Dora."

"I've got to get down to the theatre. We're having a special rehearsal. I hope you catch the fellow."

"So do I," Matthew said.

The two left the pub. Matthew got into a cab, and all the way to Trentwood House he was silent, going over in his mind the liabilities that he faced in catching the Slasher.

When he got to the house, he was admitted by Ellie and found Serafina and Dora together.

"I've been going over the clues," Serafina said. "There are so many of them, and I don't know what to make of them."

"What about the poem? Any sense about that?"

"It's just bad poetry. Maybe we should let a professor of literature see it."

"I've already done that. Professor Grey at the University of Oxford. He said he'd get back to me, but I doubt anything will come out of it."

"Have you shown it to Dylan?" Serafina asked.

"I just left him. I gave him a copy of the list and the poem. He said he'd be coming to see you." He suddenly paused and said, "He recognised the woman in the picture." He told her the story of Jael and said, "Two violent women; that may mean something." He paused, then said, "I found him at Meredith Brice's place."

"I think he likes that woman," Dora said suddenly.

"Oh, women are always after him."

"Not like this one," Dora said slowly. She was wearing a plain black taffeta dress, the severity softened only by a small onyx and ivory cameo pin at the high neck. There was an innocence about her that had caught Matthew Grant from the very beginning, and he felt that it would always be there.

"Why do you think she's different?" Serafina asked suddenly.

"The others are hunting for souvenirs or trophies. He's an actor, a famous man. Wouldn't make any difference if he were ugly, they'd still be after him. They always are. But Mrs. Brice is out of his own past. They were childhood sweethearts. That has to mean something, don't you think?"

"I think he's tired of that other kind," Grant agreed. "After all, a childhood sweetheart, that's a pretty big thing. Some men walk around with an image of a girl they knew when they were twelve years old."

"And who was your childhood sweetheart, Matthew?"

Matthew suddenly smiled. It made him look much younger. He ran his hand through his hair, which was a beautiful silver grey, not of an old person but one who is living and vital. "Her name was Ethel Grubmeyer."

Dora stared at him. "Was she pretty?"

"Except for her eyes. One of them was kind of looking off. You could never tell if she was looking at you, and she had lost two teeth right out of the middle. She wasn't nearly as pretty as you, Dora."

Suddenly Serafina laughed. "Men always lie about the women in their lives."

Dora stared at Grant, but Serafina laughed again. "He's teasing you. Tease him back.

Make up a sweetheart. It would do him good."

"Well, what do you think about that Welshwoman? Is she pretty?"

"Very."

Dora looked at Serafina, who had answered more emphatically than was necessary. "Are you jealous, Serafina?"

"No, I definitely am not!"

NINE

Grant locked his lips together, determined not to answer. Sir Herbert Welles was at his office again, and this time with the head of the Home Office, Sir Anthony Jones. He had stood there listening as they both insisted that he catch the Slasher at once, and now he managed to get a word in.

"We're doing all we can, but you gentlemen must realise that this is no ordinary murderer."

Lord Herbert Welles had to look up, for he was short, and this seemed to irritate him. His eyes were sharp and black, and his voice was stirred with anger. "You've had plenty of time to catch the fellow. From what I understand, you have sufficient clues. You should have found him by now."

"We have clues, but most of them mean nothing," Matthew said, not for the first time.

"I don't understand what you're talking

about. You can't have too many clues," Sir Anthony said.

"Yes, sir, I'm afraid you can. This fellow is very shrewd. He knows that even the slyest of criminals will leave a clue that will lead to their capture, so he's fallen on the method of leaving all sorts of clues at the scenes. He scatters them everywhere, and we have no idea which ones mean something — if any of them."

"Arrant nonsense!" Lord Welles practically screamed. "You're incapable! I demand, Sir Anthony, that you replace this man!"

"I'm afraid it's not quite that simple," Sir Anthony Jones replied quickly. Actually, he admired Matthew Grant a great deal, but he had to show some respect for Lord Welles as well. "There's something to what he's saying. Give me an example, will you, Matthew?"

"Of course. Let me show you." He went over to a table on which there were scattered dozens of objects. "These were all found at the death scene in the bedroom of Lady Margaret Acton."

"What is this?" Welles asked, picking up one of the items.

"It's a photograph of a woman."

"I can see that," Welles said. "Who is she?"

"She's the wife of General Leo Hunter."

"General Hunter? The hero of the Crimea?"

"Yes. Now, what does it mean? His wife is dead. Do I go arrest General Hunter? The newspapers would make a field day out of that!"

"Then what's it doing here?" Welles demanded.

"To throw us off the track, of course. Somebody has to go investigate the general, but he must do it very tactfully. And look, here's a letter from Gerhard Von Ritter."

"That artist fellow?"

"Actually he's a poet and a playwright."

"Why, the man's a radical!" Sir Anthony said.

"Yes, he is, but is he the Slasher? That's the question. Once again, we can't send men in with clubs to beat it out of him. It's going to take more than that!"

"Where would the Slasher get all these items?" Sir Anthony asked.

"I have no idea, sir, but I know he has found probably the best way to confuse Scotland Yard. I have men working on every one of these items."

"And what have you discovered?"

"We discovered that most of them are false leads. Somewhere we'll find the true one, but it's not going to be easy."

For the next twenty minutes Matthew Grant stood there listening to Sir Herbert Welles harangue him in a senseless fashion. Finally Sir Anthony took Welles by the arm and said, "We'll go and leave the Yard to do the work. You must see, Herbert, that this is a most difficult task."

"Put more men on the job."

"I'm afraid that wouldn't help. We don't need more men. We need men with brains."

"Well, it's certainly not you," Welles yelled and was dragged off by Sir Anthony Jones.

Matthew stood watching for a while, and then he said, "Kenzie!" He waited until Kenzie stuck his head in the door. "I'm going to see General Hunter."

"You think he could be guilty?"

"I have no idea. He may shoot me for even bringing such a thing up, but his wife's picture was at the murder scene."

Thirty minutes later General Leo Hunter was standing in front of Matthew Grant. "You're here again, Superintendent. What is it this time? You still think I murdered Lady Stephanie Welles?"

"No, sir, it's a different matter."

"What is it, then? I'm a busy man. I'm writing my memoirs, don't you see. Dashing hard thing for a soldier to write."

"Be easier if you were out slashing people with a saber, I suppose."

"Is that some sort of a trick question, Superintendent?"

"In a way it is. You read about the murder of Countess Margaret Acton?"

"Certainly. I was at the funeral. I knew the countess and her husband both. What does that have to do with me?"

"Do you recognise this picture?" Matthew took the package that he had been holding and unwrapped it. He handed the picture over without comment and saw Hunter's eyes go wide. "Well, of course I recognise it. It's my wife. Where did you get it?"

"It was in the room of Lady Acton."

Hunter stared at him. "So you think I killed her too?"

"Actually I don't, Sir Leo. You see, the Slasher has a peculiar method. We haven't let it get out to the newspapers, and I ask you to keep this absolutely confidential."

"Of course. What is it?" Sir Leo listened carefully as Matthew explained the clues that were found at the crime scene, and when Matthew was finished, he shook his head. "The bounder must be clever."

"Very clever, I'm afraid. The question is, where did he get these items? This picture. Where was it kept?"

"Why, here in my office."

"Was it on display?"

"No. Actually it was kept in this drawer over here with quite a few other pictures. Come, I'll show you." Hunter walked across the room, opened the drawer, and pulled out a handful of photographs and drawings. "You see? Most of them are of my wife." Sadness came to him, and he said, "I miss her every day, Superintendent."

"I offer my condolences, but you can see what we're up against. How could anyone have gotten this?"

"Obviously someone has had access to my office. They've taken two items that we know of. They've probably taken more."

"You think a burglar broke in?"

"That wouldn't be necessary. I have visitors all the time. My bit of fame has brought me quite an audience. People coming and going. Sometimes we're in here. Sometimes we go in the sitting room. Sometimes there are groups. One man could slip away while I was talking to the others in the parlour. All he would have to do is fill his pockets with a few mementos."

"Yes, I see that. Well, I'm sorry if I bothered you."

"You have a pretty hard job, Mr. Grant. I hope that you'll catch this fellow. He's a bad one. I saw plenty of his kind in the service."

"Why the circus! What are we doing here?" Dora asked. She was pleased enough that Matthew had come to take her away for an afternoon, and now they were standing outside the large building where the circus was held.

"Combining business with pleasure. I have to meet with Mr. Henley," Matthew answered.

"Who is he?"

"He's an acrobat who performs his act on a tightrope and on a horizontal bar. You'll see."

"That must be terribly dangerous."

"I think it is. Come along."

They made their way to the dressing rooms, and on one door "Mr. Henley" was written on a card. Matthew knocked on the door, and a lean, well-built man opened it at once. "I am Superintendent Grant, Mr. Henley. This is my assistant, Miss Newton."

"What can I do for you, Superintendent?"

"A few questions. May we come in?"

"Yes, certainly." He stepped aside, and they found a young woman in there. "This is my fellow aerialist, Miss Jeanne St. Clair."

"I'm glad to know you, Miss St. Clair.

This is Miss Newton. We are working on a case." He stared at the young woman and asked, "You look familiar . . . Oh, I remember. I saw you once at one of Miss Bingham's public meetings."

"What sort of a case?" Henley asked, interrupting. He had dark blue eyes and studied his visitors carefully.

"It's a case of murder, I'm afraid."

"Not the Slasher!" Miss St. Clair exclaimed. She was a small woman, well built, and wearing a rather tight costume with a cape over her shoulders. She had large, rather piercing blue eyes and a shining crown of strawberry blonde hair.

"Yes, I'm afraid it is about that case, although I prefer you not let it get out of this room."

"How may we help you, monsieur?"

"Do you recognise this item?"

"A ticket stub," Henley murmured. "Why do you show me this?"

"It may mean nothing, but it may be that the murderer attended one of your performances."

"Am I a suspect, Superintendent?"

"Not right now. But you may have some connection with the killer."

Jeanne St. Clair said sharply, "Hundreds of people come to the circus. Anyone could have one of these stubs."

"But not one of these." Grant extracted another item from the envelope and handed it to Henley. He waited with his eyes fixed on the man's face.

"What is it?" Jeanne demanded.

"One of our pictures we give to people."

Dora got a glimpse of the picture, which featured Henley and Jeanne in costume. Across the face was written, "To our good friend Lady Acton."

"Is this your handwriting, sir?"

"No, it is mine," Jeanne said. "I sign all such publicity material."

"Do either of you know the victim?"

"No, not at all!" Henley exclaimed. "Jeanne sells them after a performance. But she does not know the people who buy them. There are hundreds of them!"

"Is that so, Miss St. Clair?" Grant asked.

"I sign hundreds of these. Sometimes they ask me to use their name, to make it personal, and I do so. But I do not remember this name."

Grant stared at the woman, then said, "You and two other women spoke to four women at a restaurant recently. One of them was Lady Acton."

For the first time Jeanne St. Clair looked startled and made no answer.

"I know you were there, Miss St. Clair. I have witnesses."

"Oh, I remember! But I didn't know their names." She seemed flustered and added, "We of the movement see many women. I can't remember them all."

Grant studied her, then said, "I will be asking you a few more questions, but that will be all for now." He saw that questioning any further was useless. "I'm sorry to have bothered you, Mr. Henley."

"Not at all. If we could be of any help."

"Will you stay and see the performance?" Jeanne asked. She turned to Dora and smiled. "I think you would be charmed."

"I would like to, if you have time, Matthew," Dora said.

"Of course. Thank you very much for your time, monsieur, and you, Miss St. Clair."

They did stay for a performance and admired the lithe form of Jeanne St. Clair twisting, balancing, and turning alongside other aerialists. "She must be very strong to flip and tumble through the air like that," Dora remarked.

"Well, you are right. It takes fine athletes to do that."

"Do you think either one of them was the Slasher?"

"I doubt it, but I don't know what to think

anymore. It is strange, though, that the young woman is a feminist. She doesn't seem the type. Well, come along. Let's go get something to eat."

Meredith had persuaded Dylan to take her shopping. She was carrying Guin as the two were walking along the street. "How different this is from our little village, Dylan."

"I liked the village better."

"I don't see how you could like it. You nearly worked yourself to death in that mine. And your father almost died in that cave-in."

"No, I didn't like the mine, but the village was nice."

They turned the corner and saw Serafina and Septimus standing in the street and looking at a group that had gathered.

"Look, there's Serafina and her father," Dylan said. "Let's see what's going on."

The two moved up, and Serafina started when he touched her arm. "Oh, Dylan, how are you?"

"Fine. Meredith is doing a little shopping. I carry the parcels. How are you, sir?"

Septimus smiled. "Fine, Tremayne. I'm off to a meeting — boring scientists, you know. Good to see you again."

As they said good-bye to Septimus, Dylan

noticed Serafina looking away from them. "What are you doing?"

"Martha Bingham is up there."

"Do you know her?" Meredith asked.

"Yes, I've met her," Dylan responded. "She didn't like me much. Hard to believe, isn't it?" He grinned in a way that set off tingling in women. "What's she doing?"

"She's giving a speech, trying to gain adherence to her cause," Serafina said.

"Who is that young woman with her?" Dylan asked. "I've never seen her before."

"I'm not sure."

They found out later when Miss Bingham introduced her. "This, my friends, is Miss Jeanne St. Clair. She's one of the most daring women of our time. She is an aerialist with Mr. Henley. Many of you have seen her at the circus." Martha Bingham spoke loudly. "She has courage in the physical world, but what we need is women who have *spiritual* courage. Courage to stand up and demand the same rights as men have."

They were listening to Martha Bingham speak when suddenly a woman approached.

"Hello, Serafina."

"Why, Marchioness, it's you!"

"Yes, I haven't seen you in a while. How are you?"

"Well, thank you. This is my friend Dylan

Tremayne, the actor. This is his friend Mrs. Brice. This is Marchioness Rachel Reis."

"I have seen you, sir. You make an excellent Macbeth! Most Macbeths are either fat or scrawny, but you fill out a pair of tights quite well, I think."

Serafina laughed suddenly. "That's coming right out with it, Marchioness."

Dylan grinned. He liked the woman. "Did you come to hear Miss Bingham? Maybe you're one of her team."

"I think it's balderdash," Rachel Reis said bluntly. "The woman is obviously unhinged." She suddenly turned and called out in a strident voice, "Nonsense! Go home, woman, and do your cooking and washing!"

Martha Bingham stopped only for a moment. "I know you, Marchioness. You're the enemy of all women everywhere. You would have all of us to be scrubbing some pots when we're able to do anything a man can do!"

"How many children have you fathered?" Rachel Reis cried out, and a laughter went over the crowd.

"You should not make fun!" Jeanne St. Clair shouted back. "I know you're royalty, and I'm only a circus performer, but I can do more than flip through the air. I can think, and I can be the equal of a man. Let a man do what I do before you judge."

Rachel Reis had a sharp mind, and she carried on a rather vicious attack on the women who had come to promote their cause. Finally she said, "This grows tiresome. Where are you going, Dylan?"

"We're going to a religious meeting."

"Fine. I'll go with you."

"But you're Jewish, aren't you, Lady Reis?" Dylan said.

"By blood, but I have no religion at all. Not even Jewish. But I'm always ready for a new experience, so lead on. Serafina, you'll come with us?" Lady Reis did not wait for a response.

The meeting at Lorenzo's was quite usual, but Lady Reis found it amusing. She listened to Lorenzo's sermon and said to him afterward, "I like a man who believes what he says. You're totally wrong, of course, but you believe it. That is your right and your privilege."

"Thank you, ma'am, indeed. I trust that you are washed in the blood of the Lamb."

Rachel Reis blinked. She was not accustomed to being broadsided. "No, indeed, I am not! I have no religion whatsoever."

"Oh, come now, Lady. Everyone has

something they look up to."

"I look up to myself."

"Then that's your religion. You worship yourself." Gyp smiled. He made a colourful picture there with his scarlet head cloth, a gold ring in one ear, and his flashing white teeth.

Lady Reis suddenly was amused. "Gypsy, tell my fortune."

Gyp took her hand and looked at the palm. "Well, what do you see?" she demanded.

"I see a hand that one day will lie in a casket, cold and still."

Lady Reis flushed and drew her hand back. "That's the worst fortune I've ever had told."

"And the truest probably," Gyp said. "I'm sorry if I offended you, Lady."

They left soon after that, and Serafina spoke earnestly to Dylan. "I wish you'd come and spend some time with David. He misses you."

"I will. Will this Sunday be all right? It'll have to be in the afternoon, you understand."

At that moment Lorenzo came to say, "Dylan, brother, come and help us pray for this sick man."

"Excuse me, ladies."

Dylan hurried off with Lorenzo, and Meredith came to stand next to Serafina. "I suppose you recognise this dress."

"Why, it looks like one of mine."

"It was one of yours. One that you gave to Lorenzo, and he gave me first choice at it. We're about the same size."

"You look very well. Better than I did in it."

"Thank you. That's kind." Meredith was studying Serafina closely. "I'm surprised, Lady Trent, that you would let an actor get so close to your family." Her eyes glinted, and she smiled. "Actors are low class in the eyes of nobility."

"Not Dylan," Serafina said.

"You like him, I see, very much."

"We have been thrown together in some unusual circumstances. He was very instrumental in helping free my brother from an unjust charge. Naturally we grew to be friends after that."

Meredith started to turn, but Serafina asked, "Do you miss your life in Wales?"

"Not at all. Life is hard there."

"What about your family?"

"I have no family except one old aunt."

Serafina continued to ask questions, and Meredith mentioned that she had seen the Prince of Wales the previous October. "He travels a great deal," Serafina said.

"Yes, I suppose so."

Dylan came out then, and Meredith said, "I have some things to do. Guin and I should go home now."

"Yes, of course," Dylan said. He turned to Serafina. "Sunday afternoon, Serafina?"

"Yes. David will be so happy to see you." Serafina shifted her eyes to Meredith and asked, "Can I offer you a ride home?"

Meredith responded, "I can get a cab." She then reached out and touched Dylan's arm. There was something possessive in the gesture. "It was kind of you to take me shopping, but then, you're always kind." She turned and smiled at Serafina, then said, "It's good to see you again, Lady Trent."

After helping Meredith into a cab, Dylan returned to where Serafina stood and said, "That dress is one of yours, I believe."

"Yes, I think it humiliated her."

"Why, no, of course not. She was glad to get it."

There was no point in carrying on that conversation. Serafina studied Dylan and listened to him talk about Meredith and Guin a few minutes more. She thought, *Why, he's besotted with the woman. Maybe there is something to this childhood sweetheart thing. But she couldn't have seen the*

174

Prince of Wales in Ireland last October. I happen to know he was in France at the time. She filed this away and then put it out of her mind as she climbed into her coach.

"We will look forward to your visit on Sunday. David will be overjoyed to see you, Dylan. He has missed you a great deal."

TEN

Dylan leaned back in his chair and beamed at Meredith. He was holding Guin in his lap, and he said, "This is a fine meal, Meredith. I didn't know you were such a fine cook."

"I used the money you gave me to buy something special," Meredith said. She was wearing a china blue dress set off by white ribbons. Her hair was fixed in a way that made her very attractive — a French chignon — and the blackness of her hair set off the darkness of her eyes. "I like to cook."

"What is this? I don't recognise it."

"That's pickled tongue." And lifting a cover she said, "You're not going to believe this. It's turtle soup. Usually very expensive, but I got a bargain."

"I've never had turtle soup."

"Take some. You'll like it."

Dylan balanced Guin on half his lap and shared his soup with her. "Doesn't taste like anything I've had before," he said, "but it's very good."

"Here. Try some of this." She removed a cover from a deep dish and spooned out a liberal amount on his plate. "This is suet pudding. My mother taught me how to make it. Flour and suet, and the fat comes from around the kidneys and the groin."

"It's very good. Here, you sit down and eat, Meredith."

Meredith sat down across from Dylan and smiled. "Don't eat too much. I've got a special treat."

"Something sweet?"

"You'll have to wait and see. Here, I did get some small beer." She knew that Dylan did not drink, but small beer had almost no alcoholic content, and he took it without protest. The two sat there eating, and as they did, Meredith studied Dylan inconspicuously. His coat was beautifully cut, hanging without a wrinkle, and he wore a soft silk shirt open at the neck. *He doesn't know how handsome he is,* Meredith thought. *That's unusual in a man.* She studied him carefully, and finally she said, "You ever think of old times, Dylan?"

"You mean when we were children?"

"Yes, some of it's not too pleasant to remember. The mines, for example."

"I think about the good times we had."

Dylan took a bite of the fried sole that she had slipped onto his plate and grew thoughtful. Finally he smiled. "I remember those times. There weren't enough of them, were there?"

"No. I suppose there never is."

Finally she brought the dessert, which turned out to be something she called roly-poly pudding. It was jam and fruit rolled up into a sheet of pastry and cooked.

She smiled as Dylan ate two helpings and said, "You don't eat right, I'm afraid."

"No, most of the time we go out to eat after a performance, but by that time I'm usually not very hungry. Acting takes it out of me for some reason."

"You're a wonderful actor," she said. "Everyone says you're going to be the greatest actor in London."

"No, that will never happen. You have to want it, Meredith, and I don't really want it."

"You don't want to be famous and have all the money you can spend?" She smiled, and her dimple appeared in her right cheek, very faint but there. "Most people want that more than anything."

"I suppose that's true." Dylan picked up the teacup and drained it, and at once she

178

got up and filled it from the kettle. "This ought to be good," she said. "I like green tea."

"It's my favourite too."

Meredith sat down and said suddenly, "I've got to find work, Dylan."

"Oh, I don't think that's necessary. You've got a place to stay here, and your and Guin's food isn't all that expensive." He picked up a spoonful of the roly-poly pudding and extended it toward Guin. She opened her mouth and he pushed it in. "Just like a little bird, you are," he said. "Here, have another."

"I really can't go on living off of you."

"It's no trouble to me."

"It wouldn't be right for me to do that."

"We'll talk about it later."

"I've been reading some of the old papers. Are you still a suspect in that murder case?"

"No, that was all a mistake."

"How could a mistake like that be made?"

"Well, the Slasher is pretty shrewd. He must take a whole bagful of odds and ends, and he scatters them all over the murder scene. Matthew says that there is no way to tell which is a real clue and which is just something to lead them off on a false scent."

"The papers are already screaming for an arrest."

"I expect they'll continue to do that. Easy enough to scream, not so easy to catch a criminal as clever as this."

She questioned him closely for a time, and finally he interrupted her by saying, "Tell me about how you and Lewis got together."

The question seemed to trouble her. She lowered her eyes and said, "We were both poor as church mice, but we fell in love, and we married, and then we had Guin."

"He was the best friend I had as a kid. I wish he were still here."

"I miss him every day, and, of course, Guin is too young to know about death." She was quiet for a moment. Finally she said, "You know one of the things Lewis said to me just before he died?"

"What was it?"

"He said, 'I want Guin to have a father.' And then he said, 'And I don't want you to grieve over me. Find a man you love and who loves you, and make a home for little Guin.'"

She pulled a handkerchief from a pocket, wiped her eyes, and when she looked up at him, he said, "I'm sorry. There's nothing one can say about things like this."

"It's not what you say. It's the fact that you care enough to say it." She reached over and put her hand over his. "So kind to me, to us, you've been, Dylan. If you believe that Lewis is in heaven, then maybe he's looking down and sees how you are taking care of his wife and child."

"I'll do that. You can count on it." He was very conscious of the pressure of her hand. She had beautifully sculptured hands, not scarred or roughened by hard work, and he wondered about that for an instant.

"I've got to find work." Meredith hesitated. "Do you think there's anything I can do along your line?"

"You mean the theatre? Why, I'm surprised you would even ask. It's not a good life, Meredith."

"I could do anything. Maybe I could work on the costumes."

"Oh, for that matter you could be an actress." He smiled and said, "You've got a lively expression. As a matter of fact, you're probably better looking and better able to act than half the actresses onstage right now."

"Oh, do you think I could do something like that? Would you help me, Dylan?"

Dylan rubbed his chin thoughtfully and ran his free hand over Guin's hair. "I don't think it's a good idea."

"Just let me try. I'll work hard. You'll see. I can't go on living off of you. It isn't right."

Dylan was troubled by her request, but finally he said reluctantly, "I'll ask around and see what can be done." Her hand tightened on his, and he saw her eyes glow. Her lips were wide and expressive, and when she smiled it changed her whole expression. "Oh, Dylan, if I could just make a living for myself and Guin."

He saw that she was looking at him intently. He got to his feet and said, "Well, I've got to go. We've got a rehearsal this afternoon."

"I'd like to see the play again."

"Why, Meredith, you've seen it half a dozen times."

"I know, but I'd like to go again. Would you leave word for them?"

He took a piece of paper from his pocket, found a pencil, and wrote something on it. "Give this to the doorman. He'll let you in."

"And can I go out to eat with the rest of you?"

"It'll be hard on Guin," he said.

"She'll sleep through the whole thing. Please, Dylan, let me come."

"All right. We'll go out with the crew, and you'll see what a scurvy bunch we are."

"No, I don't believe that for a minute."

She was excited now, he saw, and a

thought came to him. *Why, she could be an actress. She has a glow about her, but it doesn't seem like a good idea to me.* He stood there holding Guin for a moment, looking at her and studying her fine skin and dark hair.

"You love children, don't you, Dylan?"

"Very much. I've gotten very close to Lady Trent's son, David."

"I wonder why Lady Trent never remarried."

The question troubled Dylan. "I think there was a problem with her first husband — though she never talks about her marriage."

"She's in love with you, Dylan."

Dylan's head went back, and he stared at her. "Why, don't be foolish, Meredith! Of course she's not."

"Do you think I don't know? You've been blinded by so many women chasing after you. I don't think that's good for you."

"I don't think so either, but I never seek such a thing."

She was watching him carefully now and said, "She's just like the other women who pursue you. Have you ever thought what it would be like if you were to marry her?"

"That could never happen."

"But if you did, what would it be like?"

"I don't know."

"It would be terrible for you. She'd see you as one of the servants. Oh, perhaps above the butler, but still not the man of the house. She rules the house, I understand, and she's nobility, Dylan, and you're not."

"Well, I won't worry about that because it will never happen. I'll meet you backstage after the play. We'll have a good time."

After he left the small house that he had rented for Meredith and Guin, he thought about what she had said. *Marry Serafina? Could never happen! Fine ladies like her don't marry actors. Her family would die of shame.* He put the matter out of his mind and whistled as he headed toward the theatre.

Serafina sat in Grant's office at Scotland Yard. Both of them were discouraged, for they had made little progress in the case. Serafina studied the lists of clues, and Grant exhaled a deep breath. "I tell you, Serafina, it's getting the best of me."

"You're going to catch this monster," Serafina said. "I came to tell you that I have an invitation tonight to a dinner given by Gerhard Von Ritter. Why don't you come with me?"

"Without an invitation?"

"He doesn't care. He just likes an audience. He'll be impressed that the superintendent of Scotland Yard would come."

"I'd like to learn more about him anyway. After all, one of the clues can be traced to him — that newspaper article about his recent play. What sort of a fellow is he?" Matthew asked curiously. "I've heard all sorts of stories."

"Well, as you know, he writes plays. He also writes poetry. Rather good, from what I hear. But he's a violent radical. He's German, you know, and he's got that old dramatic idea that there's a master race. He despises weak, dark-skinned people. Even the Russians he hates. I've heard him say they are inferior beings."

"What are his plays and poetry like?"

Serafina tapped her chin with her forefinger, thought for a moment, and then said, "He stresses male dominance."

"He puts women down."

"Oh heavens, yes! To him a woman is to be used, and when their use is not to be desired, they will be thrown away. We are inferior beings. He feels that Islam has the right idea about heaven."

"What is their idea?"

"The Muslims believe that if a man goes to heaven, he'll have a whole group of

185

beautiful, big-bosomed, dark-eyed virgins to wait on him."

Matthew suddenly grinned. "I believe I could make up a better heaven than that."

"Anyone could. It's ridiculous!"

"Why do the Muslim women stand for it?"

"They've been dominated for hundreds of years. They're slaves, Matthew. I feel sorry for them. But, of course, there are some slaves who have English names and walk the streets of London."

Matthew stared at her. "I suppose you're right about that. Well, I'll come. I'd like to hear Von Ritter."

"You'll get a good meal out of it anyhow. His chef is famous." She rose to her feet and said, "I'll go over the list again, and I'll study the poem. Maybe we can head this infamous Slasher off before he kills again."

"We'd better. The Home Office is practically camping on my desk. I think they may be looking for a new superintendent if I don't get some action soon."

"You'll find him," she said and smiled and left his office.

Serafina looked around the table. She was seated next to Matthew, and she saw that he was stricken silent by the ornate dinner that was being served. It had been almost overwhelming. The first course had been a bisque. This was followed by salmon or deviled whitebait. The fish was followed by entrées of curried eggs, sweetbreads, and mushrooms, and when the entrée plates were cleared away, they were served iced asparagus. There was other food that flowed steadily past them, including seven cheeses, Neapolitan cream, and raspberry water. There were pineapples, strawberries, apricots, cherries, and melons.

By the time the meal was half-over, Serafina was tired of food. It was ostentatious and gaudy and showed poor taste. She studied Gerhard Von Ritter, who sat at the head of the table. He was a tall man, lean, with blond hair and piercing blue eyes — rather the ideal dramatic superhero. His eyes glittered at times, and while he was handsome, there was a chiselled hardness about his face that made Serafina realise she would never trust this man with anything important. Her eyes went around the table, and she was impressed with the audience. Marquis Jacob Reis was there with his wife, Marchioness Rachel Reis. Across from the marquis were Baron Jacques DeMain, the French ambassador, and his wife, Baroness Danielle DeMain.

There were several other titled guests, but

the surprise of the evening for Serafina was to discover that Martha Bingham was there. She knew that the philosophies of Von Ritter and Martha Bingham were light-years apart, and she suspected that he had invited her to have a target for his philosophy. Next to Martha was Jeanne St. Clair, the young woman who worked with Mr. Henley at the circus. Violet Bates, Martha Bingham's secretary, was there also, looking very uncomfortable. She fluttered her hands and wore a timid expression on her face continually. From time to time Martha Bingham would put her arm around the young woman's shoulders and whisper in her ear — which seemed to annoy Jeanne St. Clair a great deal, for she shot angry glances at Violet.

"I think we're going to see some fireworks pretty soon," she whispered to Grant.

"What do you mean?"

"He's invited the women that he probably despises most. Any man who holds his views on the inferiority of women would despise Martha Bingham and her group. Just wait. It's going to be like a war. Explosions and death, at least the death that words bring."

"I think you're right," Matthew agreed.

Her prophesy proved to be true. As soon as the table was cleared away, Von Ritter began to speak. "I am glad you are all here," he said. "I wanted to share a few items of interest. One is the fact that interest in women's rights is dying."

Instantly Martha Bingham spoke up. "That is not true, sir. It is going well."

"You would think so, of course, Miss Bingham. But then, you are a leader of that group, and you have given yourself to this lost cause. Do you not see, my dear Miss Bingham, that a woman is inferior in every respect? Do you know a woman who can run as fast as the fastest man? Or a woman who can lift the weight of a strong man? How many inventions have been thought up by women? All by men."

Martha Bingham's face flamed, and her friend Miss St. Clair gave Von Ritter a look that would have killed, if looks could kill.

Both Grant and Serafina sat there for the next forty-five minutes. Von Ritter never lost his calm demeanour. His words were cutting and sharp, and he, at times, would glance around the table to see the effect he was having.

Martha Bingham and Jeanne St. Clair were no match for Von Ritter. At first they deteriorated to screaming rebuttals and then were silenced by his array of facts.

Von Ritter turned and said, "Lady Reis,

what is your opinion of my theories?"

"I think you know," she said. "I think there are superior women and inferior women, but to give women the vote would be futile and even stupid."

"You say that, a woman, and you deny your own sex!" Martha Bingham cried out.

"Women are not constituted for such things — except for a few."

"Oh, women like yourself."

"Exactly, and like Lady Trent there. She is a scientific person. Not at all like the women you find on the streets or washing dishes in a brothel. No, Miss Bingham, I'm sorry, but few women are the equal of men."

Lady DeMain said, more or less, the same. Her husband, Jacques DeMain, said almost nothing, and in the end Martha Bingham got up and left the room, followed by her two disciples.

"I apologise for my guests' sudden departure," Von Ritter said. "But, after all, what can you expect?"

After the meal Matthew and Serafina got into their carriage, and Matthew said, "He's a snake, Lady Trent."

"Yes, he is. I've never seen such cold eyes."

ELEVEN

One room of the Trent mansion had become a longtime favourite of Serafina's. It was more or less concealed behind several other rooms as if it had been added as a hiding place for someone seeking quietness and seclusion. Perhaps it had been originally a bedroom, and as Serafina sat in a horsehide chair, she let her eyes run around it, thinking of the many hours she had spent in this place.

The room was an interesting mixture of styles. On one side stood an old Chinese silk screen that had once been a great beauty but was now faded, and its wooden frame was scratched in places. She let her eyes rest on it, finding in its aged beauty an elegance that gave it a charm and comfortable grace. Across from the screen against the wall was a Russian samovar on a side table. A collection of Venetian glass gleamed in a cabinet, and a French clock ticked on the mantel shelf above the fireplace. In all of the furniture there was a suggestion of great age and yet of beauty that, for some reason, Serafina treasured.

With a sigh she looked down at the papers she had scattered on the mahogany desk, and for a moment a wave of sadness came to her. "I miss Margaret," she whispered aloud, and the sound of her own voice increased her sadness. Serafina did not have many close friends, and Margaret Acton had played a larger role in her life than she had realised. Now memories came trooping through Serafina's mind of Margaret in her lively, vivacious way, and her love of humour, her kindness, her generosity — all the things Serafina had treasured in this woman, this friend she had lost in such a horrible fashion.

A cuckoo clock against the wall announced the passing of the hour. "Ten o'clock," Serafina murmured and forced herself to look down at the papers. They were the history she had collected from Matthew of the known facts of the Slasher's trail of blood. She had read them over and over, and with her phenomenal memory she had no need to see the facts on paper, but still, trying to organise them into some meaningful solution had proven impossible.

Maybe I'm too close to the thing. I loved Margaret so much, and perhaps my logic has given way to sentiment. The thought passed through Serafina's mind, but she shook her head, and stubbornness appeared in her broad mouth as she straightened up and said, "There's got to be an answer here, and we'll find it somehow."

A tap at the door caught Serafina's attention, and she called out at once, "Come in." Louisa Toft opened the door and stepped inside. She had been Serafina's maid for a short period of time but had proven herself invaluable. She was a beautiful young woman of twenty-three with red hair and green eyes and a rather spectacular figure. Her eyes sparkled now as she said, "Lady Trent, Mr. Tremayne is here."

"Oh, thank you, Louisa. I'll be right down. Show him to the small parlour, please."

"Yes, ma'am."

Serafina got up, arranged the papers, and slipped them into a folder. She was encouraged by Dylan's arrival, and she knew that David would be ecstatic. Dylan had a day off, and there was no performance on this particular Saturday, it being a national holiday. She found herself hurrying along and wondered as she moved toward the stairs why she was acting so. *It's like I am a teenage girl with some sort of a wild attraction for a man,* she scolded herself.

Descending the stairway, she met Ellie coming out, and Ellie said, "I'll fix tea if you like, Lady Trent."

"Yes, and bring some of those fairy cakes that Cook made earlier today."

"Yes, ma'am, I will." She sighed, her bosom rising and falling with some sort of passion. "Mr. Dylan, he don't look half fine! You'll see," she said. "Them britches he's got on is a dream!"

Serafina could not help being irritated but, at the same time, amused. "Never mind Mr. Tremayne's britches. Go get the tea and fairy cakes."

"I'll be right back with all the fixin's, ma'am."

Serafina entered the parlour, which was often used to entertain a small number of guests. It was decorated discreetly with green velvet and rosewood furniture. There was a comfort in the space, and sunlight streamed in through the windows, lending a cheerful air to the room.

"Good morning, Dylan —," Serafina said and then broke off, for there beside Dylan was Meredith Brice, and in Dylan's arms was the two-year-old Guinivere, who turned to stare at Serafina with wide blue eyes.

"Good morning, Lady Trent," Dylan said cheerfully. He was a sight to behold. He always looked well in his clothing, and this morning he seemed to be dressed in an extra fine fashion. He wore a soft silk shirt with a meticulous, widely flowing cravat and a lightweight, casual jacket. The britches were a light fawn colour, and indeed, Dylan Tremayne was the man to wear the trousers of the period, which fit him like a second set of skin.

"I brought Meredith and Guinivere along with me this morning. I thought you two could get to know each other."

"I told Dylan it was not proper to come uninvited," Meredith said at once. "But he insisted."

"I'm happy to have you, Mrs. Brice."

"Oh, please call me Meredith." She was wearing, Serafina noticed, an outfit that looked familiar, and she suspected it was one of her own.

"I'm glad to have you," Serafina said. "Won't you sit down? My maid is bringing tea and some excellent fairy cakes."

Dylan sat down, still holding Guinivere in his lap. "I'm teaching Guinivere some nursery rhymes," he said. "She's a bright girl."

"I'm sure she is, and very attractive too,

Mrs. Brice."

"Please just call me Meredith. Oh yes, these two are inseparable. I never saw a man so able to gain the confidence of a child."

Serafina looked at Guinivere and saw that she had dark hair and large brown eyes, well shaped, and very intelligent. "She must take after her father."

"Why, yes, she does."

"I must admit I can't see much of old Lewis in her, but sometimes genes jump back," Dylan said cheerfully. "Probably takes after her grandmother."

"Yes, Lewis's mother did have dark hair and brown eyes."

The door suddenly burst open and David came flying in. "Hello, Mr. Dylan."

"Well, hello, David. Look who I've got — Miss Guinivere here. Do you suppose we could take her with us while we play soldiers?"

"Yes, let her come," David said. "Guinivere? That's the name of King Arthur's wife."

"That's right. So she's actually a princess. Come along. If you ladies will excuse us."

"What about your tea and fairy cakes?" Serafina said.

"Have Ellie bring them up to the playroom, if you will, and lots of them. We're going to be hungry with all the battles we're going to have with those men of yours, David."

Dylan left, holding Guinivere in the crook of one arm and towing David along by his free hand.

Meredith Brice sat down and smiled, saying, "He's wonderful with children."

"Yes, he certainly is. I've noticed that before."

The two women sat there speaking mostly of the raising of children until finally Ellie brought the tea and the fairy cakes. "Take tea and cakes up to Mr. Dylan and the children, please, Ellie."

"Yes, ma'am, I will."

Meredith smiled and said, "Your maid is very attractive. She's quite taken with Dylan, isn't she?"

"Why, I think she is attracted to him."

"Most women are. I've seen them at the theatre. I'm not surprised that you would be drawn to him."

Serafina was taken off guard by this remark. "We've become very good friends."

"I suppose he feels safe around you."

Serafina blinked with surprise. "What do you mean, 'feels safe'? Why wouldn't he feel safe around me?"

"Well, the women that crowd around

Dylan at the theatre and even follow him on the street, there's always a danger he could become — well . . . involved with one and then have to marry her. But that could never be a problem with you." She laughed suddenly and said, "I can understand your being attracted to him, but then, of course, nothing could ever come of it."

Serafina felt a bright flicker of anger and could not explain it. "Something has already come of it, Meredith," she said, deliberately using the woman's first name.

"I don't understand you. That sounds almost —"

"We've become very close friends. As I told you before, he was highly instrumental in saving my brother when he was falsely charged with a murder. We worked together to get him free, and since then we have worked on other things together. More than that, I depend on Dylan to help with David. Since David lost his father, Dylan has almost become a second father."

"Well, I know that's been good for your son. I simply meant that you have a title, and Dylan is a commoner. That nothing could ever come of your relationship."

"You mean marriage?" Serafina asked directly.

Meredith was taken off guard. "Yes, I was

thinking that."

"This is the nineteenth century, not the sixteenth. People with titles do pretty much as they please, and I would pay no attention to a man's social standing if I loved him."

Meredith stared at Serafina and quickly changed the subject. "I was very happy in my marriage. I was married by Rev. Clive Alridge. I suppose you've heard of him."

"Yes, I have. He became quite a famous man among Evangelicals."

"He married Lewis and me. Oh, it was a beautiful wedding. Not like any one you would enjoy."

"I don't see why you would say that."

"I mean it wasn't at Buckingham Palace or St. Paul's. It was just in a very small church, very plain, but Rev. Alridge made it so real."

"I'm sure I would have appreciated that very much."

The two women sat there, but as they did, something was nagging at Serafina's mind. It was something that Meredith had said, and she put it down for study later on.

The two women had run out of small talk, and finally Serafina said, "I usually go up and sit in on the play times that Dylan and David have. It's quite a lot of fun for me to watch. Shall we go up?"

"Oh yes, that would be nice."

The two women ascended the stairs, and when they got to the large room that had once been a nursery, they heard Dylan's voice, melodious and pleasant and filled with excitement. The two moved inside, and neither David nor Dylan paid the slightest attention. As they took their seats, Dylan flashed them a warm smile and then turned back. "Another story that I've always liked is about a wicked king called Sennacherib. He was king of Assyria. He was a powerful king with an enormous army, and he sent word to Israel that he was coming to destroy their country and make slaves of them all."

"Did he do it?" David asked.

"You wait and listen, Master David Trent! A good storyteller never gives away the end."

"Is der a girl in de story?" Guinivere piped up in her two-year-old treble voice.

"No, it's not so much about little girls. That will come later."

"What happened, Mr. Dylan?"

"Well, the king of Israel was a very good man named Hezekiah, and Hezekiah knew that his army was so small he had no chance at all against the king of Assyria. So what he did was decide that God would have to help him. When King Hezekiah heard this huge army was coming, the Bible says right here" — he pulled a Bible from a table and opened it up — " 'And it came to pass, when king Hezekiah heard it, that he rent his clothes, and covered himself with sackcloth, and went into the house of the LORD.' And he began to pray that God would save Israel."

"Didn't he get his men ready to fight?"

"No, they were helpless, Master David, but he sent his servants to see one of God's great heroes, a man named Isaiah. And when the answer came back, Hezekiah was very happy."

"What made him so happy?"

"The prophet Isaiah said, 'Thus saith the LORD, Be not afraid of the words that thou hast heard . . . Behold, I will send a blast upon him, and he shall hear a rumour, and return to his own land; and I will cause him to fall by the sword in his own land.' You see, God has promised that he will take care of problems."

"Does God always take care of our problems?" David asked, curiously leaning forward, his eyes bright.

"Sometimes he lets his people go through terrible times, but Hezekiah continued to pray. He prayed a beautiful prayer, and you'll like the ending of this story." Suddenly Dylan shifted his gaze, and his eyes met Serafina's. He was smiling slightly, and Serafina knew what he was thinking. *He knows that I was very unhappy when he told stories like this at one time, but David's so excited.* She smiled back at him suddenly.

"The army of the king of Assyria came, and they literally surrounded the whole city of Jerusalem, and everyone said, 'We're all going to die,' but Hezekiah knew better because he had the word of the Lord."

"And what happened then?" David demanded.

"Well, let's read it from the Bible. It says here in verse 36 of the thirty-seventh chapter of Isaiah, 'Then the angel of the LORD went forth, and smote in the camp of the Assyrians a hundred and fourscore and five thousand: and when they arose early in the morning, behold, they were all dead corpses.' "

"Hurray!" David shouted.

"Hurray, indeed, or amen, as we would say now."

"What did the king of Assyria do?"

"Well, the next verse says, 'Sennacherib king of Assyria departed, and went and returned, and dwelt at Nineveh. And it came to pass, as he was worshipping in the house of Nisroch his God, that Adrammelech and Sharezer his sons smote him with the sword.' "

"I'm glad. He was a bad man."

"Yes, he was."

"Anutter one! Wif boys *and girls,*" Guinivere said.

"All right," Dylan laughed. "I'll tell another story. Once there was a little girl who looked just like you do . . ."

Serafina listened as Dylan told a fanciful story, knowing that he was making it up, and she marvelled again at his imagination. She glanced at Meredith, who was staring at Dylan with the most peculiar expression. *Why, she's in love with the man already! Maybe she was his childhood sweetheart, but it looks to me as if she is ready to take up where they left off.* The thought disturbed her so much she could barely listen to the story as Dylan unfolded it.

Meredith, Guin, and Dylan stayed for dinner. It was a simple enough meal, but the family were all there, including Septimus, Alberta, Dora, and Serafina's brother, Clive. Everyone was fascinated by Meredith Brice. Clive whispered to Serafina, "She's one of the most beautiful women I've ever seen. I wouldn't be surprised if Dylan fell in love with her."

"Don't be foolish! She's just an old friend," Serafina said crossly.

"Wish I had old friends that looked like her."

"Be quiet, Clive. You're so ridiculous."

Later on, when the men had gone into the smoking room, Meredith was left alone with Serafina once again. She said abruptly, "I'm going to have to find work soon." She turned suddenly and said, "You wouldn't know anything about that, would you, Lady Trent?"

"About what, Meredith?"

"About needing to find work."

"I've always worked."

"But your family has always had money. My family didn't always know where the next meal was coming from. Dylan's was the same. I think that makes us close together. It must be wonderful to have everything you could possibly want."

Serafina stammered, "It — it's not like that, Meredith."

"What do you mean? You could buy anything."

"You can't buy peace of mind or peace of heart. You can't buy love. There are things that are not available at a local shop."

Meredith shrugged. "Well, of course, I suppose that's true."

"Believe it or not," Serafina said, and her voice fell as she spoke, "life can be hard even for those who have place and money."

Meredith stared at her as if Serafina were speaking a foreign language. "That's hard for me to understand . . . Anyway, I think I have a career. At least a job."

"Oh, in a shop?"

"Dylan thinks he can get me a place with his company."

"You mean as an actress?"

"Yes, isn't that wonderful? He says I look better than most of the actresses and that he can teach me how to act. We're going to spend a lot of time together working on this. I hope you don't mind if I take him away from you."

There was a meaning in this sentence that lay below the words themselves, and Serafina saw that Meredith Brice was staring at her in almost a feline fashion. There was something under the softness of the woman that seemed predatory, and Serafina found that it made her nervous, even apprehensive — not for herself, but for Dylan Tremayne.

"I think you're jealous, Serafina."

"What are you talking about, Dora?" The two sisters were having breakfast the morning after Dylan had left with Meredith and

Guinivere. "Jealous of whom?"

"Of Meredith Brice."

"Why should I be jealous of her?"

Dora took a spoonful of strawberries lathered with rich cream and ate them before she answered. "Why, you must see that the two are quite taken with each other."

"They're old friends, Dora."

"I know. Childhood sweethearts. Meredith told me. She said Dylan gave her the first kiss she ever had."

Serafina picked up a strawberry and popped it into her mouth without answering. Dora studied her and asked, "Doesn't that make you jealous?"

"No, it doesn't."

Dora was an interested enough girl in the ways of the world, and she knew her sister very well. "I think," she said, "you've fallen in love with Dylan."

"Don't be foolish! We're just good friends."

Dora turned to face Serafina. She reached out and put her hand on her arm. "I think it's more than that, and listen. You know more than I do about things like this. But if you love Dylan, you'd better let him know it, or that woman will get him."

■ ■ ■ ■

Dora's words stayed with Serafina all day long. When she tried to put her mind to solving the identity of the Slasher, the thought would come back to her. She could almost hear Dora's voice saying again, *"If you love Dylan, you'd better let him know it, or that woman will get him."* She found this thought extremely disturbing, but also could not seem to drive it from her mind. She went about her work that day, and when night came she still, in her bed, could hear the sound of her sister's voice.

TWELVE

"Rachel, I wish you would clean this floor properly! Look at it! It's a mess!"

Rachel Fielding, the head housekeeper, looked up in surprise. She was a beautiful woman of fifty years who had lost her husband years ago but had never remarried.

"I'm sorry, ma'am, I thought it was clean. I'll assign one of the maids to clean it."

Serafina turned back from the window and waved her hand imperiously. "Look at it. Just look at it! It's filthy!"

"Yes, ma'am, I'll take care of it right away."

Septimus turned and looked at his daughter with surprise. He had been standing at a bookcase looking at the titles, but the outburst of anger from Serafina drew his attention. He reached up with both hands and ran them through his silver hair until it was standing on end, as usual, and finally said, "You were rather hard on her, Serafina."

"She doesn't manage the household very well!"

"But, my dear, she's been one of our most dependable servants — and the floor may be my fault. I scattered some of the paper on it." Septimus moved over to stand beside his oldest daughter. He studied her face thoughtfully and then asked mildly, "Is there something troubling you, my dear?"

"No!"

"Such a big no! A simple, gentle, 'No, Father,' might have been sufficient."

"Don't try to read into my feelings, Father. I can't stand them myself," she said bitterly.

Septimus suddenly reached out and put his hand on Serafina's shoulder. He was not a man given to overt gestures of affection, but he did have a loving heart and showed it most often to Dora. Serafina had become almost like a colleague of his. He had drilled her in the elements and basics of scientific thought and practice since she was a child. They had worked together side by side, and he forgot, at times, that she was not his own age. Now he studied her and thought, *I haven't treated this daughter of mine in the right way. I made a drudge out of her, and I should have shown more love.* "I wish you'd tell me what's wrong. Maybe I can help."

"Oh, I'm just not in a good mood today."

"You never used to have moody times, so what brought the bad mood on?"

"I don't want to discuss it."

"Very well. I wish I could help you." He stood there for a moment and made an attempt to change the subject. "The Brice woman, she seems to be very attractive and reasonably intelligent, I suppose."

Serafina shot a look almost of malice at her father, and he was taken aback. "Why, have I said something to offend you, my dear?"

"No!"

"Once again, such a big no. I don't understand people very well. Anything I can't put on a dissecting table, I don't do well with. I wish it were as easy to dissect a soul or a spirit as it is to dissect a body."

"Well, it's not!" Serafina snapped.

"I suppose not. Don't you think that Dylan seems to be rather more interested in her than he usually is?"

Serafina started to shout *No!* but knew that it would only bring her father's sharp attention once again. "She's an attractive woman, and they were friends in childhood."

"I haven't been around them as much as you have, but it seems that Dylan is interested in the woman. He found her a place to live, didn't he?"

"Yes, he did, but he would help anybody."

"But he goes to see her and takes her food, and he pays a lot of attention to that adorable child of hers. I wouldn't be surprised but what something might come of that."

Serafina looked at her father with utter disgust. "Nothing is going to come of it!" she snapped.

"Why — how can you be so sure?"

Serafina could not answer. As a matter of fact, she was not all that certain that Dylan Tremayne was not interested in Meredith in an intimate, romantic way. He had shown great concern in taking care of the woman, but it seemed to go further than that. And as for Meredith — well, the look she gave Dylan, the way she would touch him in a familiar fashion, putting her hand on his arm, reaching up and touching his hair occasionally — disgusting! There was a possessiveness about her that grated on Serafina's nerves, and she turned abruptly, saying, "I have to work on these notes I have, Father."

"Very well. I'll leave you to them. If you want to talk, I'll be available."

"Thank you, Father. You're very kind."

She waited until her father slammed the door behind him, knowing he would do so. Septimus never walked through a door and shut it gently, but for some reason gave it a backhanded push that made the rafters tremble. He had been cautioned often enough by his wife, also by Serafina and Dora, but he never seemed to realise what he was doing.

She sat down and studied the notes she had made concerning the murders that the Slasher had committed. She peered at the poetry for a long time and was struck at what poor writing it was:

Hath not a Jew eyes?
If you prick us, do we not die?
The world is full of traitors,
And highborn women mere impersonators!
Better if they were off the earth —
Even those of noble birth!

For over an hour she sat there peering at the poem and the other notes she had made. Once she looked up and said, "This is *impossible!* Somehow there's got to be a clue in here that would tell us something about this madman — but what *is* it?"

Doggedly she went over the poem line by line, and then for a time she simply closed

212

her eyes and sat back in her chair. The thought came to her, *If Dylan were doing this, he would ask God to help him.* The thought disturbed her, for she had never asked God for anything, not since she was a child. Since she had met Dylan, however, the idea of God had become very real to her. She had seen him pray and had seen what appeared to be the answers. Now she came as close as she could. She spoke the words aloud: "God, you know what I am — that I have had no faith at all in you. You know I'm grieving over my friend Margaret, and you know that I'm afraid that this maniac will strike someone else. If you're there at all, help me to . . . see something in this poem that will . . . give me something to work on."

She had to force each word out. It was the first prayer she had uttered in many years, since she was a child or a young woman, perhaps. She remembered praying that she would be a good wife to Charles, and that prayer had not been answered — although she had always felt it was not her fault.

The room was silent. From the open window came the faint voice of a song sparrow making melody on the air. It was a pleasant, cheerful song that ordinarily she loved, but now she shut out the sound and concentrated on the poem.

Afterward she would never remember the train of events that took place while she sat with her head bowed and her eyes fixed on the poem, seeking desperately to find something that would lead to the Slasher's identity. At some point a thought began deep within her innermost consciousness. Down in her spirit, as Dylan would have put it. It was not a full-fledged thought, but a mere fragment of an idea so elusive that she could not lay hold on it. She remembered once grabbing at a lizard when she had been only twelve years old and wanting to keep it for a specimen. Every time she almost grabbed the tail of the lizard, he scooted away, and she had scurried after him.

Now her mind was scurrying mentally, reaching out for the hidden clue that a vicious murderer had implanted, daring someone to find the answer.

The thought was hidden deep, as if in the deep waters of an ocean cavern many miles below the surface, but as she sat there struggling, it began to rise until finally she had a glimmer that was in her mind. She could put no name to it — but then suddenly it came.

Rachel Reis.

Serafina's eyes flew open, and she made fists of her hands and slammed them on the table. *Rachel Reis is Jewish. She and her husband, and the first line of this poem is spoken by a Jew, the merchant of Venice in Shakespeare's play. The other two women have been women with titles, and Rachel Reis is a marchioness.*

Suddenly everything seemed to come together. She thought of the marchioness at the church meeting at Lorenzo and Gyp's house where she had laughed at religion. She remembered how she had mocked Martha Bingham at the outdoor meeting. She was a woman who seemed totally oblivious that she may be hurting other people.

Serafina suddenly rose to her feet, her jaw tight and her lips thin. *I've got to go see her. It may be all in my own mind, but the woman deserves to know that there's at least a possibility that she may be the next victim.* She dashed out, went to her own room, and changed clothing. She left at once and found Albert Givins sitting on a bale of hay outside the stable.

"Albert, get the carriage ready."

Albert Givins was startled. "Which carriage, ma'am?"

"The one we can travel the fastest in. And

please send someone to call Matthew Grant — have him come at once to Marquis De-Main's estate."

"Be ready in minutes, Lady Trent."

"I'll wait right here."

Serafina stood there, and as she did, Dora came out. "What's going on, sister?"

"I've got an errand to run."

"An errand? It'll be dark soon." Dora had a troubled look. "Where're you going?"

"Oh, just something I need to do." Serafina was reluctant to mention her errand or the nature of it. "I'll be all right," she said. "Tell Father and Mother I'll be back a little bit late."

Dora said, "I will," but she stood there as if she wished to add something to that. She was still there when Givins drove up in the small carriage with two of their fastest teams. He started to jump down and help Serafina in, but she leapt into the carriage by herself and said, "Go on, Albert."

"Where to, ma'am?"

"I'll give you directions."

For some reason Serafina did not want Dora to know where she was going. *It may be a fool's errand,* she thought, *and I won't have to explain it if I don't tell anyone.* As soon as they were clear of the house and beyond the hearing of Dora, she said, "Do you

216

know where the Marquis Jacob Reis lives?"

"Certain I do, ma'am," he called over the sound of the horses' hooves.

"Get there as quickly as you can."

"Yes, ma'am." Albert touched the matched bays with the whip, and they shot forward as if propelled out of a cannon.

"Shall I wait here, ma'am?"

"Yes, I think if you take the carriage around to the stables, it might be less noticeable."

"I'll do that, Lady Trent."

Serafina watched as Albert drove the carriage up the curving driveway that led to the house. She turned and looked up at the magnificent home of the marquis. It was a huge house built of pale stone, classic Georgian in style. The massive front doors were flanked by dark pillars, and wrought iron balconies dotted the windows.

She was not interested in the house, however, but in the lady of the house. She started toward the front steps, conscious that darkness had already fallen as she had made her journey. She slowed to a walk and then tried to frame into a small speech what she would say to the marchioness. *She won't believe a word I say. She's the most disbelieving person I've ever seen.* The thought troubled Serafina, and she pondered lamely, trying to find an approach that might gain Lady Reis's attention at least.

She started toward the house, and suddenly a sound caught her attention. She looked upward, and a pale sliver of a moon cast a thin silvery light over the scene, and a few pale stars shone. Again the sound, and she realised it was not coming from the front of the house but from the side. Without thinking why, she turned and ran lightly half the length of the house. She rounded the corner, and as she did she saw a dark shadow coming down from the balcony on the second floor. The person was coming her way, but then she saw the shadow drop and heard a thump. *It's him — the Slasher!* The thought crashed through her mind, and without stopping to think what she could do, she ran forward, crying out, "Stop! Stop where you are!"

What happened next was so rapid she had no time to think. The shadowy figure, clothed in completely dark clothing with a hat pulled down over the features, whirled to face her in a lightning-like movement.

"Stop right where you are!" Serafina cried, but at that instant she caught the light of something bright and glittery. Her mind only had time to realise, not in words, but in a flash of thought: *That's a knife — and he's going to stab me! Matthew, where are you?*

She took a step backward, but the dark form shot toward her. The silvery knife flashed under the pale moon, and Serafina, even as she moved backward, felt a burning sensation across the top of her chest. She cried out, "Help! Help!" but the dark figure moved toward her again. She fell backward, and the face of her attacker was muffled, only a shapeless form, but she knew that the flash of the knife would be imprinted on her memory forever.

Suddenly a dog began barking, and the dark figure turned swiftly to face two bull terriers. He whirled and disappeared in the darkness so quickly that Serafina could not follow the movement. At the sight of the dogs, the figure had wheeled and dashed away, disappearing almost in a ghostly fashion.

"What's this? Who's there?"

"Over here," Serafina called and answered the man's voice.

Serafina got to her feet and found that she was trembling. She felt the front of her dress, which was sliced as keenly as if the knife had been a razor. She knew she had been cut, and suddenly the light of a lantern covered her. "Who are you? What do you want?"

"I'm Lady Trent, Vincent. You remember me?"

"Lady Trent! Of course I do." Vincent had been the butler for the Reis household for some time. He came closer, held the lantern up, and then gasped, "Why, you've been hurt, Lady Trent!"

"I'm all right, but we must get to Lady Reis, Vincent. She's in danger."

"In danger of what?"

"Of murder, I'm afraid. Come quickly."

Vincent whirled and rushed into the house. As soon as they were inside, he held the door for her and saw that her dress was sliced and she was bleeding. "Ma'am, you're bleeding!"

"It's not serious. Take me to the bedroom of the marchioness."

"Yes, at once." Vincent whirled, and he took the stairs two at a time with Serafina right behind him. He went quickly to the second door and started to knock, but Serafina pushed him aside. She opened the door and went in. She stopped dead still. There was a candle burning, and by the light of it she saw the woman lying on the bed. Marchioness Reis had been slashed, and she lay weltering in her own blood. Her throat had been cut, and her body had been terribly disfigured.

Serafina heard Vincent begin to gag, and she turned and pushed him outside the door. "I'm expecting Matthew Grant from Scotland Yard. Is he here yet? The marchioness has been murdered. Where's her husband?"

"He's asleep, I presume."

"Perhaps you'd better go tell him that something has happened."

"Yes, Lady Trent."

As Vincent wheeled, ran down the hall, and disappeared inside another door, she looked down at herself and pulled the dress apart. The tip of the blade had made a narrow cut that was bleeding freely. She waited until Vincent came back, his face pale. "The master is speaking with someone. He'll be here as soon as he can."

"I need some clean cloth and some antiseptic, Vincent."

"Come. We'll go downstairs. The master is getting dressed." She followed Vincent downstairs, and his wife, a tall, round-faced woman, gasped when she saw Serafina.

"Lady Trent has had an accident. She needs some bandages and some antiseptic."

"I'll take care of that," his wife said. Her name was Jane, and she proved to be quite steady under fire. As Vincent left to get the coachman and the carriage ready to send for Matthew, Jane, the housekeeper, treated the cut carefully. "It's not very bad. I don't think it needs stitches. How did it happen?"

"The murderer, I met him outside."

"The murderer!"

"The one they call the Slasher."

She saw Jane's face go pale. "The mistress. Is she —"

Serafina shook her head. "I'm sorry."

She stood there looking at the shallow cut in her chest and thinking if the dog had not come when he did, the Slasher would have done to her what he had done to Lady Reis.

As she stood there, she thought about God for the first time in a very direct and intimate way. God had always seemed a vague and shadowy figure to her, but now as she looked down at the blood seeping onto her breast, she thought, *Did God bring help to save me?* Somehow the idea of God caring enough about her to save her life gave her a warm feeling, and she found herself wanting to give thanks to the God she'd ignored for most of her life.

THIRTEEN

Grant and Kenzie almost fell out of the carriage before it stopped rolling in front of the Reis mansion. "Watch out, sir, you might break a leg! That won't help anything," Sergeant Kenzie warned sharply.

Ignoring the sergeant's words, Grant dashed toward the steps leading up to the massive front door of the house. He took the steps two at a time and banged with the brass knocker as Kenzie followed him at a more reasonable pace. "Why don't they answer the bloody door?" Grant snapped with irritation.

Suddenly, as if in answer to his question, the door swung open, and Vincent appeared, looking pale and uncertain. "Yes, sir," he said, "can I help you?"

"I'm Superintendent Grant from Scotland Yard."

"Well, yes, sir. My name is Vincent. Lady Trent told me to bring you to her as soon as you arrived. Will you come this way, please?"

"Have any of the local police been brought in?"

"Not yet, sir, I believe. The viscountess suggested that you might not want help from that quarter."

Grant nodded, his lips a grim line. Indeed, it was better this way, for sometimes amateurish local policemen could destroy evidence. Vincent led them down a foyer centered beneath a curving, marble double staircase. He stopped before a door and said, "Lady Trent is in here, sir."

Instantly Matthew entered the room, followed closely by Kenzie. His glance swept the large airy space. It was an elegant and cozy room with two large burgundy couches facing each other in front of a massive fireplace. Two big wing chairs stood in an intimate reading corner directly across from a gleaming buffet. The windows were all covered with heavy, dark green draperies, but a chandelier shed copious light over the room.

"Are you all right, Lady Trent?"

Serafina had been standing beside a massive bookcase. She turned and nodded, saying, "Yes, I'm all right, Matthew."

Matthew moved closer. His eyes fell on

the blood stain on her dress, which was held together above the breast by pins. "What is that?"

"I had a rather close meeting with the killer." Serafina was much calmer than she had been immediately after the almost fatal encounter.

Vincent spoke up. "Sir, shall I bring some tea?"

"Yes, yes. That would be fine, Vincent," Grant said, nodding peremptorily. He turned and said, "Come and sit down, Serafina. You're pale."

Serafina rubbed her upper arms with her hands. "I'm all right now, but it was a frightening thing. Sit down, and I'll tell you what happened."

The two of them sat down, and Kenzie moved over to stand at the side of the room, his pale blue eyes taking in Serafina's face. He had never seen her so disturbed, which in turn caused him some anxiety. He had become quite fond of Serafina and was highly proud of the fact that Matthew Grant, his superior, was going to marry into her family.

"What are you doing here, Serafina?" Grant asked.

"I was studying the clues and the poem, and the connection between Rachel Reis and the Jewish theme came to me suddenly." As she spoke, Grant was conscious of the steadfast quality in the viscountess. There was in her a sober willfulness and imagination that often caught the colour and melody of life about her. Dora had these same qualities, which enriched her sister and made both full women — though just now there was a shadow on Serafina's face that showed the strain that she had been under. She continued telling how she had made the connection. "The marchioness was the only Jewish woman I knew, and it just came to me that the killer might be referring to her. She has a title, and she's Jewish. That was all I had, so I jumped into a carriage and came over to warn her."

Matthew leaned forward, his eyes fixed intently on Serafina. "And what did she say?"

Serafina shook her head. "I never got to see her, Matthew. I got out of the carriage and started up the steps, but as I did, I heard some sort of a muffled sound over to my left. It was dark, as it has been all evening, but I saw a shape up on the second floor. I couldn't make much out of it, but suddenly the shape somehow dropped to the ground. I cried out for him to stop, and I expected him to run away. Instead of that

I saw a flash of steel, a knife. He was on me before I could even move, Matthew. So fast. As quick as lightning, and he struck out at me with the knife." She touched her chest and said, "If I hadn't fallen backward, I think he would have cut me to bits."

"Did you try to fight back?"

"No, there was no time. He came at me again with the knife held high. I could see that much, and suddenly the dogs rounded the corner, barking. The killer whirled and ran off into the darkness. Vincent came then, and the murderer was gone, hidden in the darkness. No chance of following him on a murky night like this."

"Were you badly hurt, Serafina?" Matthew asked anxiously.

"No, it was a mere scratch. I bandaged it up, but that knife must have been razor sharp. It cut through my dress as sharply as a pair of scissors."

Matthew drew a deep breath and expelled it. He was troubled and said at once, "You shouldn't have come here alone."

"I suppose not, but I didn't have much to go on." She rose to her feet just as Vincent came into the room. "We'll have the tea later, perhaps, Vincent," she said.

"Yes, madam."

"Come along, Matthew, and you too,

Sergeant. The marchioness's bedroom is upstairs." She led the way up the staircase and paused before the door as she turned to put her full gaze on Matthew. Her look was troubled, and a quicker breath stirred her breast. She flung up her hand and said, "It's terrible beyond imagination!" She then turned quickly and walked into the room, followed by the two men. Grant walked over to the body and stared down for a long time. He made no attempt to touch anything, and when he turned to face Serafina, there was a savage expression on his face. "The same killer, I would think."

"So I thought."

"Have you looked at any of these clues?"

"No, I waited for you. We must make a list of them, as you did with the other victims."

The three of them began slowly going over the items that had been scattered at random about the room.

Kenzie began writing down the items as the two walked over them. "Here's a watch charm with the initials H. W.," Matthew said.

"I suppose that means Herbert Welles."

"And look — here's an ivory brush with L. H. on the handle," Serafina said. "That means Leo Hunter, I suppose. His items

228

have been left before."

They picked up and turned over a hunting knife with "Ritter" engraved on it, a tract about women's rights by Martha Bingham, a single bullet from a revolver, a bottle of expensive perfume, a wrapped sweet — and then Serafina held up an item and did not speak. "What is it, Lady Trent?" Kenzie asked.

"It's a page from *Macbeth*."

"Let me see," Matthew said. He moved forward and stared at it. "That's Dylan's handwriting on there."

"Yes, it is."

They did not speak, but both were troubled.

"Sir, here in the window. Look."

They both turned, and Matthew went over and picked up a single sheet of paper. It was expensive enough paper, and he said, "Here's the poem, and it's in the same handwriting as the other notes."

Sonnet to a Dead Contessa

She is the fairest of the fair
But death will close her pretty eyes
So that she will never dare
Deceive a man with sugared lies!
That form that men declare divine

Will no more deceive poor men!
That flesh will be for worms to dine
And that will pay for her great sin!
The river with a crooked arm
On the day she is born she will perish,
And none can stop the harm,
And few will her memory cherish!
In midsummer she will cease to be,
And Scotland Yard will never see!

"Blast it," Matthew said, "another one of these bloody notes that doesn't mean anything!"

"I think it does mean something, Matthew. The other one did. It led me here, but not soon enough." Her voice was sad, and she said, "I would like to have a copy of that."

"I'll make you one, ma'am," Kenzie said at once and soon was busy scribbling on a fresh sheet of paper. "As well as a list of the clues."

They went to work, finding a few more clues, and finally Grant read out the list:

- watch charm with the initials H. W.
- ivory-handled hairbrush
- hunting knife with "Ritter" carved in the handle
- tract about women's rights by Martha

Bingham
- single bullet from a revolver
- bottle of expensive perfume
- wrapped sweet
- page from Macbeth with notes in Dylan's handwriting
- picture of Joan of Arc
- queen of hearts playing card
- collection of combs and hair pins

Matthew and Serafina spent the next two hours going over the room. They thought that they had seen everything, but finally Serafina straightened up.

"Look at this, Matthew."

He came over at once. "It's a single hair. Is it yours?"

"No, although it's almost the same colour. A reddish blonde."

"It's from someone else. It could be one of the maids."

"I suppose so, but we'll keep it just in case."

They both fell silent for a minute, and finally Serafina said, "There's a clue to the identity of the killer in these poems and also to the next victim, but I can't figure it out."

"He's a maniac toying with us!"

At that moment the door opened, and a man came in. "My wife!"

Immediately Serafina and Matthew went to block his entrance. She knew him immediately as the Marquis Reis. "Marquis," she said, "you shouldn't be here. You don't want to see her like this."

"Let me see her!" he cried. He was a smallish man with sleek black hair and black eyes. His eyes were filled, it seemed to both Matthew and Serafina, with agony. Matthew came to help, and they took him out of the room. "Please, sir, you can see her later but not now," Matthew said.

"Who could do a terrible thing like this? She was not always a kind woman, but she didn't deserve this."

"Did you hear any sound at all, Marquis?"

"No, I did not. How could a thief get in?"

"He had to come in through the window," Serafina said quickly. She had already checked all of these details.

"But it's straight up, at least twenty-five feet. You'd have to be a fly to climb up that side."

"He must have been a very agile man. I saw him come down."

"You saw him? Who was he? Why did he kill my wife?"

"It was very dark, and I couldn't see his face. All I saw was a hooded figure in the darkness."

"You must find him!" the marquis called out in anguish.

They led him away, and as soon as the local doctor came, he was given a sedative and put to bed.

"He seems broken up over her death," Matthew said, "but it might be an act."

"You suspect him?"

"I don't know who to suspect," Matthew said sourly. "I'm sick of this case! If I ever catch that fellow, I'm not sure he'll have to stand trial. I might be judge, jury, and executioner."

"You couldn't do that, Matthew." Serafina shook her head.

"No, I suppose not. Well, let's get started working. We'll have to analyse all this, but we still don't know who we're looking for. Perhaps we never will."

"We'll find him. We have to. He killed my best friend and two other women. We'll find him, and he'll hang for what he's done!"

Dylan smiled down at Meredith as she bubbled over with excitement. "Do you think I really have a chance to get a part in a play, Dylan?"

"There's always a chance." The day was bright, and the sun accented Dylan's rugged good looks. He looked down to where

Meredith was holding tightly on to his arm and said, "You don't have to hold me so tightly, Meredith. Nobody's going to run off with me. They'd be more likely to run off with you."

"I can't thank you enough for trying to do this for me."

"You may not thank me. The theatre is hard work. Not the fun that people think it is. I suppose work is work no matter what form it takes."

"But it's so exciting. The curtain going up, and going out on the stage. I know I can do it." Her eyes were shining, and her face glowed with an inner excitement that could not be hidden.

"We go in here. The producer's name is Browning. He owes me a favour, and I happen to know he needs someone for a small part."

Dylan felt Meredith's hand tighten on his arm as he led her inside the building. They went to the office that was backstage at the theatre and found John Browning waiting for them. "Come in, Dylan."

"Thanks for seeing us, Mr. Browning. This is Meredith Brice. Mrs. Brice, this is Mr. Browning."

She smiled at him, and Browning suddenly laughed. "Another starstruck young woman, Dylan?"

"Oh, come now, Mr. Browning. I've never asked you a favour like this before. You know that full well."

"I know it." He looked at Meredith and asked, "Do you have any experience at all?"

"No, sir, but I know I can do it."

"Well, we do have a small part. It's just two lines, and I'm looking for someone who can do that part and help our costume mistress."

"Oh, I'm very good with a needle, sir, and I'm perfectly happy to do it."

"It doesn't pay much." He mentioned a sum, and at once Meredith beamed. "That would be very fine, sir. I'd be more than satisfied to come for that."

"Just be here this afternoon at two o'clock for rehearsal. If you'll wait just a minute, I'll get you a sheet, and you can practice on your lines."

After Browning disappeared into an inner office, Meredith turned and said, "Isn't it wonderful!"

"You think so, don't you?" He studied the rich, racy current of vitality within this woman and saw that she had a way of laughing that was extremely attractive. Her chin tilted up, and her lips curved in pretty lines. He noticed a small dimple at the left of her mouth and admired the way that the light danced in her eyes.

Browning came back and handed her a few sheets of paper. "Your character is simply called 'the maid Mary.' "

"I'm so excited."

"I hope Dylan told you that being an actress is a hard, demanding task."

"Yes, I've told her, Mr. Browning, but she doesn't believe me."

"Well, she may after a while."

"Thank you, Mr. Browning. I appreciate the favour. Call on me if you ever need me."

"I'll be calling on you, all right, but not for a small favour. I want you to star in something for me when your run is over with *Macbeth*."

"I'll be happy to talk with you about it, sir."

The two left the theatre, and Meredith talked unceasingly all the way home. She was so excited that people turned to watch her on the street. As soon as they reached her house, she said, "Come in and teach me how to say my lines."

"Well, I suppose a lesson wouldn't hurt." He entered, and she made tea, and soon the two had gone over the simple lines that she had to memorise.

"I want to do this just right, Dylan."

"We'll find some way. It's a very mundane line. It's really to move other actors around, but maybe we can put a little something extra to it."

Dylan stayed for over an hour. They had tea and cakes, and Dylan had exhausted himself trying to find something new to put into the lines that Meredith had read.

They sipped their tea, and he said, "Did you get along well with Lewis's family?"

"Oh yes. His mother, Lucy, she was a charming woman."

"You don't mean Lucy. You mean Alice."

"Oh yes, of course. Aren't I a silly thing? I can't even keep my mother-in-law's name straight. My own mother's name was Lucy, as you know."

"I suppose it's a natural mistake," Dylan said doubtfully. He was wondering how anyone could mistake the name of one's mother-in-law, but his thoughts were broken when a knock sounded on the door.

"I'm not expecting anyone," Meredith said. She got up and went to the door, and when she opened it she found Sergeant Kenzie there. He asked at once, "Is Mr. Tremayne here, ma'am?"

"Why, yes, he is. Come in, Sergeant."

Kenzie came in and removed his hat, and Dylan got up from the table. "What is it,

Kenzie?" he asked. "Has there been a new development?"

"I'm afraid there has been another murder."

"Oh no," Dylan groaned. "Who was it?"

"The Lady Reis."

Dylan shook his head sadly. "This madman must be caught."

Kenzie cleared his throat. "That's not exactly all, sir. You see, Lady Trent figured out, somehow, by reading the poem left at the last murder scene that the marchioness was going to be the victim. I don't know exactly how that worked."

"She's got a brain, that woman has. What did she do?"

"Well, sorry to tell you, she rushed right over to the Reis mansion, and she was attacked by the killer who had just murdered the marchioness."

Instantly Dylan demanded, "Is she badly hurt? Is she all right, Kenzie?"

"A minor wound, sir, but the superintendent asked me to bring you there. He knew you would want to see her."

Dylan said, "Yes. Come, man, let's go at once." He left through the door, and Kenzie rushed after him. Meredith moved to watch them go. "He didn't even say goodbye," she muttered. Then she thought of her new career, and a slow smile came to her. "I'll be a star someday. I will!"

Serafina heard Dylan's voice, and from the sound of his feet in the hall, she knew he was running. The door burst open, and he came in at once. His face was pale, and she cried out, "Why, Dylan —"

Dylan did not speak. He was, indeed, pale. The ride had seemed interminable, and he rushed over to her at once and seized both of her hands. "Are you all right, Serafina? Are you badly hurt?"

Serafina's hands were hurt by his iron grip, but his touch made her feel secure. Actually she was shocked at the show of concern in Dylan's face. *He must think more of me than I suspected.* The thought flitted through her mind and was pleasing. But quickly she said, "It was very minor."

"He slashed you with a knife?"

Serafina freed her hand and touched the pins. "I could barely see, it was so dark. I did see the flash of the knife, and I was falling backward. If I hadn't been, I think it would have been a very deadly wound. Here, sit down, Dylan." She looked up and said, "Vincent, bring some tea, please."

"It's already made, ma'am."

Serafina drew him over to the couch and

pulled him down. She sat down beside him and was pleased when he reached over, took her right hand, and held it tightly between his own. She noted that his hands were unsteady, something she had never seen in him before. She waited until Vincent had brought the tea in, and she poured and then told him the same story that she had told the superintendent.

"What did he look like?" Dylan demanded.

"I couldn't see. It was very dark."

"Well, how big was he?"

"It all happened so quickly. He was not big, not as big as you. He was wearing some sort of very dark clothing and a hood over his face."

Dylan had calmed down, and some colour had come into his cheeks. He listened as she told of their findings in the murder room upstairs, but he seemed preoccupied. Finally she said, "We have a poem that sounds meaningless. We have a group of clues. One of them is a page of a script with your writing on it."

"I'm a suspect again."

"Oh no. Matthew knows that these things are meaningless, for the most part."

She sat there studying him, not so much because of his good looks. She was accustomed to that, but she was interested in the man beneath all of this. Studying him, she saw in his eyes a shine of hard simplicity. *In fortune or in trouble he would never be much different. He could not be different,* she thought. His life had tempered him, fashioned a private world with its images and its long thoughts and its hope of what might be. She was well aware of this. She saw a tiny scar on his temple she had never noticed, and suddenly she thought, *Why, I know him so well. There is in him a loneliness and a hunger for life, and for something I thought would take its form in a woman.*

For the first time since her marriage had ended, as she studied Dylan carefully, she gave serious thought to what it would be like to be a wife. She felt as if she had never been a wife, for there had been none of the tenderness that she had longed for from Charles. As this thought came to her, Dylan reached over and took her hand, and a warmth came to her in a sense of goodness and a sense of security. She suddenly realised that these were the kind of thoughts she had had when she was a young girl and then a young woman before she married. It was what she had always longed for, and now she was seeing it in a man who was so different from who she was. But it gave her a feeling of completeness and somehow of goodness to know that this man who was good could feel such concern for her.

When he spoke, his voice was almost rough, and he gripped her upper arms so hard that she almost winced. "You will not put yourself in a situation like this again, Serafina. Do you hear me?"

"Ye— yes, I hear you," she stammered. She was very aware of the power that came out of him, of the strength of his hands on her arms and of his eyes that seemed to devour her.

"That's what you have a man like me for."

Serafina had always argued she did not need a man, but now that he held her so tightly as if she would run away and he would not permit it, she was aware that there was something in what he was saying that appealed to the very deepest part of her spirit, and she found herself saying, "Yes, Dylan, I'll do as you say."

He was pleased with her and expelled his breath. Suddenly he reached out, put his arms around her, and said, "You'll never know what a terrible thing it was when I thought you were hurt!"

His embrace almost crushed the breath from her body, but Lady Serafina Trent found herself like a mariner who had left a stormy sea and come into a safe harbor. A sense of peace and joy and happiness that she had longed for, at least for a moment, was there and was all she wanted.

FOURTEEN

As usual, the cheerful atmosphere of the breakfast table was broken by the presence of Aunt Bertha. Lady Bertha Mulvane had the ability to cast a pall of misery on any gathering that she chose to honour with her presence. The other members of the family, including Septimus, his wife, Alberta Rose, Clive, Dora, David, and Serafina, ate almost silently while Lady Bertha dominated the conversation.

Septimus spoke up, making an attempt to cut through the gloom by reading items from the newspaper. "Serafina, here's an article about Elizabeth Blackwell," he said. "It talks about her work in directing that new infirmary for women and children in New York."

"Oh, I've heard of her," Serafina said at once. "She's the first woman to graduate with a medical degree."

"The woman should stay home where she

belongs. Imagine a woman probing around on the body of a man. Disgusting!" Bertha said.

"What about a man probing around on the body of a woman, Aunt Bertha?" David piped up.

"You keep out of this, young man," Aunt Bertha warned sternly. "Young people should be seen and not heard!"

Septimus shook his head and then tried again. "You'll be interested in this, Serafina. That French chemist Louis Pasteur, who's been working on researching fermentation . . . he's just taken a new post in Paris."

"Really, Septimus, who do you think would be interested in a thing like that?" Lady Bertha snorted with disgust.

"I think the whole world will be interested in what Mr. Pasteur is doing," Septimus answered. "It's very important scientific work." Quickly, before Bertha could speak, he shook his head. "We no sooner get a war finished in the Crimea, and then we have another one breaking out."

"Another war, dear? Where in the world is it?" Alberta spoke up.

"Well, there's a mutiny in India. Been a massacre over there. Two hundred and eleven British women and children were killed."

Again Bertha proclaimed her views on the subject. "Those who did it should be caught and hung."

Septimus gave up, seeing that whatever he read in the paper would not be accepted.

"I see the newspapers are screaming for Scotland Yard to catch the Slasher," Clive said. He looked over at his sister. "What does Grant say about this, Dora Lynn?"

But Dora was not able to answer, for Bertha once more issued a proclamation. "It's vulgar for our family to be involved with such things." She opened her mouth to say more, but then suddenly caught a glimpse of Serafina's face. Lady Bertha at once shut her own mouth, for she remembered the stern warning that Serafina had given her.

David waited for his aunt to speak, and when she did not, he turned to his mother and smiled. "I think it was noble of you to try to save the woman's life, Mother."

"I wish I had been successful."

Dora picked up the paper and read what it had to say about the Slasher case. "Why, they're blaming Matthew for these murders. It's not fair!"

"It isn't fair, but very few things in this world are," Serafina remarked. She was surprised when Dora suddenly rose and walked out of the breakfast room. She disappeared without saying a word, and Bertha said, "There's manners for you! You really should speak to her, Septimus."

Septimus, who rarely spoke to any of his children about their misbehaviour, buried himself in the newspaper. Serafina watched out the window and saw Dora get into one of the carriages and drive off. *I wonder where she's going,* she thought.

Matthew Grant was talking to the marquis when suddenly he thought, *I'm getting to be quite a connoisseur of the nobility of England. All the murder victims have titles, and their husbands also.* He studied the Marquis Reis and remembered what Kenzie had gleaned in his study of the man. Kenzie had reported that the Marquis Reis had come to England as a poor boy, had worked himself up in a factory, and finally had become wealthy through the manufacture of arms. He was a small man, very inoffensive, and what seemed to be profound grief scored deep lines in his face. Matthew cleared his throat and said quietly, "I am terribly sorry to have to question you at this time, sir, but you understand that we need to catch this murderer as quickly as possible."

"Of course, Superintendent. You may go

ahead and ask me any questions you wish."

"Thank you, sir. The obvious question is, did the marchioness have any enemies that might have wished to harm her?"

"She was a very . . . outspoken woman, and her remarks sometimes irritated people. They irritated me at times, but I was accustomed to them. I knew that beneath her rough manner there was a kind heart, but others did not see that. So she did have those who were not admirers, shall we say."

"Yes, sir, but I'm not talking about minor things. I mean did she have any altercation or quarrel with anyone who might have taken this extreme form of revenge?"

The marquis stared at him blankly. "Why, no, Superintendent, nothing like that. I assume that this maniac just hunts up titled women at random and murders them. Is that not so?"

"We don't know, sir. We do know that the murderer scatters meaningless clues to throw us off the track. What about the servants?"

"Oh, they're absolutely incapable of such a thing. We research them very carefully."

The marquis answered every question that Matthew could think to ask, and finally when Matthew left the mansion, he was aware of a frustration that went to the bone.

It's impossible to think that man would kill his wife. He's just not the type. He called out to the driver an address, and within half an hour he was in the drawing room of Gerhard Von Ritter. "Ah, we meet again, Inspector," Ritter said. He smiled amiably, but there was something almost sharklike in his attitude. He was wearing expensive clothing, a suit cut especially to fit his athletic figure. He was half smiling as he studied Matthew Grant and asked at once, "I assume that this has something to do with the latest murder by the Slasher."

"I'm afraid it does, sir. Do you recognise this knife?"

Matthew had taken an envelope from his pocket and handed it over to Von Ritter. Von Ritter opened the envelope and pulled out a knife. "Why, of course I recognise it. It's my knife. Now, don't tell me it was found at the murder scene."

"Yes, sir, it was."

Von Ritter's face clouded with anger. "This is getting beyond humour."

"It certainly is — and has been. There's nothing humorous about it."

"Well, I was rather admiring the killer. He had imagination leaving all those false clues and stealing things such as this knife and other items from famous people."

Matthew Grant was irritated at the remark. "If he killed a member of your family, Mr. Von Ritter, I don't think you would find it so amusing."

A hard light glittered in Von Ritter's eyes, but he shrugged and said, "You are right, Superintendent. I spoke inadvisably."

"Do you have any family, sir?"

"No, none at all. You know the old saying — 'He that hath wife and children have given hostages to fortune.' "

"A rather cynical remark, I've always thought."

"I believe it is, but then, I'm a cynical man. What shall we do, then? Am I a suspect?"

"Well, as you know, sir, there's nothing really to charge you with. There were numerous items left there belonging to other people. We can't arrest all of you, can we?"

Von Ritter's eyes glittered, and he laughed shortly. "That would make a pretty story, wouldn't it? I'm sorry for you, Superintendent. I would help you if I could."

"Would you mind telling me where you were on the night of May the eighteenth?"

"As a matter of fact, I would mind."

Matthew's attention sharpened. "You understand that these are routine questions."

"The lady I was with all of that night is a member of the aristocracy. As a matter of fact, she's the wife of one of the members of Parliament, a high-ranking member. It would create a national scandal, Superintendent."

"We may have to ask you for that name."

"You may ask, but I will not answer. After all, I do have my standards."

An angry reply leapt to Matthew's lips, and he was certain that Von Ritter was expecting it. He bit it off and said, "Thank you for your time, sir."

"Come at any hour. We never close," Von Ritter mocked.

Matthew left Von Ritter's house and went at once to the building that housed his office. Several of his men spoke to him, but he was so deep in thought he merely muttered a reply. He found Kenzie waiting for him in the outer office and said, "What is it, Kenzie?"

"Miss Dora, sir. She came to see you, and I put her in your office. I thought it would be proper."

"Very proper. Thank you, Kenzie." Matthew walked in and found Dora standing beside a window, looking out. She turned, and he was once again impressed with the innocence of the woman. His eyes went to her face, noting her pleasantly expressive mouth, and he knew at once that though she kept it well concealed, there was a fire in this woman that made her lovely, yet she hid her rich and headlong spirit behind a rather cool reserve. As she came toward him, he saw the hint of her will and of pride in the corners of her eyes and lips, and he noted that her face was a mirror that changed with her feelings.

"It's good to see you, Dora," he said.

"I had to come, Matthew. There's something I want to say to you."

Grant saw the seriousness of her face and said, "Come and sit down."

"No, I want to stand." She came to him and put her hands out, and he took them and held them. They were small but strong, and there was an earnestness about her that told him to hold his peace and let her speak.

"What is it, dear?" he asked quietly. "Just tell me. You can tell me anything."

"Remember that you said that, Matthew," Dora said. She hesitated, cleared her throat, and said, "I want us to get married."

"Why, we're going to get married. I've already asked your father's permission."

"No, Matthew, I mean *now*. Right away."

Matthew, for a moment, could not think of a proper reply, and then he said, "Well, of course, I would like that too. But there are . . . disadvantages."

He struggled over the last word, and she said, "I want us to get married. Don't you love me, Matthew?"

"You know I do." He put his arms around her and kissed her, and she clung to him. When he lifted his lips, he said, "I love you as I never thought a man could love a woman."

"I want a life with you. I want us to have our own home. I want us to have children. Those are the things I want, and I don't want to wait any longer."

Matthew Grant was a hard man. His had been a difficult life. He had mixed with hard company in his job as policeman, inspector, and now superintendent, but this girl brought a light of gentleness and a taste of something he could not even identify. He wanted to call it heavenly gentleness. Whatever it was, he knew that it was the one thing he thanked God for every day of his life. Suddenly he laughed and said, "All right. Shall we go today?"

"Oh no," she laughed and hugged him, putting her face against his neck. "No, I think we ought to announce it. Maybe in two weeks."

"Your family won't like it."

"Aunt Bertha won't, but I can convince the rest."

"I won't take anything from your family — money, I mean. We'll have to live on my salary."

"I don't care."

"It will be hard," he warned.

"I don't care, Matthew, as long as I have you. This Slasher case has made me realise just how short life can be, and I want to be by your side every moment of every day."

He laughed and then embraced her, and as he did, the door opened, and he saw Kenzie walk in. A look of shock touched Kenzie's dour Scottish face, and Grant laughed again. "A man can hug the woman he's going to marry in his office without shocking you, can't he, Sergeant?"

Kenzie did not laugh often, but he did now. Pure pleasure came to him, and he walked forward. "My congratulations to you both. I'm so happy."

Dylan had come to Serafina's house, and they had gone over the clues they had found. It had gotten to the point that they could not even call them clues. "False scents" was the term that Serafina had given to them. They went over each one of them and then over the poem, which told little enough about the killer.

"This is a terrible poem — and makes no more sense than the others," Dylan said. He read it aloud, slowly and carefully:

Sonnet to a Dead Contessa

She is the fairest of the fair
But death will close her pretty eyes
So that she will never dare
Deceive a man with sugared lies!
That form that men declare divine
Will no more deceive poor men!
That flesh will be for worms to dine
And that will pay for her great sin!
The river with a crooked arm
On the day she is born she will perish,
And none can stop the harm,
And few will her memory cherish!
In midsummer she will cease to be,
And Scotland Yard will never see!

"I don't get any sense out of it," Serafina said. "But it's not like the other poems."

"How is it different?"

"The others were in no set form, but this is a sonnet. Four quatrains and a couplet."

"I wonder if there's a key to the identity of the next victim. We've got to figure this out! 'On the day she is born she will perish'?

How could that be? And what does a river have to do with a murder?"

"Yes, this one is tough. And the rest of the clues are meaningless."

"I think he's toying with us, Serafina."

Serafina seemed preoccupied, for she was still walking in the glow that she had felt when Dylan had come to her so full of concern. It had told her more about his feelings for her than he would ever speak out loud. As she watched him, she became aware of something. *He would never tell me he loved me because I have a title and he's an actor. And besides that, he's a devoted Christian and I'm not.*

The thought saddened her, but she could think of no way to speak of this to him.

"Have you thought any more about what you saw of the killer, Serafina?"

"Well, I've tried to think of something, but he had to be a strong, active man to climb the side of that wall and then to come down without breaking his neck."

"And you didn't see anything of his features?"

"No, nothing. I wish I had."

The two talked on about the case, and finally Serafina asked, "How is Meredith doing with her new job?"

"Very well. She has hired a nanny to keep

Guin. The acting isn't much, but she's do- ing it very well. The producer is quite pleased. She's talked him into giving her a bigger part in the next play."

"Do you think she'll become a success?"

"She has some talent. Certainly she has the looks for it. I've tried to talk her out of it though."

"You have? Why?"

"It's not a good life, Serafina."

Serafina continued to ask questions about Meredith Brice but could not make any- thing of Dylan's answers. He was fond of the woman, she could see that, but they were old friends.

Finally Dylan said, "I'm going to ask you something that will probably offend you."

"Go ahead, Dylan. What is it?" She turned to face him fully. "Don't be afraid of of- fending me. We're better friends than that."

"I can't tell you how frightened I was when I heard you had been attacked. The thought that scared me green was that you'd been killed."

"That thought came to me too," Serafina said tersely. "I could have been too. It was only the dogs and Vincent coming at that moment that saved me."

"If you had been killed, it would have been terrible for me."

"Would it, Dylan?" she asked softly. "Really?"

"Of course. For two reasons. First, because you and I are such great . . . friends." He struggled with the last word, and then he said, "I would have missed you in the flesh, but I would be devastated to think that you went out to meet God without any preparation."

Serafina had known this was coming. It had been coming for a long time now, and she was quiet for a moment. When she looked up, she saw, to her surprise, that there were tears in Dylan Tremayne's eyes. He was such a strong man that she did not think of him ever weeping, and it went right to her heart. She whispered, "Why, Dylan, I didn't think —"

"You need Jesus in your life. I don't know any other way to put it. Will you think about it, Serafina?"

Serafina did not hesitate. "I've already thought about it, Dylan. As a matter of fact, it's been a constant thought recently."

Dylan pulled out his handkerchief, wiped his eyes, and took a deep sigh of relief. He reached forward and took her hands, and to her amazement he lifted them and kissed the backs of them, something he had never done before. "I couldn't do without you,

Serafina Trent," he whispered. Then he turned and left the room as if afraid he would say more.

Serafina was greatly moved by his tears and his words and by the fact that he cared about her so much he could not stay in her presence and talk about such things as death. She sat there for a long time, then went over to the table, picked up the Bible that he had given her, opened it, and began to read.

Fifteen

The evening meal had been good, but Serafina had noticed that neither Matthew Grant nor Dora had much to say. This was not unusual, for they were both rather quiet people, but somehow Serafina felt that they were either despondent or keeping something back. She was not at all surprised when, after the last course had been served, Dora looked around the table and said, "Matthew and I have made a decision. We want to get married very soon."

"Impossible!" Lady Bertha snorted. "It takes months to get ready for a wedding for a family of our station."

Since Lady Bertha had only the faintest connection with the Trent family, the "our station" sounded out of place, but Bertha never minded being out of place. "There will be a great deal to do, and I'm sure you will not want to do anything that isn't in keeping with our position."

Matthew had been watching Dora. Serafina saw his jaw suddenly grow tense, and he turned to face Bertha squarely. There was a steely quality in his voice when he said, "Lady Bertha, this is not something we have come to debate. We have talked about it, prayed about it, and we feel that it's time for us to start our married life." He turned away to face Septimus and said quietly, "Sir, I hope this meets with your approval."

"Why — why, it's somewhat surprising, but I have no objections. What about you, my dear?"

Alberta stared at her husband and then at her younger daughter. She shot one nervous glance at Bertha but then said firmly, "I think it should be exactly as you two plan it. It's your wedding after all."

"It is not her wedding! It is *our* wedding!" Lady Bertha burst out. "I insist that this wedding not take place for at least six months!"

"I don't want to be argumentative," Matthew said, and though his voice was low, there was an adamant quality in it, "but this is something we feel that we want to do. I might as well tell you the rest of it. You know my position. I'm not a wealthy man. Dora is accustomed to better things than I'll be able to provide, but I have already told her that we will live within my income."

"Which doesn't matter," Dora added quickly. She was seated next to Matthew and suddenly reached over and took his hand. Her eyes were starry, and her gentle features revealed the state of her heart. "We'll be like any other young couple. We'll get by."

Septimus looked fondly at this younger daughter of his. "That was the way it was with your mother and I when we got married," he said. He looked across the table and smiled at his wife. "You remember that, dear? Hard times, wasn't it?"

"Yes, it was, but we didn't mind. We were so in love that though a mere pittance was all we had, we didn't care."

"You never told me that, Mother," Dora said.

"Well, that's how it was. You may not believe it, but your father was a very romantic man. He even learnt how to play a guitar and sing love songs to me."

Clive, who had been taking all this in, suddenly laughed. "Do you still have that guitar, Father?"

"I don't believe so. I think I hocked it once when we were struggling to make ends meet."

"I would love to hear you sing one of those songs." Clive grinned broadly. Then he turned and said, "Sister, count on me. Matthew, anything I can do, I will."

Serafina smiled. She saw Aunt Bertha was puffed up like a large toad, but she gave her a warning look and turned to Dora and Matthew, saying, "I think it's wonderful. And, Matthew, it's very good of you to take all the responsibility on your own shoulders. I think I'd be proud to have you as a brother-in-law."

"At least we have two weeks. We can make some preparation," Alberta said. "After all, we don't lose a daughter every day in the week, do we, Septimus?"

"We're not losing a daughter. We're gaining a son. Someone to support us in our old age, I'd say." He winked at Matthew, and Matthew laughed. "It'll be quite an honour having the superintendent of Scotland Yard in our family. Don't you think so, Aunt Bertha?"

Lady Bertha Mulvane did not think so, not in the least, but when she looked at the happy faces around the table, she was at least smart enough to see that her cause was lost. "I'll be available to attend to any of the details of the wedding."

"Thank you, Aunt Bertha." Dora smiled

at her. "I'm sure we'll be calling on you." She turned to Matthew and reached out to hold his hand. "I have you trapped now. You can't get away."

"I'll never get away from you, not in a million years," Matthew Grant said. His fellow workers at Scotland Yard would have been shocked and amazed at the tenderness in their superintendent's face as he looked at his bride-to-be.

Dylan was lying flat on his back in the middle of the floor, and Guin was crawling all over him. He laughed, suddenly seized her, got to his feet, and tossed her up. "You're a charmer, you are."

"Stories! More stories!" the child cried.

"Oh, you want more stories, do you? Well, you'll have to give me a token of your affection. Here, give me a kiss right here." He touched his cheek, and Guin threw her arms around him and kissed him.

"Now, more stories," she commanded.

Dylan plopped himself down in a chair and began telling some wild, outrageous story. He had discovered that the child loved stories of any kind, and at the age of two, he soaked them in. He found it was impossible to shock her, for when he told stories of ogres who devoured little children in the woods, that was no more shocking to her than the Little Red Riding Hood tale that she demanded very often.

Meredith had been making tea, and she said, "Put that child down and talk to me."

"I'm sorry. I can't do it. I have a previous engagement."

Meredith pouted. "I declare. I believe you think more of Guin than you do of me. I'm absolutely jealous."

"Well, she's prettier than you are."

Meredith glared at him for a moment and then burst out in laughter. "You're a fool, Dylan! You say the wildest things I ever heard."

"Well, I like younger women, you see."

Meredith came over and tugged at his hair and brought a cry from him. "You behave yourself or I'll pull all your gorgeous hair out. Then where would you be? A bald-headed Macbeth? I don't think it would work.

"It's time for your nap, Guin." Meredith ignored the protest of her daughter, picked her up, and disappeared. She came back soon smiling and saying, "She wants more stories, but she's so sleepy she'll go right off."

"She's a beautiful girl. Going to be a beautiful woman just like her mother."

"Don't try your wiles on me," Meredith said. "I'm so excited, Dylan." She pulled him over to the couch and was now pressing against him. He was extremely conscious of the scent that she always used in her hair and in her clothes. She was giddy, for she had been given a larger role in a playhouse down the street from the theatre where Dylan was performing. Dylan had felt somewhat guilty about introducing her to the acting profession, for he was not an advocate of women actresses. He knew too many of them for that. But he had been instrumental in finding her this new role, and she had done well in the rehearsals.

"It's so exciting!" she exclaimed, and her eyes were sparkling. "Just think, I could be a star one day!"

"You could, but I'm not sure you'd like it."

"Not like it?" Meredith stared at him. "I would love it. You just don't appreciate what you have, Dylan. I can't understand it. You know what it's like to be poor, and now you're making lots of money, and people admire you. I just don't see how you can say it wouldn't be the best thing that ever happened to me."

"I've seen too many actors and actresses go wrong, and sometimes the more success you have, the easier it is to stray. That's why I'm a little bit afraid of success. It takes your mind off important things."

Meredith stared at him in disbelief. "Important things? What could be more important than having a successful career?"

"God." Dylan spoke at once and shrugged his shoulders. "If we don't love God and give him first place, all the success in the world will turn to ashes. I've seen it happen."

Meredith smiled and moved closer to him, and Dylan was well aware of her touch. She was one of the most beautiful women he had ever seen, and he noticed the smooth ivory shade of her skin where her blouse fell away from her throat. Her eyes were wide and coloured a blue shade of grey. They seemed to have no bottom, and her black hair lay rolled and heavy on her head. Her best feature was the curve of her mouth, which was ripe and self-possessed. Her figure as good as any woman's in England. He was well aware of the way the light from the window touched her and ran over the curve of her shoulders, deepening her breast.

Suddenly her nearness within him set off shocks, and his vision was narrowed down until he saw only the full swell of her lips and their increasing heaviness. Her breath quickened, he saw, and her lips made a small change and became soft with the caught interest of a woman. Her delicate fragrance slid through the armour of Dylan's self-sufficiency, and Meredith sensed it at once. She turned toward him, putting herself against him, and her hand went up behind his neck. She pulled his head down, and without meaning to he laid his lips on hers. The kiss affected Dylan powerfully. It seemed to fan close-up hungers that had been in him many years. He knew he would remember, for a long time, how soft and sweet her lips were, and the vibration of her voice as she whispered his name. She whispered, "Do you care for me at all, Dylan?"

The question caught Dylan off guard. She was nestled within his arms, and her eyes had caught his.

"I've always thought you were a sweet and beautiful child, and you haven't lost that."

"That doesn't answer my question."

"I don't know how I feel. We're going in different directions. You want to get into the theatre, and I want to get out."

"But if we care for each other, that wouldn't matter, would it?"

"I don't know, Meredith. You're tempting to any man. Certainly I know that." All at once Dylan recognised that he was falling under her spell in a way that he had not responded to a woman in years. It frightened him, and he did not know why. He suddenly moved and got to his feet. "I think I'll have to go. I have to be at the theatre in an hour."

"Stay awhile longer." The invitation was clear in her voice and in the set of her lips and the glint of her eyes.

"I'd better not, Meredith. I'm happy you got the part. We'll talk about this some other time." He turned quickly and left the house. As soon as he was outside, he took a deep breath. He felt as if he had just had a close escape. She was a very tempting woman, and he knew she had opened a door of invitation to him. He had almost walked through it, and now he felt like a man who had just escaped falling into a trap. It troubled him, and he could not get it out of his mind as he turned and hurried down the street.

"I don't know why you're fussing so much, Dylan. After all, it's only an art exhibit."

The two had turned and were headed into a large public building. On the outside was a sign that proclaimed an art exhibit was being held. Dylan stared at it moodily. He still was troubled over the scene with Meredith. Of course, he had not mentioned this to Serafina.

"We've got to get Matthew and Dora some wedding presents, and I would like to get them a picture for their new place together, whenever they get one."

"I don't know anything about art."

"Well, I don't know much, but I know when I like a painting. Come along and don't argue with me."

"You're getting to be a bossy woman."

"I always was. You just never noticed."

Suddenly Dylan laughed. "I noticed, all right. It was one of the first things that I noticed about you."

They entered the art gallery, and Dylan felt out of place. There were pictures on the wall that he didn't understand and people he didn't know, and he stayed by Serafina's side. She knew many people and stopped once to introduce him to a couple. "Baron DeMain and Lady DeMain, may I introduce you to my friend Mr. Dylan Tremayne."

"Oh, I've seen Mr. Tremayne on the stage." Lady DeMain's French descent showed itself in her accent.

Her husband, the French ambassador, smiled as he nodded toward Dylan. "I'm not happy to meet you, sir."

Dylan and Serafina stared at the baron,

and Serafina asked, "Why do you say that, Baron?"

"She insisted on going back and seeing that play three times." The baron chuckled. "I must admit it was not a painful duty. I admire your interpretation of Macbeth very much."

"Thank you, Baron," Dylan said. He never knew exactly how to talk to nobility, so he let Serafina and the baroness do most of the conversing. He suddenly looked across the room and said, "Look, there's Martha Bingham and that protégée of hers, Jeanne St. Clair."

"You're acquainted with them, right?" the baroness asked at once, speaking to Serafina.

"We've had dinner recently. She has been after me for some time to join her crusade 'to set women free,' as she puts it."

"She is a nuisance, isn't she? Oh, dear me, here she comes, along with her two followers! We'll have to listen to her views again on the superiority of women and the inferiority of men."

Martha Bingham was, indeed, set on a mission. "How do you do, Baroness and Baron, and you, Lady Trent." She paid no attention whatsoever to Dylan, which amused him.

"I didn't know you were an art fancier, Miss Bingham."

"Oh, she is!" Jeanne St. Clair spoke up quickly. She moved closer to her employer and took her by the arm as Violet moved aside to stand by the wall. "She loves beautiful paintings." Serafina had noted that Jeanne and Violet were never far from their leader.

"Yes, I do," Martha Bingham said, "but I'm here to do more than look at paintings. I want to ask you two again to join me in my crusade to set womanhood free in England."

Serafina knew this was coming. She stood there as Miss Bingham presented the entire case for the emancipation of women, and her eyes met those of Lady DeMain. The baroness just rolled her eyes upward in despair — a gesture Martha Bingham caught at once. "I can see," she said, "that you are still determined to live in the Dark Ages. Now, come along, Jeanne. Come along, Violet. If you ladies change your mind, please let me know." Martha strode away, with Jeanne by her side and Violet bringing up the rear.

"What a bore," Baron DeMain said after the two had left. "Are there many of her kind in England?"

"A few," Serafina said. "Come. Let's select a picture. We're buying a painting for my sister, who is going to marry Matthew Grant, the superintendent of Scotland Yard."

"Oh, you'll have a policeman in your family."

"More than that, dear." The baron smiled at his wife. "The superintendent of Scotland Yard. You'll have to be on your best behaviour, Lady Trent. And you, sir, must be careful too."

They left the two, and Dylan said, "They're a lovely couple, aren't they?"

"Yes, they are. Very popular for the French. They have a hard time since we've had so many wars with them, but I like them both very much indeed."

They circulated and found General Leo Hunter speaking with Gerhard Von Ritter. "Look at those two," Serafina said. "Two of the biggest egos in the world, I suppose. I don't know which one is the worst."

"Both suspects in the murders, aren't they?"

"I'm not sure. Some of the effects were theirs, but there were so many others involved that it would be hard to say. Come. I like that picture over there." They stopped before a canvas of horses jumping over a fence chasing a fox.

"Does Dora like foxhunting?"

"She hates it. She always feels sorry for the fox."

"So do I." Dylan grinned. "I'm for the underdog."

"Come along. We'll find something else . . ."

The two had looked at every painting at the exhibit when suddenly Dylan said, "Look, there's Matthew."

"Oh, he mustn't know why we're here. Don't say anything about buying them a gift."

"He looks excited." The two waited, and Matthew came toward them at once. His eyes were flashing, and he said, "Well, we've made an arrest."

"You've found the murderer?" Dylan said.

"We think so. He killed a woman a few years ago in exactly the same manner."

"Who is it? Anybody that we've been suspecting all along?"

"No, someone you may never have heard of," Matthew said. He was excited, and his eyes glowed as he said, "Did you ever hear of Rian Felan?"

"I don't believe I ever have," Serafina said.

"Nor have I. Who is he?" Dylan asked.

"He's a criminal, and he was arrested and

tried for slashing a woman. He was convicted, but it was later overturned. Some irregularity."

"Has he been out of prison long enough to have done the murders?"

"Indeed, he has, and we found him in the same block where the latest murder was committed. We can put Rian in the area at the same time she was killed."

"At the right time?" Serafina asked quickly.

"Yes, at exactly the right time. We need you to look at him."

"You mean to identify him as the one I saw at the Reis mansion?"

"Yes. That would be the clincher."

"But I've told you, Matthew, it was so dark I couldn't see anything."

"Come and take a look at him anyway. Maybe something will come back to you, something about his form, the way he walks, something like that."

Serafina shook her head doubtfully. "I'll be glad to do that, but I doubt that I'll be of any help."

"Good! Come along." As they left the exhibit, Serafina turned and found Martha Bingham and her followers watching them leave. She did not like the woman and wished that she had no contact with her, but there was something determined about her group. They were standing close together, and she thought, *They make a strange trio. I can't see what they have in common.* But she put it out of her mind and looked forward to meeting the man who was possibly the Slasher, who had brought such misery to highborn families.

SIXTEEN

Serafina had been in Old Bailey, the most notorious prison in London, before. It had been that time when her brother, Clive, had been under suspicion of murder and had spent the days before his trial here. As she walked down the long corridor following a guard and accompanied by Matthew Grant, she felt the same touch of fear that the prison had given her then. It was like being buried alive, and a shiver went over her as she saw the cells where the men were kept caged in a fashion that would not even be suitable for animals.

"Right this way, sir," the guard said. He was a tall, sallow-faced man with a mournful expression. He opened the door and gestured inside. "You and Lady Trent must wait here. I will go bring the prisoner to you."

"Thank you very much," Grant said. He stepped aside and gestured toward the room. Serafina walked in and found it was a bare room with nothing but a table and two chairs, one on each side. "You sit there, Serafina. You'll get a good look at him, although the light is bad in here."

Indeed, the light was bad, a flickering gas lamp that cast shadows of their figures onto the stone floor.

They waited silently and finally Serafina heard footsteps. The steel door opened, and the guard stepped inside. "Here is the prisoner, sir. I'll have to lock you in, you understand."

"Of course."

"I'll be right outside, so just bang on the door when you are ready to leave."

"Thank you very much."

Serafina looked at the man who stood there. He was not a large man, rather under average height. The prison clothes could not disguise that he was a strongly built individual, and he had a striking face and jet-black hair that set off a pair of yellowish-hazel eyes that gave him a catlike appearance. His mouth was very broad, his chin was stubborn, and his hands looked strong enough to break steel. One chain joined his feet together, allowing him to take only short steps, and another joined his wrists, which in turn were attached to a belt.

"You can sit here, Felan."

The prisoner looked quickly at Grant. "You know my name, but I don't know yours. Now what do you want with me? You're not reporters, are you?"

"I am Superintendent Grant of Scotland Yard. This is Lady Trent."

Felan's yellow eyes went at once to Serafina, and she felt as if he could see straight through her clothing and even deeper than that. He had a penetrating gaze, but he smiled and looked almost gentle for a savage. "Lady Trent, is it? Well, I must be going up in the world to be visited by nobility."

"Sit down, Felan," Grant said sharply. He pulled the chair back, and the chains made a musical tinkling sound as Felan moved forward in short, mincing steps and sat down. The chain that bound his wrists to his waist was too short to allow him to put his hands on the table, so he sat there, leaned back, and studied the two. "Scotland Yard, is it? What is it you want with me?"

Serafina was studying the criminal's face carefully. There was something frightening about it. If she had met him alone in an isolated place, she knew she would have been terrified. He had that sort of dangerous look about him.

"Well, Serafina?"

"I'm sorry, Superintendent. I can't help you."

"Oh, you're trying to pick me out for a job, are you? Well, I tell you right now I had nothing to do with it." He suddenly smiled, and his teeth were surprisingly white against his dark skin.

"You killed one woman in the same fashion."

"Ah, but they reversed the verdict." He leaned back and said, "Gives me a satisfaction, Superintendent, to talk about my crime. Yes, I killed Lenora Hensley. I enjoyed it too. She was my woman, and she went with another man, so I slashed her to bits." He looked up at the ceiling thoughtfully, then his eyes locked with Serafina's. "I enjoyed it. I did. I was ready to swing for it."

"I've always thought it was one of the greatest miscarriages of justice when you were released on a technicality."

"I'm sure you'd think so, but you can't try a man twice for the same crime, and you can't prove that I killed anyone, whoever it is."

"You were seen in the same vicinity."

"So were other people."

Matthew Grant leaned forward and said,

"You were also seen in the same neighborhood as Countess Margaret Acton, and we're looking for a witness that will find you outside the residence of Lady Rachel Reis."

Suddenly Felan began to laugh. "Oh, you think I'm the Slasher! Is that it?"

"That's exactly what we think," Matthew said grimly. "We're going to prove it."

"You won't prove it. You might put me in the neighborhood, but we both know that's not enough, don't we, Superintendent?"

The interrogation went on, and Serafina sat there saying nothing. She had seen a piece of paper in the breast pocket of his prison uniform. At one point he took it out and waved it. "Look, I wrote this. This isn't what a murderer would write, is it now, Lady Trent?"

Serafina took the piece of paper that he handed her and saw that it was a poem, a sonnet, and very well done too. "Did you write this?"

"Yes, I did. I'm a poet. One of the many facets of my character."

"The Slasher leaves a poem wherever he kills."

"I bet they weren't in my handwriting." Felan grinned. "You got a sample of it, Superintendent?"

Matthew fumbled into his pocket and came out with a notebook. "Yes, here is one of them."

Felan read the poem that had been found by the bedside of the marchioness and snorted. "This is pure garbage! I wouldn't be caught dead writing trash like this!" He tossed the book back, and Matthew caught it, his face reddened. "We can put you in the vicinity of two of the murders, and you write poetry. We searched your house too, Felan."

"I'll bet you did. Find any clues?"

"We found a knife with bloodstains on it, and on one of your jackets and a pair of trousers."

"Of course you did. I'm a poacher. That's rabbit blood on the knife and on the trousers too."

Serafina saw that Matthew was disgruntled and was relieved when he turned and banged on the door. "Guard — guard, open the door."

Serafina rose, and when the guard stepped inside, Felan said, "Better do all your talking to me. You'll never pin any of these murders on me."

"I'm going to try," Matthew said grimly. He took one last look at the prisoner and then followed Serafina out.

They did not speak until they were out in the clear sunshine, and she turned to him. "What do you think, Matthew?"

"Be almost impossible to prove anything unless we get more evidence. We'll keep checking though. We know he is a murderer. We know he killed a woman once in the same fashion that three women have died, so he's our best suspect for the moment. I hope he's guilty. He deserves to hang."

When they got to her carriage, she suddenly turned and said, "I just had a thought, Matthew. It was too dark for me to see the murderer's face that night the marchioness was killed, but I did see him come down from a considerable height. It would take quite a strong man, and agile, to do that, wouldn't it?"

"I would think so. That window is at least twenty-five or thirty feet high. A man would break his neck if he slipped and fell." He studied her. "What's your idea?"

"I think we ought to get an expert to look at the Reis mansion and see if it's possible to climb up that way and then to come back down."

"That's not a bad idea. You have someone in mind?"

"Monsieur Henley. He's more or less a suspect himself, but I don't think he's guilty."

"Neither do I. Come along. We'll go to the circus."

The sun was high in the sky as the four people stood looking up at the window on the second floor of the Reis mansion. The ceilings of all the rooms were very high, probably twelve to fourteen feet each, so by the time you accounted for a raised structure allowing windows to shine into the basement, Serafina estimated that the window of the marchioness's room was at least forty feet off the ground. She turned and studied the face of Henley, who had come without argument, and then her glance shifted to his partner, Jeanne St. Clair.

"What do you think, Mr. Henley?" she asked. "Could a person climb that wall?"

Henley walked over to the stone house. There were crevices, and some of the stones protruded enough to get a handhold. He looked up thoughtfully and said, "This is really not my area, I'm afraid, Lady Trent. You should find someone who has done mountain climbing. That would be the kind of skill you would need here."

But Serafina turned and pointed to a huge oak tree that grew some forty feet from the house. Branches spread in all directions. One of them, a large, strong branch, extended its length until the tip was within ten or twelve feet of the window. "Would it be possible to climb that tree, go out on that branch, and leap to the window?"

They all turned and looked. Matthew was surprised, for he had not thought of this. "I doubt if that could be done," he said.

"I will try," Henley volunteered. He walked over to the tree and grasped the lower branch. He climbed easily up to the limb in question, and then, standing upright, he walked out along the limb, but by the time he had gotten three-fourths of the way there, his weight pushed the limb down so that the tip was well below the level of the window to Lady Reis's room. He moved farther, and the branch dipped still more. He looked down and called out, "Could not be done, I think. If the branch was higher, it might be possible." He came skidding along the branch as if he were walking on a sidewalk, came down the tree, and then turned to say, "What do you think, Jeanne?"

"No, not on the branch. Couldn't happen. The farther you get along there, the more it dips. Even my own weight would pull it down. There would be nothing to push off against. The branch would give."

Henley was thoughtful. He stroked his chin and said, "Well, you're from Switzerland. You've done some climbing in the Alps. Do you think you can climb that wall?"

Jeanne St. Clair turned and looked at the wall. She walked over slowly and began to feel the crevices. She gripped the stones and moved upward, but before she had gone more than four or five feet, her hands slipped. She fell backward but caught herself — hitting the ground on her feet but rolling over backward and coming to her feet lightly.

"There's not enough to hold on to. It would be impossible to climb that wall."

Serafina looked upward and studied the house and the window. "If you were in the room, Miss St. Clair, could you climb down?"

"No, no, that would be even more difficult. Climbing down is far more dangerous to a mountain climber than climbing up. I think it would be totally impossible to take a chance."

"I'll have the carriage take you back. We're going to stay for a time," Grant said. He accompanied the two to the carriage, saw them in, and walked back to where Serafina was looking up at the window. "Well, that didn't help much."

"I'm not sure," Serafina murmured softly.

"There was something odd about the way the Slasher came down. I can't quite think of what it was. I can't get it straight, but I remember just a moment's thought before he hit the ground that there was something strange about the way he came down. Let me think on it."

"You think on it, and I'll work on finding some way to put Rian Felan's neck in a noose."

The following Sunday there was no play at the theatre, so Dylan came out to be with David. He brought Meredith and Guin with him, which irritated Serafina considerably. She spent the afternoon having to entertain Meredith — mostly listening to her talk about how wonderful Dylan had been to her and how she was excited with her new career.

At one point she began speaking of her early days in Wales and grieving over the fact that the police had not been able to find her sister. "She was at my wedding, Angharad was. I remember it so well."

"When were you married?"

"Just four years ago in May. Guin was born two years after that, and then I lost my dear husband." She took out her handkerchief and dabbed at her eyes.

"How did you make a living?"

"Oh, we come from a coastal town, Dylan and I. I shucked oysters for a living. A hard job it was too."

"That must have been very hard."

"Hard it was, Lady Trent. I'm glad you've never had a job that difficult."

A thought entered Serafina's mind. "I've got to go do something about the meal for supper tonight. Will you excuse me?"

"Certainly. I'll just go find Dylan and the children."

"I'll bet you will," Serafina mumbled under her breath as she turned and left. She made her way into the kitchen and found the cook, Nessa Douglas, already making preparations for the meal.

"Nessa, didn't you tell me you and your husband were in the oyster business for a while?"

"Yes, ma'am, we were, and a hard life it was."

"What was the hardest thing about it?"

"Oh, your hands, Lady Trent. Look at my hands." She turned her hands palms up, and Serafina saw that her hands were criss-crossed with old scars that made white lines across her palms. "There's no way to avoid getting cut. Many a day I shucked oysters with bleeding hands."

"Couldn't you wear gloves?"

"No, that wouldn't work. You've got to feel the oysters." She laughed suddenly and said, "This is a vacation for me after a thing like that. What would you like for supper?"

"Surprise us. Your food is always delicious, Nessa." She turned and walked away, and went at once to where she found Meredith with Dylan and the children. He had rigged up a swing and now was pushing them gently.

"Supper will be ready in a couple of hours. Should Guin take a nap, Meredith?"

"Indeed. She's played hard all day. Come along, Guin." She reached her hand out to get the girl, and Serafina stole a quick look. She saw the inside of Meredith's left hand, and it was smooth and without sign of a scar. *So much for oyster shucking!*

The dinner was a fine one, starting with shrimp bisque and deviled whitebait. Later there were curried eggs, sweetbreads, and crisply fried quail. For sweets there were ices and fairy cakes.

All during the meal Meredith was quick to speak. She seemed very cheerful, and once Septimus leaned over and whispered to Serafina, "She's quite a happy lady for a widow."

"Yes, she is."

As the adults finished up their meal, David was getting restless at the table. "Did you know my grandfather was a sailor, Mrs. Brice?" he piped up.

"Oh, not really a sailor. Not in the Queen's Navy," Septimus protested. "But I did serve a summer on a yacht as a deckhand."

"Did you learn to steer the boat?"

"Oh, dear me, no. The owner did that." Septimus laughed. "I did learn to tie knots though. Here, let me show you." He went over to a side table with drawers and pulled out a piece of rope.

"Why are you keeping a piece of rope in here?" Serafina asked.

"Never know. Rope comes in handy." He began to show them the knots, including a bowline, a granny, and other simple knots. Then he said, "Let me show you my favourite." His hands moved quickly, and he began forming loops. When he had finished, he had three strands tied together at each end. He held the ends of the rope and said, "You see how tight this is? See if you can pull it apart, Dylan."

Dylan took one end of the rope and said, "No, don't think so. What's it used for?"

"Well, sailors use it to take up slack when a rope is too long and they want to hold something. But it has another feature too. It's called a sheepshank, though I don't know why that would be. You see this middle rope here?"

"Yes, sir, what about it?"

"Let me show you something." He reached into his pocket, came out with a knife, and sliced the middle rope. "Now pull."

Dylan pulled while Septimus held the other end, but the other two loops held fast. "You see. Now give me some slack." When Dylan loosened his grip on the rope and let it fall slack, it suddenly parted. "That's the strange thing about a sheepshank. You can cut that middle one, but it'll hold fast until the rope goes limp and then it comes apart."

"Teach me how to do that, Grandfather."

Septimus laughed. "I will, but at another time."

Suddenly Serafina straightened up. "Come with me, Dylan."

"Come where?"

"Just come with me." She turned and said to Meredith, "Mrs. Brice, I'll have our coachman take you and Guin home." Meredith glared at Serafina, but she got to her feet, for she had no choice. "Come along, Guin," she said stiffly. "I think we've been dismissed."

As they were preparing to leave, Meredith said to Dora, who was standing nearby, "You should speak to your sister. She's so jealous of Dylan that she won't let another woman near him."

Dora, with her gentle spirit, could find no answer to make, but she decided it would be best not to repeat this to her sister.

Serafina would not speak to Dylan about her purpose. She sat deep in thought beside him in the carriage, and when they finally pulled up in front of the Reis household, she went at once to the front door, and he hurried to keep up with her. Vincent answered the door, and she said, "Vincent, I need to get up on the roof."

"On the roof, ma'am?" Vincent said, shock and amazement covering his face.

"Yes, on the roof."

"Certainly, ma'am, if you insist. May be a little bit dirty."

"That doesn't matter. Come along, Dylan."

"You are quite bossy today," Dylan said. "What is all this about?"

"I may not tell you, but it's something I had to check."

The two followed Vincent up the stairs to what amounted to a third floor, which was an attic room. From the attic room a door led out to the roof.

"You're not going out on the roof," Vincent cried in alarm.

"Yes."

"But you might slip and fall."

"Take off your shoes, Dylan."

Dylan laughed. "I think you've lost your mind, Serafina." Nevertheless, he did what she said and saw that she had done the same. They edged out of the door that led out onto the roof, and Serafina moved carefully as Dylan followed. "Don't fall. You'd break your neck. What are you looking for?"

"I'm looking for this." She pointed to a chimney that pierced the roof of the mansion. Around it was a piece of rope that had been knotted. "That was the sheepshank knot. That's the way the murderer got down. He tied that knot and cut the one. That's the way he came down, and he must have pulled the rope after him. That's what I was trying to remember, Dylan. He seemed to come floating down. Not climbing step-by-step, but I was too frightened to think about it at the time." She looked at the rope and said, "We've got to tell Matthew about this, and we've got to check the roofs of the other victims. We may have a pattern here."

"Well, if he knows how to tie a sheep-shank knot, he's probably got the background of a sailor. Come along. Be careful now." The two made their way back, put on their shoes, and descended. As they were on their way to Scotland Yard to find Matthew, Dylan reached over and took her hand. "You're some woman, Serafina Trent. Who would ever have thought of a thing like that?"

"I never would've if my father hadn't mentioned that sheepshank and shown us how it worked. You think it will help?"

"Might be the very key we need. I hope so. I want this monster brought to justice!"

SEVENTEEN

At the end of a long day at Scotland Yard, Dylan and Serafina waited an inordinately long time for Matthew. The Slasher case had taken its toll on him, and he entered his office looking tired. He stood there without expression while they told their story. When Serafina had finished, he said, "We'll have to find out which suspects could tie a knot that ordinarily only a sailor could do."

"Well, he wouldn't admit he could tie the knot, not the murderer," Dylan said.

"No, we'll have to find out who's been in the navy or had boating experience."

Serafina said, "Well, this explains how he got down, but it doesn't explain how he got up on the second floor of all three houses in the first place."

"No, it doesn't, but my guess is that he came in whenever he could without being seen," Grant said. He gnawed his lower lip nervously and said, "We'll have to give this some thought. Go home. I'll go out in the morning and check what you said."

"You'd better check the other roofs too, for Lady Welles and Margaret. Somehow," Serafina said, "I think this killer is a very formal being."

"What do you mean, 'formal'?" Dylan asked.

"I mean he likes to do everything the same way every time."

"I believe you're right," Grant said. "And he'd have to be able to climb out on the roof, tie the knot, and climb down the rope. Not everybody could do that."

"No, but do you think Felan could do it?"

"Yes, I do. He's very strong and not a very large man. I still say he's our man."

Meredith was walking along the lane with Dylan. He had taken her out shopping, and he stopped and said, "Look, there's an eel pie stand."

"You always loved those things," Meredith said. "Are you hungry?"

"Yes, I'm starved." They moved over to the booth and found a thin man with a stovepipe hat sitting crookedly on his head and a filthy apron around his waist. But the smell was delicious, and Dylan bought two pies. They both ate with enjoyment — the hot pastry crunching and flaking and eel flesh delicate on the tongue. "Better than cucumber sandwiches," Dylan said.

"You just wait until I cook your supper," Meredith said. "I'll make you a pie that the old devil himself would want to get his hands on."

The two continued down the street, and finally they wound up back at the house. Guin ran at once to Dylan, and he caught her up and hugged her. "A story! A story!" she chanted, pulling at his coat.

"Dylan, you've stolen her heart away. You're a devil with women of any age." She turned and said, "Thank you for watching Guin, Mrs. Fellows."

Dylan laughed and at once sat down with Guin in his lap as Meredith walked her landlady to the door. Later when Meredith fixed supper, he found she was indeed a fine cook, but he knew that already. "You're going to make some man a fine wife. A good cook, a good-looking woman like you. Men ought to be standing in line."

Meredith gave him a strange look, and he saw that she was troubled. "What's the matter?" he asked. "Something wrong?"

"I've been wondering whether I should tell you more about Lewis's last words. He talked about you."

"Well, we were such good friends. What did he say? Sometimes a dying man's last words are important."

"He'd been very ill and had a high fever, but almost the last thing he said was, 'Go find Dylan. Marry him if you fall in love. Let him be a husband to you and a father to our daughter.' " She suddenly looked down, and he saw tears in her eyes.

"You should have told me this before."

"It sounded too — forward. Women are chasing you all the time, and I sound just like another one."

"No such a thing. There's soft you are. It's the finest compliment Lewis could have paid."

"He loved you dearly, Dylan, but, of course, you pay no attention to what he said."

But Dylan was quiet for a long time. Meredith stole glances at him and saw that he was deep in thought.

Finally he said, "I'm going to leave now, Meredith. I've got some things to think about."

"Go you, then," she said. She came close to him, put her hand on his cheek. "Thank you for all the goodness that you've shown to me and my poor daughter."

"I'll — I'll see you tomorrow."

Dylan left Meredith's small house and went at once to Grant's office. *I've got to have some help with this, and Grant's the one I ought to ask. For a man as young as he, he's got a lot of wisdom.*

He met Sergeant Kenzie, who said at once, "The superintendent isn't here. He's gone out to talk to Septimus about the autopsy on Lady Reis. You'll probably find him there if it's important."

"Thank you, Sergeant. I think I will go look him up."

He left the office and walked the streets for a while indecisively. Meredith's words had shaken him greatly. He had given some thought, as a single man will, to marriage, and he knew that deep down in his heart the thing he wanted most in this world was to have a wife and family. Sometimes when he would pass a house at night and see the lights in the windows and hear the sounds of merriment coming out, he would think, *Those people have everything.*

Finally he set his jaw and turned and called for a cab. "Take me out to Trentwood House. I'll tell you how to get there, and don't spare the horse."

Serafina had crawled out onto the roof of her house. It had a steeper pitch than the

Reis mansion, and she had to move very carefully. She reached the chimney and with some difficulty managed to get a rope around it. She tied a knot that Septimus had showed her and tugged at it. It made a good, tight fit and seemed in no danger of breaking. Then, sitting flat, she tied a sheepshank and tossed the rest of the rope so that it dangled to the ground. She had deliberately gotten a rope sixty feet long so that there would be plenty. She reached into her pocket, took out a pair of scissors, and began hacking away at the rope, cutting one of the strands. Finally the scissors dug their way through, and she kept the tension on the free end, the part that dangled over the roof. Slowly she lowered herself to the edge, and when she came to look over the edge, the ground seemed very far away. She was a determined woman and had never been fearful of much of anything. Now, however, the thought of what would happen if she fell frightened her. "Broken legs. Maybe a broken neck," she murmured. She hesitated for a moment and then did a strange thing. She was very still, and then she said, "Lord, don't let me break my neck as I try out this theory."

She lowered herself over the edge of the roof and for a moment hung dangling there, but as she hung on, she found out how difficult it was. The rope seemed to be slipping between her hands, and fright came to her then like an armed man. She heard her name called and glanced downward to see Dylan, who had rounded the corner of the house and was running to where the rope dangled. At that instant the rope suddenly gave way, and she felt herself falling.

I'm going to die!

She fell through the air, half turning, hoping to land on something besides her head, and then she suddenly struck, not the hard ground she was expecting, but something that was yielding. She heard a whooshing sound, and her own breath was knocked almost out of her, but she rolled over and saw that Dylan had run underneath her to break her fall. He was lying now on his back and did not seem to be breathing.

I've killed him! She pulled him up into a sitting position and clutched him, holding his head against her breast, and began to weep deep, gasping sobs.

Dylan came out of unconsciousness, finding himself struggling simply to take a breath. He was aware that he was leaning against something soft, and there was a familiar smell of lilacs. His mind whirled, and he could not remember for a moment what he was doing here — or even where he was — and then he felt the movement of the softness beneath him and he heard sobs.

Wildly he opened his eyes and looked up to see Serafina bending over him. Her eyes were closed and great tears were running down her cheeks. She was holding him tightly, and he heard her murmur, "Oh, Dylan — Dylan, please wake up. Don't be dead."

Dylan found he could not move. For a moment he simply lay there trying to draw in breath, and finally air did begin to filter into his lungs. He coughed and looked up and whispered, "What — what's the matter?"

He saw her eyes fly open, and they were filled with tears. "Dylan," she cried, "you're alive!"

Dylan was aware that she was holding him as you would hold a baby close, and there was a delicious sensation for a moment, and then memory came flooding back. He pulled back and put his hand on his chest. Gasping for breath, he said, "Why, with no thanks to you! Were you trying to commit suicide, Serafina?"

Serafina was wiping her eyes, but he saw that her hands were trembling, and so was her chin, as if she had gotten a tremendous shock.

"What were you doing coming down that rope?"

"I wanted — I wanted to see if a woman could do it. I fixed a sheepshank like my father said, and I must have cut the wrong knot."

"Well." Dylan slowly was experimenting with his breathing and found out it was much better. "I'm going to be sore all over tomorrow. How much do you weigh?"

"Oh, Dylan, I thought you were dead." Her hands were trembling, and her voice was unsteady.

He got up, pulled her to her feet, and said, "I thought we had straightened out that you're not going to try dangerous things anymore." But then he saw that she was really broken. She could barely stand. He leaned forward and pulled her against his chest, and she put her head down on his shoulder. "Well now. If you're having my opinion, Lady Serafina Trent, you're a foolish woman. But it came out all right. You didn't kill yourself or anybody else, not this time."

The two stood there, and once again Serafina felt that curious and unusual, almost unique, sense of security when Dylan held her. She had never felt this with a man before, and now after the terrible experience and the fear that she had actually killed him, she could only let him hold her up and cling to him with all her force.

"What do you call this?"

Dylan didn't know how long he and Serafina had been standing there, but he turned to Grant, who had come up on them. He could not answer for a moment, and Serafina pulled away and gave Grant a wild glance. "It was my fault, Matthew. I wanted to see if a woman could come down a rope."

"You think the Slasher might be a woman?"

"I don't know. I guess I wasn't thinking very clearly."

She told him the whole story, and then she reached out and touched Dylan's arm tentatively. "If Dylan hadn't broken my fall, I think I would have been killed."

"As it was, it was only me that nearly got killed," Dylan said and managed a smile. "I wish you'd stop crying. You're making enough noise to have the house down."

"I was never so frightened in all my life — except, perhaps, when I saw the Slasher," Serafina said.

"Well, could a woman come down that rope?"

"This woman couldn't. It would take a very strong man or woman to do that. Come in. Let's have some tea to calm my nerves."

Dylan said, "I came out to talk to you, Matthew."

"Then I'll let you men talk while I go in and change attire." Serafina smiled as she walked past Matthew into the house.

"All right. Come along. Let's walk through the garden. I don't suppose the roses will be shocked by anything you've got to say."

Serafina watched the men go from a window inside the house. She was still trembling. She could not forget holding Dylan to her breast and how he had held her and kept her from falling apart. She knew she would treasure that moment in spite of the terrible circumstances.

"You mean the woman told you her husband wanted you to marry her?"

"That's what she said. It was his dying word that I'd be her husband and a father to Guin. I've got to have some help here, Matthew."

"I don't think anyone can help you with this."

"You've got to tell me *something!*"

"All right," Grant said firmly. He gave

Dylan a straightforward, almost harsh look. "Don't do it, man."

"But why not?"

"I don't have a good feeling about it."

"Well, you must have more than just a feeling."

"That's all I've got. I don't feel right about it. How do you feel about it?"

"I feel a debt to Lewis."

Matthew stared at Dylan. He could not believe what he had heard. "Buy him a fancy headstone if you want to show respect, but don't marry the woman just to please a dying man's request — if there was one."

"What do you mean, 'if there was one'?"

"Women have tried tricks before to get a halter around your neck. I've seen it. This may be another one of those."

"No, she's not like that."

"I've told you what I think. Don't do it, Dylan." He turned and walked abruptly away, and not wanting to speak to Serafina after that, Dylan went back to his carriage and got in.

Matthew watched him go, and as he walked toward the house, Serafina came out.

She had changed clothes, and he asked, "Did Dylan tell you about this business with Mrs. Brice?"

"What business?"

"She told him that it was her husband's dying wish that she marry Dylan and let him be a husband to her and a father to that girl of hers."

"You're joking!"

"I wouldn't joke. He asked me my advice."

"What did you tell him?"

"It was short. I said, 'Don't do it.' "

"You told him exactly right!"

"Well, what do you think, Serafina?"

Serafina looked confused and then angry. "He's a grown man."

"Grown men are pretty helpless sometimes when beautiful women get their hands on them. He's just a man like the rest. Remember they were childhood sweethearts, and Lewis was his best friend. You'd better talk to him, Serafina."

"No, you talk to him."

She turned and walked away, and Matthew watched with surprise. "Well, Dylan, my boy, I think you really spit in the soup this time!"

EIGHTEEN

"Here you go, Mrs. Fellows. You take Guin and your daughter out and show them a good time. It's kind of you to keep her for me tonight."

Mrs. Fellows, who owned the house that Meredith and Guin lived in, smiled. She was a heavyset woman with a sprinkling of grey in her blonde hair, but she had a daughter only a year older than Guin. The two girls had become good friends, and Mrs. Fellows had been a good landlady.

"Why, it's my pleasure, ma'am. You don't worry about little Guin now. I'll bring her about ten o'clock in the morning if that's all right."

"That would be fine. Here's a little extra. You might want to take them to some sort of entertainment. You enjoy yourself."

"I'll see you tomorrow at ten. Come along, Guin."

Mrs. Fellows picked Guin up, and Meredith said, "You be a good girl now," and watched as Mrs. Fellows carried the girl out.

As soon as the door closed, Meredith went into a frenzy of activities. The first thing she did was take a bath. This involved heating water on the stove, and since it was hot it made a fog in the room. She filled it up with hot water, undressed, and sat there and soaked and washed her hair, using a fragrant soap that she had splurged on.

Finally she rose, dried off, put on a robe, and went out into the sunshine to let her hair dry. All the time she was humming a little, and her mind was working. There was a calculated look in her eyes, and finally when her hair was dry enough, she went inside. She glanced at the clock over the mantel and saw that it was nearly six o'clock. "Dylan will be here in an hour. I'll have to hurry." She moved to the bedroom, put on a shift, put on new drawers made of silk, and then slipped into a dress that she had spent all of her excess cash on. The gown was green, elegant as water in the sun, and stitched with silver beading and seed pearls. The waist was tiny and the bodice was very low cut and crossed over at the front. There was no bustle with this one, and the fullness was replaced by a new frilliness at the top of the sleeves. She looked at her reflection, tugged the dress down somewhat lower over her breast, and turned around to try to see what she looked like from the back. Finally she nodded with satisfaction at her reflection. She spent the rest of the time fixing her hair and dusting lightly with rice powder and touching her lips with a little carmine. Finally she used some of her favourite scent, on which she had also overspent. When all was done, she said, "Well now, Mr. Dylan Tremayne, you've been running like a scared rabbit since I told you that Lewis wanted you to marry me, but tonight we'll see who holds the best hand, won't we?"

As soon as possible, Dylan got away from the theatre. The performance had gone well, and he had stopped to buy a present for Guin. He reached the house and knocked, and when the door opened, his eyes grew wide. "Well, a new dress, is it?"

"Oh, I found this one on sale, so I had to buy it. I knew you liked green so much. Come in."

"I brought this for Guin." He held up the box containing the toy.

"Oh, Dylan, I'm sorry. She's been begging to spend the night with her little friend Helen — you know, my landlady's daughter.

So I finally let her talk me into it. She gets lonesome for children."

"Well, you can give her this tomorrow."

"Yes, it'll be just the two of us tonight."

Dylan handed her the package, and she smiled at him and said, "You're so good to Guin. You don't know how I appreciate it. I've cooked you the best dinner I know how. Are you hungry?"

"Oh yes. I've been thinking about this meal all day. It provoked my hunger."

"Oh no, it's much more than that. Here. You sit down while I put it on the table. I'll call you when it's ready."

Dylan settled himself, put his head back. He was very tired, for he had missed a great deal of sleep. The near brush with death he'd had when he caught Serafina had hit him hard. He had been unable to sleep, having bad dreams, and she had told him that she'd had the same experience. Now as he sat there, memories came floating back, and he suddenly thought, *What if I had been five feet farther away? I wouldn't have been able to have gotten under her. She might have been killed.*

The thought troubled him, and he sat up and rubbed his eyes. At that moment Meredith came in. "Come along. It's all ready."

"It smells delicious."

"I hope you like poached salmon and vegetables."

"I've always liked them. Remember in our village how many salmon we would eat?"

"You still remember that?"

"Oh yes."

She put out cold salmon, sliced cucumbers and potatoes with herbs, and beside it she set a glass of a pinkish-looking nectar. "I know you don't drink alcohol," she said, "but this is a new kind of fruit juice."

"What sort of fruit?"

"Oh, it's a mixture. Part of it is pineapple juice. Hard to get in this country."

He tasted it and said, "It's very unusual. It's good though." He drank half the glass, and she brought the rest of the food, which included a plate full of hot boiled mutton and horseradish sauce.

Dylan ate, and twice she refilled his glass with the juice. Finally she brought out sweets, including a steamy pickled pudding with syrup and brandy sauce.

"It's all I can eat."

"Well, have some more juice." She filled his glass again, and he noticed that she wasn't drinking.

"Don't you want some?"

"I tried some, and it didn't seem to agree with me."

"Well, it agrees with me. It's delicious." He finished the glass, and she immediately filled it once again.

"Let's go sit on the couch."

"No, let me help you do the dishes."

"No, that's not something a man should do. Come along." She pulled him to the couch, and they sat down together. She talked more than he, mostly about their days back in Wales.

Dylan found that he was overwhelmed with the meal. "A full meal like that always makes me sleepy."

"Well, just put your head back and rest a little bit. You can listen to me talk."

Dylan did put his head back and closed his eyes. Her voice droned on and on. She was speaking mostly about her life with Lewis and their childhood days.

Dylan suddenly awoke with a start. He felt groggy. "Can't keep my eyes open," he said. "I've got to go home and go to bed."

"Oh, it's too early to leave yet."

"I don't know what's the matter with me. I've missed a lot of sleep lately." He got to his feet, but suddenly the room seemed to reel, and he swayed from side to side.

"What's wrong, Dylan? Are you ill?"

"I think I am. I ate too much, I believe. Maybe the salmon wasn't good." He took two steps and lurched to one side. Meredith caught him and said, "Come. You'd better lie down for a moment. You can't go home like this."

"Got to get home."

But Meredith took him by the arm and guided him out of the dining area. She led him to the bedroom and said, "Lie down."

"I'll — I'll mess your bed up."

"Doesn't matter. Here, lie down. You'll feel better soon." He sat down and then fell backward. Meredith looked down at him, and a smile turned the corners of her lips upward. She reached down and put his feet up on the bed. He was breathing erratically, slowly, then quickly.

"Can you hear me, Dylan?" she said, standing right over him.

He did not move, and she nodded with satisfaction. She moved down and removed his boots, then his socks. It took some time, but she got him out of his clothes, all except the white drawers that he wore. Then she undressed and put on a new white shift that she had bought, made of soft cotton. It struck her above the knees and clung to her figure. She got into bed next to him, and then she rolled over and laughed softly. She reached up and touched his coal black hair. "Sleep well, husband," she whispered.

■ ■ ■ ■

Dylan seemed to be struggling to get out of some dark hole. His head was splitting, and he could not remember where he was. There were strange smells, and he knew he was in bed, but it did not seem to be his bed. He struggled out of the unconsciousness and opened his eyes. Suddenly a woman's voice said, "Good morning, husband." An arm came over him, and a soft form pressed against his side. He turned quickly, shocked to find Meredith lying in bed beside him. She was stroking his arm, and she laughed, saying, "Maybe I should call you husband-to-be."

Dylan was utterly confused. He knew something had gone terribly wrong, and his one thought was to get out of that bed and get away. He rolled over and sat up, and his head seemed to split.

"Where are you going, Dylan?"

"I've got to go." He looked at her once and then away, for the shift revealed her figure very plainly. He began to pull on his britches and his shirt, and in the meanwhile she got up and came around and said, "Why are you leaving?"

"I've got to get away from here. This —

this shouldn't have happened."

Suddenly he pulled on his socks, his boots, and she pulled at his arm. "You're not going to leave me now, are you, Dylan? Not after last night."

"Yes, I've got to get away."

"You're just like all other men." Her voice grew sharper, and he turned and saw that her face was twisted. "You used me to get what you wanted. You made promises, and I wouldn't let you in my bed until you told me you cared for me."

Dylan had no memory at all of that. "I don't remember."

"Well, I'm sure you don't, but you told me you wanted to do what Lewis asked. You wanted to marry me and be my husband and Guin's father."

Dylan was horrified. He knew he had made the most serious mistake of his life, and she suddenly collapsed and began to weep. "I thought you were a Christian man, Dylan. I thought you were the one man who wouldn't betray a woman. You're just like all the rest — except for Lewis."

Dylan's heart smote him. He had obviously taken advantage of this woman, although he had no memory of it. He came over and stood beside her. She was sitting on the bed, but she was bent over, and her body shook as she wept. He put his hand on her shoulder. "Meredith, we'll work this out somehow."

"You had what you wanted. Now you'll leave Guin and me forever."

Dylan tried desperately to remember, and finally he asked in a hoarse voice, "I asked you to marry me?"

"Of course you did. I would never have let you make love to me if I didn't think we were going to be married."

And then Dylan Tremayne knew there was no way out. He had quick thoughts of trying to figure out something, but nothing came. In the end he said, "Don't cry, Meredith. It will be as you say."

At once she looked up, and her eyes were wet with tears. She whispered, "Do you mean it, Dylan? We will really be married?"

"Yes. We'll be married, just as Lewis wanted."

She came up then and threw herself against him. There was no desire in him. He simply wanted to get away. "I've got to leave now. I've got to think. This is sudden."

"You'll come back later?"

"Of course I will." He finished dressing and left as quickly as he could. But as he stepped outside the door, he stopped dead still, and the thought came as clearly as printed black letters against a white background. *What am I going to tell Serafina?*

NINETEEN

The entire audience was standing up, and the theatre rang with applause and loud cries of acclamation. Dylan had come out for the sixth time to take a curtain call, and now he stood there smiling slightly. He bowed gracefully and gave a final wave of farewell as he stood before the audience. For one second he stood there savouring the smells, the sounds, the brilliant lights, the kaleidoscope of colour created by the dresses of the women and augmented by the flashing of diamonds and precious jewels at their hands and necks. He glanced to his left and saw Meredith there applauding, her eyes glowing and a smile on her lips. He inclined his head toward her slightly, and she threw him a kiss. Some of the audience saw it and turned to stare at Meredith. For the occasion she had bought a new dress of a turquoise colour with such a high sheen that light shimmers shot across it with every movement she made.

Finally Dylan held his hands up, and when the applause had subsided and quiet reigned in the theatre, Dylan said, "It has been an honour for me to entertain you for this brief time tonight. I want to take this opportunity to thank you and to express my gratitude for your generosity, for your kind words, and for your prayers as my life takes a new turn."

A whisper ran around the room, and Dylan smiled slightly, noting that his remark had caught the curiosity of the crowd. He said simply, "Good evening to you, and may God bless you all." Turning, he left quickly, hurried through the cluster of actors that had gathered in the wings, and made straight for his dressing room. He was not in a mood to hear the adulation that always came after a good performance, but he could not avoid Hugh Edwards, who stood in front of his dressing room door. Edwards was a tall, thin man with a pair of small glasses that enlarged his blue eyes. His reputation as a producer was admirable, and Dylan was genuinely flattered by his attention. "Mr. Edwards, it's good to see you."

"Dylan, I wanted to speak with you for a moment."

Dylan knew exactly why Edwards was

there. "I'm afraid it would do no good for you to press your offer, Mr. Edwards."

Edwards stared at Dylan and shook his head. "You can't mean it, Dylan! Why, you're at the top of your profession. This role I'm offering you will make your reputation, which is already great."

"Thank you for your offer, Mr. Edwards, but my mind is made up. I'm leaving the theatre."

"What in the world are you going to do?"

"I'm not at all certain about that, but God knows. Good night, sir."

Dylan darted into his dressing room and locked the door behind him. As quickly as he could, he disrobed, put on street clothes, and then faced the door. He knew it would be a battle to get through, and as soon as he opened the door, voices calling his name rose and hands pulled at him as he squeezed through. He made his apologies continually. "I'm sorry, I have a previous engagement. Thank you very much — I appreciate your kind remarks." Finally he reached the street door, stepped outside, and then, to the amazement of those who followed him, broke into a dead run.

Since most of the men were in dress suits and the women in ballroom gowns, no one pursued him, but one of his admirers said angrily, "Well, he's got the big head, all right! He forgot that we're the ones who made him who he is today."

Dylan did not hear that remark, but he knew that it was a common opinion. It was impossible to make anyone understand, it seemed, that he was truly leaving the theatre, even at the very peak of his popularity. He had not made a public announcement, but three different producers had tried to entice him to sign a contract to do a production with them, and he had turned them all down. This sort of thing could not be kept secret, and soon even the newspapers were asking, "What's Dylan Tremayne up to? Is he going to start his own troupe, put on his own play?" The articles went on to surmise that something big was brewing in Dylan Tremayne's head, but no one came close to expecting the simple truth: he was sick and tired of the theatre and could not bear it any longer.

He paused at the corner of Thirty-second Street and waited. He had told Meredith to meet him here as quickly as she could after the performance. He had not been there five minutes before she came hurrying along the street. It was late, and the gaslights cast a golden tint over her face. Coming up to him, she cried, "Dylan, it was wonderful!

322

Everyone loved you!"

"I suppose they did, but it's the performance they love, not me. Come now, there's a cab." He guided her quickly toward the hansom and threw up his hand. The cabbie drew the horse to a standstill. Dylan handed Meredith in and then walked around and got in and sat beside her. He gave the driver the address, and the driver said, "Yes, sir. Get you there quick as a wink."

Dylan leaned back and put his head against the cool leather. Meredith began speaking almost at once. "I talked to so many people, and all of them are wondering what you are going to do, Dylan. Some of them think you're going to start your own company."

"I won't be doing that, Meredith."

Meredith stared at him with apprehension. "You're not still thinking of leaving the theatre, are you?"

"I'm determined to do it. I can't stand this life anymore."

Meredith stared at him with disbelief and not a little anger. He had told her repeatedly that he intended to leave the theatre, but she had thought it was a phase. Now all the way to her house she began mustering reasons why he ought to stay in his profession. They reached her house, and he got out without a word and helped her step down to the pavement. When they came to the door, she reached up and put her arms around his neck. Her eyes were glowing, and her lips parted slightly. She pulled his head down, and the kiss was a long one. She held tightly to him, for she knew her power over men. This one was a man; therefore, he was no different from other men! She pressed herself against him and knew that she had stirred him. Moving her head back, she put her cheek next to his. "We've got to think about ourselves, Dylan."

"I am thinking about us. If I stay in the theatre, it will ruin me. I've seen it spoil too many men already — and women too, for that matter."

Meredith Brice was a woman of some experience with men. Now she moved with an impulse. "Come in. We'll talk about it."

But Dylan read the invitation in her voice, and he knew that she was asking him for more than talk. There was a sexual overtone to her words, and the invitation gleamed in her eyes and was obvious in every line of her body. He shook his head and said, "I'm going to make a public announcement to the newspapers tomorrow."

"Come in and spend the night."

"No, it would be wrong."

"I don't see why. We've already been there, and we're going to be married."

"It's the way I feel about things," Dylan said.

Suddenly Meredith said, "Have you told Lady Trent about our engagement?"

Meredith noticed that there was a hesitation and a moment's pause before Dylan answered, "No. I haven't said anything to her about it."

For some reason his answer displeased Meredith. "Are you ashamed of me?" she demanded.

"Why, not at all."

"I think you are. If you weren't ashamed, you would have told everyone."

"We can't be married right away. It's impossible."

"Why is it impossible?"

"Because I'll be a man with a family, and a man without a profession. I've got to find something to do with myself."

"Dylan, we'll talk about it."

Meredith was growing desperate now, but Dylan stepped back and said, "No, I need to think. I'll see you tomorrow." He turned and left, and Meredith stared after him, anger evident in her countenance. Her lips drew into a thin white line, and her eyes narrowed. When he disappeared around the corner, she whirled and went into the house, slamming the door behind her.

"It's strange how much time and care and money women put into weddings," Dora said. "Matthew said if he had his way, we would just elope."

She and Serafina were working on the plans for Dora's wedding, and Serafina smiled. "You couldn't do that. It wouldn't be fair to your family. Think how sad Aunt Bertha would be."

Dora laughed with delight. "I am so glad I'm marrying Matthew — if for no other reason than to put Aunt Bertha in her place. You must have scared the life out of her when you threatened to turn her out if she said anything mean about him."

"She turned absolutely pale." Serafina smiled fondly at the memory. "She hasn't said anything to you when I wasn't there, has she?"

"No, I don't think so. She wouldn't dare."

The two went over the list of guests and the details of the reception, and finally they stopped to have a cup of tea. The morning sunlight was shining through the window, and Serafina leaned back, noting how the motes seemed to dance in the bars of pale yellow light that filtered through the glass.

It suddenly occurred to her. "Dylan would say that God knows about every one of those motes. He's already told me that God knows every fish in the sea and every bird in the sky. How wonderful to have that kind of belief in God! I wish I did!" She shook her head and said briskly, "Well, we seem to have this wedding pretty well planned. We have to let Mum have a part in it though."

"Oh, we'll make her think she did it all." Dora leaned back in her chair and looked thoughtful for a moment. She had on a pale yellow dress in a fine muslin weave. It was trimmed with off-white Austrian lace and fitted tightly at the waist and hips and gathered to a fullness in the back. "You look about sixteen years old, Dora." Serafina smiled. "You're more beautiful than I've ever seen you. I hope Matthew appreciates you."

"Oh, he does! You'd be surprised how eloquent he can get when there's no one around. He's afraid someone would make fun of him, but now I've gotten used to it, and I tell him if we're married for fifty years, I expect to hear those pretty speeches every day."

Serafina laughed, pleased with her younger sister and pleased also with the husband she was getting. She had always admired

Matthew Grant, and she was convinced that he loved her sister as much as a man could love a woman.

"I just don't know how to be a wife."

Serafina looked up suddenly over her cup. "What do you mean, Dora?"

"I mean — I don't know anything. Some girls have already had — well . . . experience."

"You mean they've slept with men before they were married."

Dora's cheeks grew pink. "I suppose that's what I mean. At least they'd know *something.*"

"You wouldn't want that. You're coming to Matthew innocent and pure. He knows that, and the two of you will make out fine."

"But I don't know what to do."

Serafina put her cup down and reached out and took Dora's hand. "Do you love Matthew?"

"You know I do!"

"And he loves you. So when two people love each other, they'll find a way to express that love. Matthew probably has had the experience you talk about. Most men have, but he's a gentle man, and he'll teach you. It's only right that he should."

The two women talked, and finally Dora got up looking relieved and left the room.

Serafina thought about how much she herself had been like Dora before she married Charles. She had known literally nothing about sex, but if she had known something, it would have been spoiled, for her husband had been a brutal and abusive man with her. Serafina had been shocked to eventually learn that he was a pederast.

Dissatisfied and unhappy at the past memories, Serafina got up and left the room. She went upstairs and found David playing with his soldiers. "Let's go outside and play croquet, David."

"Yes, and I'll beat you, Mum."

"We'll have to see about that. I'm acknowledged to be quite an expert player."

"I beat you the last time."

Serafina said, "I wasn't feeling good that day."

David laughed. "You made that up. Come on. Let's go."

Fifteen minutes later the two were out in the bright sunlight. For the next half hour they knocked the balls over the emerald green grass. May had brought a beauty to the English countryside. The grass was trimmed as level as a carpet, and the house itself was ornamented with plants and flowers, vines and blossoms of all kinds, some of them giving off a delicious fragrance.

Suddenly David cried, "Look, there comes Mr. Dylan!"

Serafina looked up quickly, and sure enough Dylan was walking toward them. He had a serious look on his face, and Serafina knew, somehow, that this was not just an ordinary visit. "Let's go say hello."

They walked toward the front lawn, and David ran to Dylan, who picked him up at once. "How's the old man today, David?"

"I'm not an old man."

"Well, you will be someday." He looked over and said, "How are you, Serafina?"

"I'm fine. I've been going over the details of the wedding with Dora. She's so happy I'm afraid she's going to explode."

"Come on, Dylan. Let's go work on the tree house you're going to build me."

"We'll have to do that a little bit later, I'm afraid."

"No, let's do it *now.*"

"David, don't nag Mr. Dylan. You go inside and play with your toys. We'll come and get you after a while."

David kicked at a clod, but he gave a smile. "Don't be too long. Grown-ups talk too much."

Serafina smiled at that last remark. "I don't know where he gets those ideas. He's very firm though. Come along, let's get in the shade. It's getting warm." She noticed he did not speak as she led the way to some chairs underneath a spreading chestnut tree. She sat down, and as he took a seat opposite her, Serafina waited for him to speak. His hands were clasped tightly, and there were two vertical lines between his eyebrows — a sure sign that he was thinking hard and trying to put words in order. To make him at ease, she said, "I'd like to go to Mr. Spurgeon's church with you next Sunday."

Dylan looked up at once and said, "I'd like nothing better than to take you, but I'm afraid that won't be possible."

"Why, are you going out of town?"

Dylan rubbed his forehead. "No, Serafina, I'm not going out of town, but I'm in a position now where I can't —" He broke off and looked down at the ground and shook his head in despair.

"What's wrong, Dylan?"

Serafina watched as he lifted his head. She saw that his eyes were cloudy with some sort of doubt. When he spoke, his voice seemed almost harsh. "Meredith and I are going to get married."

Serafina could not think of a single remark. She stared at Dylan and realised that she had seen the possibility of this, but she had always put it out of her mind. "I'm —

surprised to hear that."

"It's something that's out of my past."

"I don't understand, Dylan."

"My best friend was Lewis Brice. I've told you about him. He and Meredith married after I left Wales. He was dying, and Meredith said his very last request was that she find me and tell me that he would like very much if I would be a father to Guin — and a husband to her."

Bells went off in Serafina's mind. She analysed what he had said and saw that he was terribly unhappy. *I can't tell him she's lying because I have no proof.*

Dylan waited for her to speak, and then he said, "I hope you understand my position."

For one moment Serafina did not speak, and then she decided to speak the absolute truth. "Dylan, I thought — I thought you felt something for me."

"I did, Serafina, but you're of nobility, and I'm just a plain man."

"That doesn't matter. Do you love her, Dylan?"

"Not like —" He paused then and swallowed hard. "Not like I should, but I owe Lewis a great deal. And I can help Meredith and Guin."

She stared at him and could not identify

her feelings. She knew there was anger there and also jealousy. She had felt it before. "I don't know much about real love, Dylan. I didn't have any of it in my marriage. You know I haven't believed in romance, that I fought against it because I thought that all the romances in books were made-up things." She paused, then made a decision. "I want to tell you about my husband — and about my marriage."

"Are you sure, Serafina?" He was watching her closely, for he had long known that her marriage had been unhappy, though he knew only a few details. He was aware that her parents knew little enough, though they had seen that Serafina was miserable. "You don't have to tell me if it will hurt you to say it."

"I — I think I need to speak of it, Dylan. I know I told you that Charles liked . . . boys . . . and I was afraid for David, though, as far as I know, he stayed away from him because David was the heir he desperately wanted. But I have never told anyone how he treated me." Her voice was unsteady, and Dylan was aware of the pain in her eyes. From the time he'd met her, he had guessed at her depth. No woman could show the world so much pride without harboring somewhere the power of great emotions. He was startled as he sensed the undertow of her spirit. There was a richness, a completeness in her that he had always admired, and he was still while she gathered her thoughts.

"You've seen how I resist anything romantic, but I wasn't always like that. Before I married, I had wonderful dreams about how marriage would be — like a storybook romance, with a prince and a princess. I was so happy! And then the dream became a nightmare. I knew almost nothing about the physical details of a marriage, but I assumed I would learn. But — he came to me, and he did — things I can't —" She broke off, and tears came to her eyes. "I was so innocent. He tortured me, physically and emotionally. Oh, Dylan! He killed the innocence that was in me, and I grew afraid of romance of any kind. I determined never to marry again, but then I got to know you."

Dylan was looking down into her eyes, and he saw the longing and the love that had been held captive by a beast. He touched her cheek, and she came to him, leaning against him and sobbing. Finally she grew still, and taking out a handkerchief, she turned and wiped the tears away. She said, "You know how I feared anything romantic, how I fought against it, but you came, and you've opened my eyes to what a man and a woman ought to be."

Dylan's eyes opened wide, and he stared at her with incomprehension. "What is it you're saying, Serafina?"

Serafina said, "I love you, Dylan."

Tears came to her eyes then, and she whirled and ran away. Dylan stood and watched her helplessly, and finally he turned and walked slowly away. When he got to the driveway, he kicked viciously at a rock, then he got into the cab he had come in and said, "Back to London, driver," in a dead voice.

"What happened to Dylan? I saw him coming."

"He had to go back, Dora."

"Why didn't he stay? I know David was looking forward to his visit. They've been making big plans about that tree house."

"He came to tell me something."

Something in Serafina's tone caught Dora's attention. She came closer and peered into her sister's face. "What is it? Can you tell me?"

"He's — he's going to marry Meredith Brice."

"No, that's impossible!"

"I'm afraid it's very possible."

"You can't let that happen."

"How can I stop it?" Serafina said sharply.

She felt the tears rising, and despite herself she could not keep them back. She yanked a handkerchief out, wiped her eyes, and said, "There's no help for it. She's told him that her former husband, who was Dylan's best friend, was dying, and he asked her to find Dylan and ask him to be a father to Guin — and a husband to her."

"I don't believe that for a minute!"

Serafina shook her head. "It doesn't matter, apparently, what you believe or what I believe."

"But you love Dylan. I've seen it."

"Well, he'll never love me. I asked him to take me to church. It should have pleased him, but he said he couldn't do it because he was an engaged man."

Dora started to speak, but Serafina cut her off. "I can't talk about this." She fled to her room, shut the door, and threw herself across the bed. She felt the sobs rising and was shocked at her own feelings. She did not know that she had this kind of emotion stored up in her, and for a time she simply gave way to it. Finally she said in a muffled voice, "This won't do." She got up from the bed and walked back and forth. Her eyes fell on the Bible, and she said, "Dylan's always saying that God leads people, that he hears them when they pray. But how can

I expect God to help me when I've given him nothing?"

For half an hour she paced back and forth, and her mind kept going back to the Bible that lay on the table. Finally she stopped and realised that she knew deep down that Dylan was making a big mistake, and she whispered, "God, I don't have any right to pray to ask you for anything, but Dylan Tremayne is a good man, and he's about to throw his life away. If you would tell me some way to help him, I would be so grateful." She was amazed at her own action, for prayer was as foreign to her as Sanskrit. She finally sat down, picked up the Bible, and held it. She did not know much about the Bible; she had read parts of it, and now she wished desperately she had studied it more carefully. "God, please help me with this. I don't know what to do." She began to turn the pages, and for a long time it seemed useless. There were stories there of kings long dead, of wars, of men and women who were so alien to modern people, they seemed like creatures from another planet.

Finally she turned a page, and her eyes fell on a verse that had been underlined. It had been her grandmother's Bible and was very old. The paper was yellow, but the underline was plain enough. She read it aloud very softly, noting that it was in the Thirty-second Psalm: "I will instruct thee and teach thee in the way which thou shalt go: I will guide thee with mine eye."

At that moment Serafina Trent was as convinced that God had spoken to her and promised to guide her as she had ever been in any scientific experiment she had ever performed. She closed the Bible, and a sense of purpose came to her.

"All right, God. You promise to teach me the way I should go, and I promise you that I will go any way you show me." She sat there for a long time, her head bowed and waiting, and finally she arose with a look of determination on her face and left the room.

TWENTY

Septimus sat in his favourite chair, and as Alberta came in he did not even look up. Glancing at her husband, she asked, "What's the matter with you, Septimus? You haven't said ten words all day."

Septimus reached up and grabbed his hair with both hands, pulling as if attempting to lift himself out of the chair. It was a strange gesture that Alberta had tried to break him of, but he seemed to be unconscious of it. "I'm worried," he muttered. "Don't know when I've been so worried."

"What are you worried about?"

"About Serafina, dear. She's not acting right."

Alberta sat down across from him on a horsehide-covered chair. "I know. She's abnormally quiet." Her face mirrored the worry on her husband's. "Has she said anything at all to you?"

"No, but then I'm not the sort of man that

people confide in when they have troubles."

"That's not so. I always confide in you."

Septimus gave her a thin smile. "Yes, my dear, but I haven't been able to establish that kind of communication with our children. I'm just not — I'm not loving enough, I suppose."

"Why, Septimus, our children know you love them!"

"Yes, I do love them, and that's why I'm worried. She hasn't said anything at all to you?"

"Not a word."

"What about Dora?"

"She may have spoken to Dora, but Dora won't say anything about it. Maybe she's ill."

"She doesn't look ill. She looks as healthy as ever. She's a deep thinker, that girl is! I don't think we know how deep. Something's gnawing away at her, and I can't just go in and demand she tell me."

"No, I'll talk to her. Maybe it will all come out."

"I hope so, dear."

Meredith was obviously angry. "I can't see why I wasn't invited." Dylan was on his way to a reception for Dora's wedding. Matthew had pressed Dylan into duty as best man, so naturally he would attend the affair.

"They wanted to keep it as small a party as possible."

"They're a bunch of snobs is what they are!"

Dylan started to respond and saw the futility of it. He had endured Meredith's bad humour, for there was nothing he could do about it. "I didn't make up the invitation list, Meredith."

"All right. You come over as soon as it ends."

"Well, I'll do my best. Sometimes they want to talk for a little bit."

"You can talk to me."

He saw that there was an adamant expression on her features and said, "All right. I'll be here as soon as I can." He heard the carriage pull up and looked out the window. "There's Matthew." He turned to go, but she caught him and turned him around. "You never kiss me good-bye."

"I'm sorry, dear." He leaned over and kissed her lightly, then left.

"That's not much of a kiss," she called after him.

Dylan did not answer. He got into the cab with Matthew, who said, "We're a little bit late."

"I suppose that doesn't matter too much

for these things, does it? I've never been to one."

"Neither have I. We'll do the best we can, won't we? Don't lose the ring."

"You haven't given it to me yet."

"I'll give it to you just before the ceremony. You've been so absentminded lately I wouldn't trust you with it."

"Have I been?"

"Yes. You have." Matthew had been thinking hard about some way to approach Dylan. He felt that Dylan was making a terrible mistake in marrying Meredith, but it was against his nature to interfere with another man's choice. He was very fond of Dylan Tremayne, however, and now he said tentatively, "I hate a busybody."

"Well, so do I."

"Hate me, then, because I'm going to meddle in your affairs."

Dylan turned to stare at Matthew. "What do you mean?"

"I mean I hope you've thought about what you are doing marrying Meredith."

"Of course I've thought about it."

"Everybody thinks you're making a mistake."

"Well, *everybody* is not making my decisions for me." Dylan's tone was sharp, and he turned to stare out the window. "I'm doing what I feel is the right thing."

"You're marrying the woman because a dying man had a desperate notion to ask you to care for his wife and his child. I can't blame the man for that. From what you say, he was a fine chap, but he was in no condition to make decisions that would so influence your life."

"I think he would do it for me."

"You'll never know that. The only person that you can handle is yourself. You need to think through this. For example, you don't have a profession."

"You're right about that. Not much money either."

"You're determined to give up your acting career?"

"Yes, I'm leaving."

"You could make a lot of money there."

"It's just not what God wants for me, Matthew. I've explained all that to you."

Matthew was silent for a while. The clatter of the horses' hooves made a symphony of sound on the hard surface of the road. Matthew turned to glance at Dylan and saw that he was in a deep, depressed state. Finally he said, "I've been meddling in more ways than one about you."

"I don't understand."

"I've gone over the budget at the Yard.

We've been talking for some time about putting on a new man, and I put your name forward. I think you can have the job."

Dylan straightened up and said, "An inspector at Scotland Yard?"

"You won't be an inspector." Matthew grinned. "You will be as close to a dishwasher as you can get at the Yard."

"A dishwasher? What does that mean?"

"It means the position that you would be filling is to do the dirty jobs that the rest of us don't want to do. There are a lot of them. They are boring, they take hours, but I convinced my superiors that you have great experience with criminal classes. I told them about how you know people and how they'll talk to you — especially if you put on a disguise. So you may have to get dirty and smelly and grow whiskers in order to get information. The money's not much either. As a matter of fact, it's a sorry job."

"Thank you, Matthew," Dylan said at once, with relief. "I'll take it."

"You haven't even asked how much it pays."

"Pays more than I'm making now. And besides, I think I might be quite good at it."

"You've proved that with Lady Trent. We're counting on that. You're smooth enough to get along with the upper class, and you can get along with murderers, prostitutes — whoever you have to. I think if you take this job, you won't be at it long. Your quality will show forth. You'll just have to eat a lot of dirt before you rise."

"You're a good friend, Matthew." Dylan reached out and grabbed Matthew's hand.

"Hey, you're breaking my fingers! Don't be so happy, man! It's not that great a position."

But Dylan was happy. He had been worried about which direction to go, and this was something he felt he could do and do well. He sat back and began to pepper Matthew with questions until they reached Trentwood House.

Dora was happy, and Serafina stood beside her as they prepared for the dinner. "Where will you go for a honeymoon?"

"To Ireland."

"Ireland? It's beautiful there."

"Matthew says it's beautiful." She suddenly turned and said, "Serafina, I want to thank you for the wedding gift."

"Why, that was a family wedding gift."

"No, it was you. We're so excited."

Serafina had talked with her parents, and together they had decided to give the newly married couple a small house. It was not a fancy house, but it was handy to Scotland Yard and not too far from Trentwood. They had made a ceremony out of it, and for once Matthew Grant had been totally silent. They had made the presentation, and Septimus had handed him the deed. He had swallowed hard, and despite the hard life he had led, tears had glittered in his eyes. "No one," he had said huskily, "ever did so much for me before."

Now Serafina said, "We're going to have to fix it all up, you and me."

"Of course we will."

She would have said more, but at that moment Matthew and Dylan came in. Matthew kissed Dora, but Dylan stood back. It was an awkward moment for him and for Serafina. He looked at her uncertainly, then nodded and said, "Good evening, Serafina."

"Hello, Dylan. I'm glad you could come."

More company arrived for the dinner then, and Serafina moved to greet them. It was a small group, only family and very close friends, and when it was finally over, Dylan found himself alone with Serafina for a few moments. He said awkwardly, "I saw you at Mr. Spurgeon's church Sunday."

"Yes, he's a marvelous preacher. How are Meredith and Guin?"

"They're fine."

His answer was short, and she sensed he was unhappy. "I heard that you're not going to act anymore."

"That's true, but I have good news." His eyes lit up. "Matthew has obtained a position for me at Scotland Yard."

"How wonderful!" Serafina beamed. "I'm so happy for you."

"Yes, he's a fine man, isn't he? It's the lowest position in the Yard, of course, and doesn't pay much."

"But you'll be doing something you're good at. We've proved that, haven't we?"

"Yes, we have, but you're the brains in our little crime-solving expeditions."

The two stood there face-to-face, and for one moment there was something that bound them close together. Dylan, as always, was struck by her beauty, and he knew that she was intelligent, sensitive, with a depth that most women did not have. Her body was full-shaped against the folds of her dress, and there was a rhythm and a vitality about her that affected Dylan powerfully. It fanned the flame of the close-held hungers that had been in him for so many years. He well knew that all men, even the toughest of them, had an ideal woman somewhere in their hearts, fashioned out of deep desires, and he was no different. He knew that few men ever had such a picture materialise, and now it came to him with a profound shock that this was what he was giving up. This thought hit him hard. *I am giving her up. I know she loves me. She said so.* The thought had been with him ever since, and now he realised that her nearness, as always, nearly set off shocks within him. His vision was like the lens of a camera narrowing until he saw only the full swell of her lips and their increasing heaviness. "But — I'm going to miss you, Serafina."

At that instant Serafina's eyes widened. Colour came to her cheeks, and she leaned toward him with a sudden intent. Her hand came up uncertainly and touched the lapel of his coat. A rose colour stained her features, and he said, "I wish it could be different. There's a poem I've always liked about a man going off to war. His sweetheart criticised him for leaving her, and the last line says, 'I could not love thee, dear, so much loved I not honour more.' "

"That's why you're marrying her, isn't it — your honour?"

"Yes."

Serafina would have said more, but at that moment her father and mother came in. Matthew was with them. "It's time to leave, Dylan."

Dylan said his good-byes, and when he walked out, he felt as if he had been wounded. He had been shot once in action when he was a soldier, not seriously, but he remembered the bullet striking him, knocking him down, and he remembered how little he felt. All he could think of was the numbness that had come to him. At the door he turned and looked back, and Serafina was watching him with an expression he could not identify. He turned and walked out into the night with Matthew, unable to think and unable to reason, knowing somehow life had become far too complicated for him.

TWENTY-ONE

David stared up at his mother with a troubled expression, and finally said in a small voice, "Does that mean that Dylan won't be able to come here anymore?"

Serafina had known that breaking Dylan's news to her son would be difficult. David had often said to her, "Mom, if you would marry Dylan, he could stay here all the time." She had smiled at his childlike hope for such a thing, but now that she knew she loved Dylan Tremayne, there was a special poignancy to David's grief. He knew with a childish wisdom that he was losing Dylan.

"He won't be able to come here as often as before, but we'll do what we can to invite him."

"I don't like Mrs. Brice."

Serafina almost said, "I don't either," but she withheld it. "Why, you mustn't tell Dylan that."

"I won't, but I wish he wouldn't do it."

Serafina tried to change the subject as gracefully as possible. She left soon after that. It was Sunday morning, and she had gone to Spurgeon's church for three weeks in a row. When she arrived, she gave her ticket to the doorman, thinking it was strange that a preacher would be so popular that you would have to have a ticket to get in to hear him. She had been investigating the church where Spurgeon was pastor and had discovered that some people gave up their tickets to non-Christian people. Spurgeon had urged them to do this. "Let the unsaved in. You can worship Jesus in your home, but today the lost sheep need to hear the gospel."

She moved inside and found a seat next to a poorly dressed couple. The woman looked to be in her sixties at least, and was frail, but she had a bright smile. "God bless you, Lady," she said.

"And God bless you too." It was the first time Serafina had ever said a thing like that, but she felt good about it. She looked over the building, which seated thousands of people and was already packed. In earlier days she would have said that this was mass hysteria, but there was a strange power in the pastor. There was much singing, but not like singing she had heard before. It was full-throated and filled the auditorium. There were no musical instruments, but she had learnt a few of the tunes and was able to join in.

Finally the pastor, Charles Spurgeon, stepped forward. He began to preach in such a different manner from usual clergymen. Most clergymen in this day read from a full manuscript. Some even had a prompter with the manuscript in hand if the preacher stumbled over a word. They were, in effect, perhaps great literary writers but not very communicative or practical.

But when Charles Haddon Spurgeon stepped forward, things changed. A message burned in his heart, and above all he wanted to communicate it effectively to the common people. He got warmed up in his message, and his text was "Behold the Lamb of God, which taketh away the sin of the world." He walked back and forth and pulled out a handkerchief and flourished it about when he made a point. He stopped once and prayed, "Oh, Lord, take us and mold us as the clay, though there is so much grit in us that it must hurt thy fingers."

Serafina had laughed at that but knew some would be offended. She settled down and listened to the preacher, and, as always, he was able to hold her attention and the attention of everyone in the room. She listened as he went over his points, and every word seemed to sink into her.

"The beholding of the Lamb of God," he said, "is a thing to which men cannot readily be brought. I know many whose consciences are truly awakened, and who see themselves as sinners in the sight of God; but instead of beholding the Lamb of God, they are continually beholding themselves. I do not think that they have any confidence in their own righteousness, but they are afraid that they do not feel their guilt as much as they ought."

This might be true of some, but Serafina Trent felt her guilt sharply. She was shocked at how her heart began to pound, and she began to know that the Spirit of God was in this room, and over and over again Spurgeon would cry out, "Behold the Lamb of God. That means to believe on the Lord Jesus Christ. Trust in him as your Saviour; accept God's revelation concerning him. Trust him to save you. That's the way of salvation."

He went on to talk about Jesus, how he loved people, and how he died on the cross, and without really knowing it, Serafina knew that God was working on her heart.

She lost track of the sermon and considered the years she had spent ignoring God, and now she was finding out that Jesus was as real today as he had been in the days when he walked the earth. Finally they began to sing a song that she knew well:

Rock of Ages, cleft for me,
Let me hide myself in Thee;
Let the water and the blood,
From Thy riven side which flowed,
Be of sin the double cure,
Cleanse me from its guilt and power.

Not the labours of my hands
Can fulfil Thy law's demands;
Could my zeal no respite know,
Could my tears forever flow,
All for sin could not atone;
Thou must save, and Thou alone.

While I draw this fleeting breath,
When my eyelids close in death,
When I soar to worlds unknown,
See Thee on Thy judgement throne,
Rock of Ages, cleft for me,
Let me hide myself in Thee. Amen.

When the song was over, she got up and left with the rest of the congregation. She felt as if she had been somehow beaten, not physically, but she knew that in her heart something had taken place. As she walked away from the church, the thought came, *I must learn to behold the Lamb of God!*

"Well, here you are — the newest Scotland Yard wonder!"

Dylan had entered the Scotland Yard offices and found Sandy Kenzie as he had been instructed to do. Grant was on his honeymoon, and now Dylan was ready for a new career.

"I'm glad to see you here, Dylan. You have a lot of talent we can use in this place."

"I hope I'll be of some use."

"Come along. Let me introduce you to the rest of the men. Some of them are fine chaps, and some of them are not. You'll be able to sort that out."

Most of the inspectors were, indeed, able men and accepted Dylan's new position eagerly since it would take some work off their shoulders. There was one, however, named William Lacey, who had sneered at him and refused to shake hands. "An actor? I don't see what good you'd be."

Sandy whispered, "He's lazy and not much of an inspector. We'll put him where he won't do any damage."

"I hardly know where to start, Mr. Kenzie."

" 'Sandy' will be fine. Let me show you the building, and then we'll get to work."

The two went through the entire office building, and finally in Sandy's office they went over the list of suspects and victims and the so-called clues in the Slasher case.

"This last poem has got us all baffled. Neither Superintendent Grant nor Lady Trent can make anything out of it. Why don't you take it and study it? Then we'll start talking to the suspects again.

Dylan took the single piece of paper and studied the words carefully. A scowl came to his face, and he muttered, "Sounds like nonsense to me — but it means life or death to some poor woman!"

Hugh Edwards stood at the door and introduced himself. Meredith knew Edwards was a famous producer and said with regret, "I'm sorry, sir, but Dylan's not here."

"Sorry to hear that. By the way, I hear that you and Dylan are to marry."

"Yes, sir, that's true."

"My congratulations to Dylan, and to you too, of course. You must help me persuade him to be in my new production. It's *Henry V.* Dylan would be just perfect for the role."

"Oh, he would be excellent in that!"

"Then you must persuade him. If anybody can, I think it would be you."

"I'll try, sir."

Edwards frowned. "I can't think why he wouldn't want to go on. He's doing so well in the theatre."

"I hope he does. He gives pleasure to so many people."

"Well, here's my card. If you have any success, let me know at once."

"Thank you, sir. I'll do my best."

As soon as the door was closed, Meredith leaned back against it. "He's got to do it! He's just got to do it!"

The prison was much like an underground coffin, at least to Dylan. He had been there before, twice as a prisoner, other times as a visitor to his friends when he had been investigating a crime scene. Now he waited until the guard brought the inmate in. He looked up and said, "Hello, Felan, have a seat."

Rian Felan stared at him. "Do I know you?"

"We met once, but I'm sure you wouldn't remember it."

"What's your name?"

"Dylan Tremayne."

Rian threw himself down and grinned. "I do remember you, I think. You were part of the Hanks family."

"For a while, yes."

"What are you doing here now? You're not a lawyer, are you?"

"No, I'm with Scotland Yard."

Amazement spread across Felan's face. "But you were a criminal yourself."

"I was only twelve years old, Felan. I didn't even know the Hanks were thieves until they took me off the street almost starved to death."

"Well, they made a good thief out of you. I remember the old man would shove you through windows. You were so skinny then. Like a snake," he said. "And you would let them in and they'd strip the place." He laughed.

"Things have changed, and I need to talk to you about these murders."

"You mean the Slasher? I killed one woman, Dylan. She was my woman, and she cheated on me. I cut her up, and I enjoyed it. I'd do it again too."

Dylan shook his head. "It's a miracle you didn't hang."

"Well, maybe God's looking out for me. What do you think?"

"I don't think so. I want to ask you a few

questions."

"I bet I've heard them before. Superintendent Grant has asked me every question he could think of — and so did that inspector with the Scottish accent. Go ahead though. I'll give you the truth."

For the next hour Dylan shot question after question at Rian Felan, but by the end of that time he was convinced that Felan was not guilty. He was guilty of murdering a woman and then getting off by some form of miracle, but if he was telling anywhere near the truth, and Dylan knew he would check it out, Rian was not the Slasher.

Finally rising, he said, "Well, I'll be going now."

"When is Grant going to give up and let me out of this place?"

"Can't say about that. Need anything?"

Rian Felan was surprised. "Yes, I do. I need some money. I could buy some food if I had it."

Dylan had very little money, but he pulled out two pounds and handed it over. "Old times' sake," he said.

"You're all right. You'd better stick with your playacting though. It pays better than this detective business."

As soon as Dylan stepped inside the house,

Meredith came to him.

"I've had a good day. Scotland Yard detective now."

"Listen," she said, ignoring his opening remark. "Hugh Edwards came here."

"I can guess what he wanted."

"What do you mean?"

"He's been trying for weeks to get me to star in *Henry V.*"

"You've *got* to do it, Dylan! He's a rich man. We didn't talk money, but he'd pay well."

Dylan pulled off his coat and draped it over a chair. He turned to her and said, "I thought you understood, Meredith. I'm not going to be an actor."

"You've got to, Dylan! You have to. How are you going to take care of a family?"

"I've got a job. It won't be easy, but we can do it."

The argument went on until finally Dylan could stand it no longer. He got up and said, "Meredith, we can talk about some things, and I'm willing to listen to your ideas, but this is my decision and it's final. I'll never go on the stage again." He turned and walked out, and he heard her screaming at him as he hurried away, glad to be out of her range.

TWENTY-TWO

"Well, behold, the husband cometh."

Matthew Grant had come into the office, a big smile on his face, and he seemed to literally glow with happiness. "Yes, I am back, Dylan. I'm an old married man now."

Dylan smiled at his friend, pleased to see him so content. "A week doesn't make a marriage, but I suppose it's a good start."

Matthew seemed to be unable to contain himself. He walked around the office, paused to look out the window, then threw his arms apart in a gesture of utter happiness. "I'm the happiest man in the world, Dylan! All my life up to this point has been wasted. I should have gotten married a long time ago."

Dylan laughed at Grant's exuberance. "That wouldn't have been possible. God was getting you a bride ready."

"You really believe that, don't you?"

"Of course I do. You think God's not

interested in whom we marry?"

"I think you've been reading those Calvinistic sermons too much. The next thing I know you'll be parking your carriage on the railroad track."

Dylan laughed. "Not so bad as that. Now, tell me about your honeymoon."

The two men sat down in the office, and for the next twenty minutes Dylan listened as his boss told him almost every detail. "She's the sweetest, prettiest woman that ever lived."

"Good that you should think so."

Grant suddenly lifted his head, and a more sober light came into his face. "What about you, Dylan? Anything new on your own marriage?"

"No. Nothing."

There was a flat quality in Dylan's voice, and the light of happiness seemed to have faded. Matthew watched him, thinking, *He's miserable, but he won't admit it.* Aloud he said, "When's the date?"

"We haven't set one yet. Got to find a place to live, and money's rather scarce."

"I wish we could pay more, but this is all the budget affords right now."

"No, Matthew, you've really saved my life giving me this job. I'm perfectly content with the wages."

"You'll do well, I'm sure. Won't be long before you'll be a full-fledged inspector. Now bring me up to date on what's been going on these last few days."

"At the present moment it looks as if Rian Felan is the best candidate because of his past history and witnesses who can place him near the residences of two of the murders."

"What do you think?"

"I don't think he did it."

Grant looked at Dylan with surprise. "You say that with a lot of confidence. What makes you think so?"

"Oh, a lot of things. In the first place, Felan has no motive at all. He didn't even know any of the murder victims. But we know he killed one woman in exactly the same fashion that all these women suffered. That ought to go for something. Still, I don't think it'll ever get him convicted. Another thing is his attitude. I knew him a long time ago, and I can tell a little bit about him. He's no good, but I don't think we're going to be able to pin this on him."

The two men talked for fifteen more minutes, and finally Grant threw up his hands. "Everybody's impatient. They want this case solved, and so do I, but I don't see any light at the end of the tunnel."

"Something will turn up, Matthew."

"Well, I hope so." Matthew suddenly brightened and said, "By the way, Dora is cooking a dinner tonight. Her very first for guests, and you're invited."

"That sounds wonderful."

Matthew hesitated, then said, "You think Meredith would like to come?"

"I'll ask her. I'm sure she would."

"Come along about six o'clock. We'll have time, and the women can get better acquainted."

The house that Serafina's family had given Matthew and Dora was not terribly far from the house where Meredith lived with Guin. Meredith had gotten ready for the dinner saying little, but when it was time to go, she said, "We're going in a coach, aren't we?"

"I think we might as well walk."

"Walk! But it's been raining."

"Not raining now."

"Why not take a cab? My dress will get all wet."

"Well, Meredith, to be truthful, I don't have the money. I haven't gotten paid yet, so we'll have to walk."

Meredith gave him a disgusted look. "All right, let's go." He opened the door, and she stepped outside. The rain was gone now, and there was a clear fragrance in the air that always pleased Dylan after a rain. It was early enough so that the sun was still casting its beams down through tattered clouds that drifted along overhead. The city seemed washed and clean and pure, and since it was summer, there was not a great deal of smoke in the air. The city was often so cloaked with yellowish fog from thousands of coal fires that it had achieved a name: such a fog was called a "London particular."

But that was not so now, and Dylan said, "That fresh air smells good. I hope Dora has a big dinner. I'm hungry."

Meredith did not answer, and glancing at her, Dylan had a moment's intense depression. They had been at odds about his leaving the theatre, and he knew before they reached the house she would mention it again. They were only halfway there when she said, "Dylan, you must see how foolish this is. You're not going to make enough money to support a family."

"We'll get by. I saw a house today over on the east side. It was —"

"I imagine I know what it was like. A grubby and dirty place with no yard and terrible smells. Stopped-up drains, no doubt."

"Well, actually it was a little rough, but when I get to be an inspector, things will be better."

"That may never happen. Oh, Dylan," she said, "I'm so tired of arguing about this. I can't understand you at all."

Dylan did not answer, and the two did not speak until finally they got to the house. When they paused in front, she said, "This is a nice house. It's wonderful of Serafina's family to give it to Matthew and Dora."

Meredith looked at the house, which was a neat cottage with beautifully tended flower beds in the front. It was half timber and half stone and was indeed an attractive house.

Dylan knocked on the door, and almost at once Dora opened it. She smiled and came to him, holding out her hands. "Dylan, how wonderful to see you."

"Well, it's good to see you. You look like a blushing bride." He leaned over and kissed Dora on the cheek and saw her grow pink. "Just a friendly kiss from your husband's best friend."

"You are a charmer," Dora cried. She turned to Meredith and managed to keep her smile. "Meredith, I'm so glad to see you. Come in. Maybe you can help me get the meal on the table."

"Of course," Meredith said in a spare tone.

Dora turned to Dylan. "You and Matthew wait in the parlour while we get the meal ready."

At that moment Serafina walked through the door that led to the kitchen. Dylan had not known she would be there, and as had been true in recent days, he felt a sense of awkwardness. "Hello, Serafina," he said.

"Hello, Dylan. Hello, Meredith. How are you today?"

"Very well, thank you." Meredith's reply was hard as rock, and she had no smile on her face.

"You go on and spend this time with Matthew while we get the food ready."

Dylan walked into the parlour, which was small, indeed, compared to the rooms at Trentwood House. Matthew greeted him with a big smile. "Glad to see you, brother. Come in and have a seat while those women slave over the food." He threw himself into a chair and waved Dylan toward another one. "I do love to be waited on."

"And how does your wife take that?"

"Well, the glow is still on. I suppose sooner or later I'll have to come off of Olympus, but as it is, we're doing fine."

The two men sat there but not for long, for ten minutes later Dora came to say,

"Come along now. Dinner is on the table. I'm a little bit nervous. It's the first meal I ever cooked by myself."

The table was spread with dishes, no doubt brought from Serafina's home. There was an exquisite bone china service, hand-painted with blue harebells, and as they sat down, Matthew said, "Why don't you ask the blessing, Dylan?"

"Of course." They all bowed their heads. Dylan prayed a brief prayer and ended by saying, "We thank you for this new union, and we pray that it will be a glory to your name. Amen."

He looked around the table and said, "This looks delicious."

"I hope you like it."

There was cold poached salmon with fresh vegetables and young potatoes. Later there was a shoulder of lamb and even a plate of stuffed breast in pastry.

The talk went around the table, mostly from Matthew and Dora. The other three members were quiet, but Dora talked more than Dylan had ever heard her. From time to time he would steal a look at Serafina. There was always a guilt in him, and at the same time there was a longing to explain to her what was happening to his life.

Finally Matthew said, "That was a lovely

meal, my dear."

"Thank you, Matthew."

Matthew looked at Dylan and grinned. "I have to mention how well Dylan is doing at the Yard. You're going to be proud of him, Mrs. Brice."

"I was proud of him before, when he was in the theatre."

Her remark brought a silence to the room, for all of them were aware that Dylan and Meredith did not agree on this.

"You won't believe how many offers he's turned down," Meredith said. "With enormous amounts of money. I don't like to say this, Superintendent, but the job that Dylan has is beneath him."

"Don't say that, Meredith," Dylan said quickly. "It's generous of Matthew to help me."

Meredith glanced around the table, and her face had an angry expression. She said no more, however, and finally they ended the supper with fresh strawberries and cream.

The men went into the parlour, but at one point Dora came out and asked Matthew to help. He left immediately, and almost as soon as he left, Serafina came in.

"Dora's taken Meredith out to see the garden." Her voice was strained, and it was evidently a hard thing for her to make conversation. "When do you think you'll be married?"

"Our plans aren't fully made. It's a little difficult to put everything together."

There was an awkward silence, and Dylan knew he had only a few moments before the others returned. He said quickly, "Serafina, I have to say that you have meant a great deal to me. I can't really tell you all that's on my heart, but whenever I think of what a woman ought to be, in every way I think of you. I wanted to tell you that before."

Serafina was watching him steadily. "Thank you for those words, Dylan. David is going to miss you."

"I'll try to come and visit." They both knew that he wouldn't, couldn't, in fact, and then Serafina said, "I'll miss you, Dylan Tremayne."

As soon as the words were uttered, Matthew came back, and the mood was broken between them. They all gathered in the parlour for a final tea and some ices, but just as they sat down, a knock came at the door.

"Who can that be?" Matthew said. He got up at once and went to the door, and those left in the parlour could hear his voice. He came at once, with Sandy beside him. "There's been another murder," he said.

"Is it the same as the others?" Serafina asked quickly.

"Not really. It's not one of the nobility this time."

"Who's the victim?"

Matthew shook his head. "You know her. It's Violet Bates, the young woman who works for Miss Bingham."

"Well, that's a strange one," Dylan said at once. "She was a very inoffensive woman. Why would the Slasher break his pattern like this?"

"I don't know, but we'll have to go at once and look at the crime scene. You ladies must excuse us."

The men left, and Meredith said almost at once, "I must be going too."

"My carriage is outside. I'm going home. Let me take you by your place," Serafina offered.

"That would be kind of you," Meredith said, but her words were gentler than her expression. The two women said their thanks and farewells to Dora, went outside, and got into the carriage. Meredith gave instructions to Albert Givins before she got in.

When the two women were settled, the

horses moved forward at Givins's command, and a silence settled in for a few moments. Finally Meredith turned and gave Serafina a calculated look. "I know you're sorry to lose Dylan," she said abruptly.

"I never had him," Serafina said, for there was something suggestive in Meredith's charge.

"You can't fool me, Lady Trent. You care for him. Anyone can see that. You'll never have him now, though, and he won't be coming to your home 'to spend time with David.' I saw through that from the beginning. I hope we never have to mention this matter again."

"I certainly won't, but you're wrong about Dylan. He's a good friend."

"I don't believe that," Meredith said flatly, and not another word was said. Finally, when she got out, she did not even thank Serafina for the ride but turned and walked toward the house.

"Take me home, Albert," Serafina said, and she sat back and felt drained. It had been a stressful evening, and she knew that Meredith was telling her she would not tolerate any relationship whatsoever between her husband and Serafina Trent.

"Where is Serafina?" Dora asked her

mother, who was sitting outside in the garden.

"She's gone, dear."

"Gone? Gone where?"

Alberta shook her head. "She wouldn't say. She just said she had to get away for a while, and that she wasn't sure where she was going, but she'd let us know by post when she got there."

Dora was puzzled. "That's not like her, is it?"

"No, she's very meticulous in her ways. I'm worried about Serafina. She's been unhappy lately."

Dora knew more than her mother what the problem was with Serafina, but it was not her place to say anything. "Did she say when she'd be back?"

"No, she didn't mention it. I hope she's not getting ill or anything like that."

"I'm sure she just needs a little rest," Dora said quickly. She turned and left the garden and thought for a long time about her sister and about Dylan Tremayne. "She loves him," she whispered to herself, "and she doesn't want us to see the pain she feels."

TWENTY-THREE

"There is a man here to see you, Dylan."

Dylan looked up from the papers gathered all over his desk and asked, "Who is it, Kenzie?"

"I have seen him before, but I can't place him. He insists on seeing you though."

"Well, let him in."

Dylan frowned and rubbed his eyes. He had spent hours on the evidence that had been gathered by the Yard, and the more he went over it, the less he seemed to know about the Slasher. He was not sleeping well, and he knew part of this was because Meredith could not seem to leave him alone about his decision to leave the theatre. He stood up as the man entered and exclaimed, "Why, Albert!"

" 'Ow are you, sir?" Albert Givins pulled his hat off and tugged at his forelocks. He was a small man with Cockney in his speech and a pair of bright blue eyes underneath a sandy thatch of hair.

"I'm surprised to see you, Albert."

"I 'ave a note for you, sir."

"A note from whom?"

"Why, from Lady Trent."

"I thought she was gone on vacation."

"She come back last night, sir, late. Got me up first thing this morning and gave me this note and said I was to give it to you as soon as I could. 'Ere it is, sir."

Dylan took the envelope that had the Trent crest on it and opened it. He pulled out a small, single sheet of paper and recognised Serafina's handwriting at once. The note was simple:

Dylan, come at once and bring Mrs. Brice with you. It is very urgent that I speak to both of you. Albert will bring you here and take you home again after our meeting.

He looked at the last line and could not think for a moment, for it said:

I have missed you very much.

With affection,
Serafina

The personal note threw Dylan off, and

he looked up to see that Albert was waiting. "Did she say anything?"

"She said for me to be sure that you and Mrs. Brice come. It's very urgent, she said."

"How did she seem? Was she sad? Angry? What?"

"Couldn't tell much about it, sir. I was so sleepy when she rousted me out, but she did tell me more than once to make sure you came." He suddenly grinned broadly. "I asked her 'ow she thought I'm going to make a Scotland Yard detective do anything I says."

"Well, I'm not exactly a detective yet, but let me tell my superior where I'm going, and we'll be on our way."

Fifteen minutes later Dylan, having gotten permission from Sandy to be gone for an indeterminate period, leapt out of the carriage and walked up to the door of Meredith's house. He knocked, and she appeared at once.

"We have an appointment, Meredith."

"An appointment?" Meredith stared at him. "With whom?"

Dylan had already decided that it would not do to tell Meredith of the details. She had no patience with him anytime he mentioned Serafina, so he thought it best just to get her in the carriage.

"I'll explain on the way," he said briefly.

Meredith stared at him and then shrugged. "I hope this means you've gotten some sense. Let me get Guin, and we'll go."

Dylan did not enlighten her. He waited, and soon she came out carrying Guin. He took the child, and the two went outside. For a moment Dylan was afraid she'd recognise Givins, but she did not even look up. He opened the door of the carriage, helped her in, handed her the child, and then got in beside her. "All right, let's go," he said.

The carriage started at once, and almost instantly Meredith began asking him for more details.

Finally, when he saw that it was useless but also was aware that she could not jump from the swiftly moving carriage, he said, "Lady Trent's been gone for almost a week. She sent me a note saying she needed to see both of us. That it's very urgent."

"Stop the carriage! I won't go see that woman."

"Yes, you will, Meredith. I'll have to insist on this. I don't know why she wants to see us, but I owe her a great deal."

"You owe her nothing! Let me out!"

For once Dylan was firm. He took her arm and squeezed it. He had a strong grip, and she winced. "Be still, Meredith. I'll see that you're brought back as soon as the meeting is over. I don't know what it's about, but we'll find out."

That was the last word that Meredith said. He noticed that she was pale, and Dylan spent the rest of the time telling a story to Guin, who was always ready for such.

When the carriage pulled up to the Trent estate, Dylan was surprised to see Givins guide the horses not to the front door but around to the outside laboratory. It was where Serafina and her father performed autopsies when the occasion arose. He could not understand why this would be where Serafina wanted to meet the two of them, but when the carriage stopped, he opened the door and jumped down. He took Guin and reached up to help Meredith out, but she came down without his aid.

"Thank you for coming, both of you."

Dylan turned quickly to see that Serafina had come out of the laboratory. She was wearing a simple white dress, and he could not read her expression. She seemed very sober but not at all sorrowful. "We came as quickly as we could."

"And I protest at your high-handedness, Lady Trent! You may be nobility, but you have no manners! I've been practically kidnapped," Meredith said furiously. "I demand that you take me home!"

"You'll be going there shortly, but come inside first. I have something to tell you both." They moved inside, following Serafina, and Dylan closed the door. No one was in the laboratory, and everything was put away in an orderly fashion. A door at one end led to the supply room, and there was a silence in the place that seemed, for some reason, ominous.

"My reason for getting you here," Serafina said, "will be obvious. It has to do with you, Mrs. Brice."

"What could you possibly have to say to me?"

"I have been making a list of mistakes that have cropped up in our conversations."

"What are you talking about? What kind of mistakes?"

Serafina turned to face Meredith. The two of them almost set off sparks, Dylan saw. He and Guin were left out. This, whatever it was, was between Serafina and Meredith. He could not imagine the issue, and he listened carefully as she spoke.

"When I first met you, you remarked that your sister, Angharad, came to England, and that your reason for coming here was to locate her."

"It's the truth."

"No, it's not. Angharad Evans, your sister, never came to England. She died in Wales."

"It's not so!"

"I'm afraid it is. I stood beside her grave, and I spoke with the minister who spoke at her funeral. He knew both of you well. His name is Allen. You remember him, I trust?"

"I don't remember that."

"I do. I wrote it down because it seemed important to me."

"Dylan, don't let her say these awful things to me."

Dylan stared at Meredith. "I'd like to hear what she has to say."

"Last April you told me that you had seen the Prince of Wales in October of '57."

"That's right, I did."

"You could not have seen him. He was in France all that month, the month before, and the month after."

"I — I made a mistake."

"I grew suspicious. There are several more but minor things. You claim to have worked shucking oysters, but your hands are not scarred — as are the hands of all who have done that sort of work."

"Don't listen to her, Dylan! She's lying!"

"I've just come back from Wales. I went to the village where you grew up."

"That doesn't prove anything."

"No, but here is a sworn statement from the pastor of the local church. He keeps the records of all marriages, and there is no record of a marriage between Lewis Brice and Meredith Evans. I talked to other people who knew you without telling them why I was there. They all said, in one way or another, that you had never been married. In fact, most people said you two never had a relationship."

"It's a lie! I was married to Lewis!"

"No, you were not. Because on the date you said you were married, Lewis was not in Wales. He had gone to Africa the year before as a volunteer to work with David Livingstone. He died there and is buried there."

Suddenly Meredith turned to face Dylan. "You see what she's doing, don't you, Dylan? She wants you for herself. She's been in love with you for a long time."

Dylan stared at her, unable to reply. Serafina spoke up at once. "I won't dignify those accusations with a response. Dylan, read this."

Dylan took the documents and the letter that stated that there was no record of a marriage between Lewis Brice and Meredith Evans. The pastor had added, "I knew

Lewis until he left for Africa, and I'm certain he never married in this village or anywhere else."

Dylan looked up and stared across the room at Meredith. "Why have you done this, Meredith?"

Meredith cursed. Her face twisted, and she vowed it was all lies. "You'd believe whatever she says!"

Serafina said, "I have one more bit of evidence, and it will prove one thing: that Guinivere is not your child."

"You're a liar! That's what you are, a bloody liar!"

Serafina did not answer. She walked over to the door, opened it, and said, "Come in, please."

Dylan stared at the man who looked like one of the roughs. He was staring at Meredith, and he said, "Didn't expect to see me, did you?"

"Who are you?" Dylan asked at once.

"Me? I'm Caradoc Price, the lover of that there woman."

"I never saw this man!"

"Tell your story to Mr. Tremayne, Price," Serafina said.

"There ain't a whole lot to tell." He was a big man, bulky with a pasty complexion as if he had not been outdoors a great deal.

"Me and Meredith, we never married, but we lived together. She found out I had another woman named Gladys. She turned me over to the law. I was a poacher, among other things. So I went to prison until I could pay the fine. She laughed at me. Somehow she heard about Dylan here being a star on the stage. She took Guinivere and come to England."

"How did you get out of prison to come here?" Dylan asked. He had a heaviness in his spirit, for at one time Meredith had been a true friend and his first love, even though it was childhood love.

"Why, Lady Trent there got me out. She paid my fine, after I told her my story, and got me out."

"What is it you want, Caradoc?" Dylan asked.

"Me? I don't want nothing but to get a little bit of my own revenge on Meredith. She sent me to jail, so I breaks up her little game. And the girl? She's an orphan. I reckon Meredith just grabbed her to use when she decided to come here and take you for what you've got. She ain't no kin to Meredith."

"We can find a home for her here," Serafina said at once. "You'd like to stay here with Dylan, wouldn't you, Guin?"

"Yes!"

Meredith stood staring at Dylan, and he said gently, "I think you'd better go back to Wales, Meredith."

"All right, fine. I'll go back," Meredith said. She turned away and faced the wall as if she could not bear to look upon any of them.

Dylan stood, heartbroken, staring at Meredith's back for a moment. He opened his mouth and tried to speak, but he struggled for words. He closed his mouth, then willed himself to try again. "Meredith . . ." he began, his voice barely a whisper. He stopped, closed his eyes, swallowed his tears, and went on. "Meredith, I'm — I'm s-sorry I dishonored you."

"You fool!" Meredith spat, whirling around to face him, her face red and her eyes flashing. "You never *touched* me!"

"What do you mean? You said —"

But she wouldn't let him finish. "I *know* what I said!" she hissed. "But it wasn't true. I put something in your drink to make you pass out, so that when you awoke the next morning, you wouldn't remember anything. And then I lied and said you'd made love to me — but I only said that so you'd marry me, because I thought you'd be worth marrying! Little did I know. Oh, little did I know." Bitterness dripped from her every word.

And Meredith's venomous words were more than Serafina could take. "He's twice the man, Meredith, that you'll ever deserve!"

"As if you would know," Meredith said with her eyebrow raised, then turned her back on them both again.

Serafina started to say something in return, but before she could, she felt Dylan's hand on her shoulder. Turning, she saw that he was shaking his head.

Serafina called Ellie, the tweeny maid, who had been waiting outside the door. Ellie enticed Guin to go to the house for cookies, and then Serafina moved to the desk, opened the drawer, and removed a purse. She handed it to Caradoc, saying, "There's enough for her passage, and your fee is in there. I'll have my coachmen take you back." She turned and said, "Meredith, I think you'd best go back to Wales and try to find yourself there."

Dylan watched in a stunned fashion as Meredith and Price walked outside. Meredith did not say a word but gave him a poisonous look. The carriage rolled away, and Meredith looked out and pronounced a curse on Serafina, who did not answer.

Serafina turned back to Dylan and said, "I'll take care of Guin and will look into the legalities of adopting her. You can come see her when you feel up to it, but I know this is hard for you right now."

Dylan turned to her. "Not as hard as it would have been if I had married her. I would have found out sooner or later, I suppose."

Serafina came, stood close to him, put her hand on his arm, and said gently, "You wanted to do a good thing, Dylan. I knew all the time you didn't love her. You just wanted to help her and the child."

"No, I didn't love her, but I thought I could do something good."

"You tried to save what was left, and I admire you for it. Would you like to come to the house?"

Dylan felt that he had taken a blow to the midsection. He could not think properly. "I'd like to go back to town, if you don't mind."

"Of course not. I'll have Peter hitch up the small carriage and take you back."

She turned to go, but he reached out, took her arm, and held her for a moment. "I don't know what to say, Serafina, but I know that when this all sinks in, for the rest of my life, I'll be grateful to you for saving me from making a terrible, terrible mistake. Thank you very much. You've been my good angel."

Serafina's eyes lit up, and her lips trembled. "I'm happy for you, Dylan. You're going to pull through this. It may take awhile, but you'll find your way."

Ten minutes later Dylan was in the small carriage along with Peter Grimes, the footman. He was curious, Dylan could tell, but he asked no questions. Just made a few remarks about the weather. When they reached the city, he drove at once, at Dylan's direction, to the office that held Scotland Yard. Dylan got out and said, "Thank you, Peter."

"You're welcome, sir."

Dylan walked inside, and when people spoke to him as he made his way through the small office that he shared with Sandy Kenzie, he responded automatically. He sat down at the desk and stared at the papers blindly. Over and over again he thought about what he had just experienced, and finally Matthew came in and said, "Kenzie tells me you had an errand."

"Come in. Let me tell you something."

Curious, Matthew came in and shut the door. He listened as Dylan told him what had happened, and then he said, "Well, I know this hits you hard. It's bad news to find out someone has betrayed you, but personally I'm relieved that the truth came out."

Matthew came over, put his arm around Dylan's shoulder, and said, "Come on, man. Work's the best thing. We'll talk about this later. Maybe you can have supper with me and Dora tonight."

"That would be nice, but I don't think I'm fit to work. Can't think of anything very logically."

"Take the day off. Go for a walk. Go down to the river. Do something to take your mind off of it."

"Thanks, Matthew. I'll do that."

Dylan had returned to the office, and dusk had fallen. He sat there at his desk going over the evidence on the killings and read again the last poem that the Slasher had left.

Sonnet to a Dead Contessa

She is the fairest of the fair
But death will close her pretty eyes
So that she will never dare
Deceive a man with sugared lies!
That form that men declare divine

Will no more deceive poor men!
That flesh will be for worms to dine
And that will pay for her great sin!
The river with a crooked arm
On the day she is born she will perish,
And none can stop the harm,
And few will her memory cherish!
In midsummer she will cease to be,
And Scotland Yard will never see!

Dylan had stared at the poem for more than an hour. He had gotten up and walked the floor until he had it in his memory. He had always been a quick study, and now the poem went through his mind over and over and over again.

Finally he began to pray. "Lord, my mind won't handle this. I need help. Somebody will die if we do not stop it." He continued to pray, and then suddenly a thought came to him that he had never had before. He stared at the poem, then quickly left the room and went into Matthew's office. Matthew was working late, and he looked up in surprise.

"What is it, Dylan?"

"I need to look at your map of England, the big one."

"There it is on the wall. What is it?"

Dylan did not answer. He darted over to

the map. He looked over it quickly, and almost at once he put his finger on a section of the map. "I've got it, I think, Matthew! I know who the next victim will be."

Matthew came to his feet, his eyes bright. "What do you mean?"

"Look, the poem says the river holds the town with a crooked arm. Look at this. See this small town of Trent? A river surrounds it."

Matthew gasped. "You don't mean you think Serafina will be the next victim?"

"I think so. It says a noble lady will die on the day she is born. Today is Serafina's birthday. The last two lines say, 'In midsummer she will cease to be.'"

"Midsummer — that's a quarter day." The two men stared at each other, and Dylan said, "Look at the last line. 'Scotland Yard will never see.' He's daring us. He's telling us what he's going to do."

"We've got to get out there before it's too late."

The two men rushed out, and Matthew bellowed loudly until a cab stopped in front of them. "I'll tell you how to get there."

The carriage raced down the road, and from time to time Matthew stuck his head out the window. "Hurry, man! Kill that horse if you have to!"

Dylan had not said a word. The Slasher had given them the information, but they had been blind and had not seen it.

"God, keep her safe. Keep her safe," he murmured over and over again, and a great fear came into his heart as he realised how much Serafina meant to him.

Twenty-Four

Serafina had spent the afternoon playing with Guin and David, and then after dinner she put both children to bed, David in his room and Guin in the room they'd prepared for her. She was glad the little girl had gone to bed easily, but Serafina could not sleep. The situation with Meredith Evans had disturbed her. She had worried also about Dylan, for she knew he was a sensitive man and would not take this well.

Finally she closed her eyes. The room was bright with moonlight coming through the large windows, but she finally drifted off to sleep . . . or almost so, at least.

In one of those twilight experiences when one is neither awake nor asleep but some of each, she heard a slight muffled sound, and for a moment she lay there confused. Then suddenly her heart seemed to stop, for in the bright moonlight she turned her head to see a shadowy form.

The Slasher!

At once she realised that she was a dead woman if she didn't do something. She rolled out of bed and cried out, but the figure came toward her. She reached about wildly and picked up the kerosene lamp from her dressing table. She threw it, and it hit the killer and soaked his garments with whale oil.

"You cannot escape. I'll kill you like I killed the others."

The voice of the Slasher was high-pitched. Serafina backed away and picked up the box of matches. She lit one immediately and cried loudly, "If I toss this match, you'll burn to death."

"Not before I kill you."

Serafina had time to toss the match. She backed away and saw it catch on the sleeve of the killer. It blazed up, and as the killer beat it out with his free hand, Serafina moved to the fireplace and grabbed a poker from the rack that was there.

The Slasher laughed and moved closer. There was a maniacal sound in the laughter, and suddenly Serafina saw the glint of a knife. He laughed again and made a pass with the knife. Serafina jabbed the poker and caught the killer in the chest, but he made no sound and circled to stand in front of the door. The Slasher was moving gracefully, toying with Serafina. Serafina cried out again, but he jumped, and Serafina felt a strong hand on her throat. She collapsed backward. The dark figure was muffled. She could see a pair of eyes staring at her from underneath the dark hood.

"The great detective! You fool! I gave you the names of the victims, and you couldn't catch me. Before you die, I want you to see what you missed, you stupid woman."

The killer threw the cloak back, and Serafina stared — for it was a woman who held her there!

"Jeanne St. Clair!"

"Yes, it's me, Jeanne St. Clair. All of Scotland Yard couldn't catch me, and it was so clear. How many people would be able to go up and down a wall like a cat? Only an acrobat or an aerialist like me could do it."

"Please let me go."

"You'll be going somewhere, but just as the other women did."

"Why did you kill all those women, Jeanne?"

"Because Martha told me to, of course."

"Why would she want those women dead, and why would you kill for her?"

Jeanne St. Clair had glittering eyes. She

held the knife at Serafina's throat, but she was enjoying this moment of triumph. "Because none of you would help with the movement. You are all fools! You are slaves to men, and you don't even know it."

"But why would you kill for her?"

"You're too stupid to see that, aren't you? She's been my lover for years." The laugh came again and had a madness in it. "That shocks you, doesn't it?"

"But Violet Bates? Why kill her? She had no title, and she was a supporter of Miss Bingham."

"Why, she loved Martha. Always had. She wanted me out of the way. I found out she was going to tell the law that I was the Slasher. I couldn't have that, could I? Now — you want to say your prayers?"

"Yes, I do."

"They don't mean nothing. Say them quick. I'll finish the amen."

Serafina felt the knife at her throat, and she began to pray. "Lord, help this poor woman —"

"Keep your prayer. I don't believe in no God!"

"But Jesus loves you, Jeanne."

Suddenly there was a sound of wood smashing, and Jeanne St. Clair whirled and saw two men come in. She had no chance to move, for Dylan grabbed her, and Matthew was right behind him.

"Jeanne St. Clair," Matthew said. "I should have known you would be the one who was able to climb walls and get away like a bird . . . almost."

"You're all fools!"

"Maybe we have been," Matthew said, "but you're going to pay for it." He produced some cuffs and restrained her hands behind her back. A piece of paper fell from her sleeve.

"Maybe so," the woman said. Her eyes had madness in them, but there was triumph in her voice. "But I won't be alone."

"You killed those women."

"Yes, I killed them, but Martha ordered me to do it. Paid me good money too."

"You'll swear to that in court?"

"Of course I will." The laugh again, and the woman sounded demented. "But she thought she was rid of me with that plain frump of a Violet! Now we'll go to the pit together. Take me when you arrest Martha, Superintendent. I want to see her face!"

Matthew said, "I'll just do that. You want to come, Dylan?"

Dylan had picked up the piece of paper and was studying it carefully. "It seems that Miss St. Clair intended to leave another poem — for another victim."

Matthew took the paper and read it. "Who did you intend to kill next?"

"You'll never figure it out, stupid policeman."

Dylan saw Serafina's troubled expression and said, "Matthew, take this woman down to the station. I think I'll stay here. Serafina may need some company."

"Well, you solved the case, Dylan. I think this will get you in full status at the Yard. You'll be Inspector Dylan Tremayne if I have anything to say about it."

"He's as stupid as the rest of you!" Jeanne said.

"We'll see who's stupid. Come on." Matthew pulled her out the door.

Serafina turned to Dylan. He came to stand close to her. He held his hand out, and she saw that it was trembling. "I didn't think anything could do that to me."

She put her hand lightly on his chest. She was wearing only a thin nightgown, but it never occurred to her. The threat of instant death had taken everything else out of her mind. She was aware that he had put his arms around her, and she looked up and said, "I found out about Meredith in Wales, but I found something else too."

"And what was that, Serafina?"

"I found God in Wales. I went out on the moors all alone. I walked and I cried out, and the Lord came to me. That's why I could pray for Jeanne instead of myself when she was about to kill me."

Dylan listened as she told, with her face alight, how she had found Jesus to be real, something she had always run from in the past.

He held her close. She pressed her face against his chest, and he whispered, "Now you are a true handmaid of the Lord."

TWENTY-FIVE

Septimus and Serafina were looking through the window watching David and Dylan. They were engaged in building a tree house for which the two had made great plans. Guin played on the grass with two dolls and the mastiff Napoleon lying beside her.

"I hope they don't fall out of that thing and break their necks," Septimus said.

"They won't," Serafina replied and added, "God wouldn't let that happen."

Septimus turned to face her. "You're serious about this faith of yours in Jesus, aren't you?"

"Yes, I am."

He was silent, and Serafina saw that there was a sadness in him. "What is it? Is something bothering you?"

"I can look back, and I see now that I was the one who kept you away from God all your life."

"I don't want you to have any guilt

about that."

"I can't help it." His face softened, and he whispered, "Maybe you'll find time to tell me what it's like — believing in God."

Serafina reached up, pulled him close, and kissed his cheek. "I think I can find the time for that," she said, and light shone in her eyes. "I think I'll go out and see if I can help with the tree house."

She left the house at once, and when she neared Guin, she reached down and picked her up. They looked up at the ladder that led to the tree house. "Is this house reserved for males?" she called out.

"No, come on up, Mum and Guin!" David's head appeared, and his eyes were shining. "Don't fall."

Serafina put Guin back on the grass and asked her to wait there. Awkwardly Serafina climbed up. "What a nice house." They had built the floor and walls and two windows, and David was speaking very loudly. "We're going to put some bedding up here so we can spend the night."

"It will be a little bit cold, won't it?"

"No, it's going to be fun. We're going to have a secret code too, for members only."

Serafina turned so David could not see her face and winked at Dylan. "Can I be a member, David?"

"Can she, Dylan?"

"Well," Dylan said, "our membership rules are strict. You've got to pay dues."

"How much?"

"A big platter of fairy cakes every day."

There was, in fact, a light at the end of this dark tunnel, she saw. The case had been closed. Dylan had received full credit. The papers had made a great deal out of the fact that a famous actor had now become a famous detective. Matthew had seen to it that he had gotten full credit for the arrest of the Slasher. The trial had lasted only two days, for with Jeanne St. Clair's giving full testimony of her guilt and implicating Martha Bingham, both women were sentenced to hang.

Now Dylan had passed out of gloom, and his relationship with Serafina was different. She had always avoided talk about the Bible, of God, and now she eagerly listened as he told her things about the faith that she now embraced.

"Well," Serafina said fondly, "what's the purpose of your club?"

"To save people," David piped up, "and animals too."

"Oh, I like that! But, by the way, I think Nessa has made some cake and lemonade. Why don't we go get some?"

"Yes! I'll go first." David scooted down the ladder and ran across the yard, yelling something that Serafina could not understand.

"What's he saying, Dylan?"

He turned to her and came close. "I can't tell you until you're a member of the club. You'll have to go through the initiation."

"Well, I'm ready."

He moved forward and took her in his arms and kissed her. "There, that's part of it."

She laughed, and he brought her to him again with a quick sweep of his arms. When he kissed her and felt the desperate hunger of her lips, a feeling raced through him like fire shaking his mind. She had this power over him, and he saw that he had the same power over her. This woman was capable of lifting him to wild far heights, and suddenly he saw that her lips were trembling as if she were weak.

"What is it?"

"I nearly lost you."

"I've loved you a long time, Lady Serafina Trent."

"You never said so."

"Well, you're a viscountess. I'm a simple policeman. I don't have anything to offer you."

"You can offer me yourself."

"If I had money and a title and you had nothing, it's easy what the decision would be."

Suddenly lightness came to Serafina Trent. She knew that she was beginning a journey. She could see in his eyes that he could no more keep away from her than she could keep away from him. "Doesn't this club have rules about being courageous?"

"Indeed, yes," Dylan said.

"Then show some courage, man."

"All right, I will. I want to be David's father."

"Well then?"

"The only way I can be that is to be married to his mother." He was smiling now, and she loved the way he teased her at times like this.

"Is that a proposal? It's the worst I ever heard! Where's all that romantic talk, the poetry, the fire you Welshmen are supposed to have?"

Dylan laughed, and wrapping his arms about her, he lifted her off her feet and swung her around. "The day I stop loving you will be the day I die."

Serafina was in his arms, and he was saying the sweet and lovely and wonderful things that she had always longed to hear —

but never had. When he put her down, she pulled his head down and kissed him. As he lifted his head, he saw there were diamonds in her eyes. "David will be glad," she whispered.

"And what about his mum?"

"She's only a viscountess, but she'll soon be much more than that! A wife she'll be. Never let me go, Dylan."

"If you're having my opinion," Dylan whispered, "I'll be married to a queen. And any man married to a queen is a king, isn't he?"

They both laughed and climbed down the ladder. He took her hand as they walked toward the house.

Dylan suddenly laughed. "Aunt Bertha will be pleased that you've decided to marry a policeman."

Serafina giggled like a teenager. "She can be one of the bridesmaids." Then she reached up and grabbed his ear and tugged it. "We're going to shock the world, Dylan Tremayne. Aunt Bertha will have to get used to my new name. Serafina Tremayne — wife and mother."

And then David came running toward them, and Serafina bent over and whispered in his ear. David looked up at Dylan and laughed. "See, I told you she liked you. Now let's go have cake and lemonade."